*Heartwarming stories of true friends . . .
and true love!*

A TASTE OF HONEY
DeWanna Pace
(November 1998)

Toya and Betina have been friends forever. But can their friendship survive when Toya is promised to the man Betina secretly loves?

WHERE THE HEART IS
Sheridon Smythe
(December 1998)

Orphans Natalie and Marla were like sisters. And now as adults, when the orphanage is destined to be sold from under Natalie, Marla has plans—to match her up with the orphanage owner!

LONG WAY HOME
Wendy Corsi Staub
(January 1999)

Cira Valentino and her best friend, Lucia, are desperate to reach America. But when disaster strikes, can a handsome American heir save Cira, and make her and Lucia's dreams come true?

Jove titles by DeWanna Pace

SUGAR AND SPICE
BECKONING SHORE
A TASTE OF HONEY

A Taste of Honey

DeWanna Pace

JOVE BOOKS, NEW YORK

If you purchased this book without a cover, you should be aware that this book is stolen property. It was reported as "unsold and destroyed" to the publisher and neither the author nor the publisher has received any payment for this "stripped book."

FRIENDS is a trademark of Penguin Putnam Inc.

A TASTE OF HONEY

A Jove Book / published by arrangement with
the author

PRINTING HISTORY
Jove edition / May 1999

All rights reserved.
Copyright © 1999 by DeWanna Pace.
This book may not be reproduced in whole or part,
by mimeograph or any other means, without permission.
For information address:
The Berkley Publishing Group,
a division of Penguin Putnam Inc.,
375 Hudson Street, New York, New York 10014.

The Penguin Putnam Inc. World Wide Web site address is
http://www.penguinputnam.com

ISBN: 0-515-12387-0

A JOVE BOOK®
Jove Books are published by The Berkley Publishing Group,
a division of Penguin Putnam Inc.,
375 Hudson Street, New York, New York 10014.
JOVE and the "J" design
are trademarks belonging to Penguin Putnam Inc.

PRINTED IN THE UNITED STATES OF AMERICA

10 9 8 7 6 5 4 3 2 1

This book is dedicated to

BRENDAN NAPIER WIMBERLY

*—talented author, samurai critiquer,
psychic decorator.*

*You're right, friend.
Laughter is the remedy.*

And the song,
From beginning to end,
I found in the heart of a friend.

—Henry Wadsworth Longfellow,
"The Arrow and the Song"

Prologue

**Nassau, Germany
1838**

"*Ach, du liebe Zeit!* I wish our papas would not argue!" The grown-ups' disagreement saddened nine-year-old Toya Reinhart. She wrapped her arms around her knees and rested her chin upon them. The gathering at the river was supposed to be fun and full of good wishes. But suddenly, the farewell party given to families leaving for America had become a sparring match.

"We will never argue," Betina Bram assured her, grasping one of Toya's hands and threading the tiny fingers through her own.

"Or forget each other," Toya whispered, making a solemn pledge as she faced her friend. "No matter where we live."

Tears shimmered in Betina's brown eyes. The slight wind off the river buffeted the blanket the girls sat on and ruffled the dark curls that framed Betina's face. "No matter where."

"Here, this is for you." Toya dug into the pocket of her skirt and retrieved the embroidered kerchief she had hidden there. Though she tried to give the surprise to Betina all afternoon, the right moment had eluded her. Giving the gift meant it was time to say *auf Wiedersehen.*

Tilly, Toya's identical twin, broke through the circle of parents crowded around the musicians' stand and ran toward the girls. Her strawberry-blond braids bounced against her shoulders as if they were reins flicking a swift-footed mare. "Papa says come now, Toya!" she yelled. "We are leaving."

Toya's and Betina's gazes met. Toya blinked hard, fighting back the burning sensation in her eyes. With all the effort she could muster, she smiled a smile that slowly eased the stranglehold on her heart. She would not let Betina's last memory of her be one of tears. She would be brave for both of them. "They're only pfeffernuss, but the kerchief belonged to my mother."

"I cannot take it . . . *them.*"

Betina refused to accept the spiced cookies, leaving Toya no other choice but to place the kerchief in her friend's lap. She gently squeezed Betina's hand. "You have to . . . so when you come to America, you can give it back to me."

"But you need all you have. Papa says it is a long voyage."

"That's Mother's handkerchief!" Tilly halted in front of them and frowned. "What is she doing with—?"

"I can give it to anyone I want," Toya challenged. Their beloved mother had sewn one for each of them the last Christmas of her life. "You have your own."

Her eyes softened as she faced Betina again. "If the pfeffernuss get hard, dip them in milk or chocolate. They will last a long time."

Toya glanced at the crowd's solemn faces. "Papa says every family must soon make a choice or die in poverty. Herr Bram will decide to follow *später,* I just know it. And

I will pray every night that he chooses to join us in Texas."

"*Danke schön.*" Betina accepted the gift and slid it into her own skirt pocket. "I will pray for you too, Toya. Never will I forget you."

"Dreamers you are ... both of you." Tilly plopped down beside her twin, her green eyes full of scorn. "And you, Toya, are worse. You will not look at things the way they are. Papa told Herr Bram he refused to listen to any more nonsense. We will leave the fatherland and never see Betina again."

"We are *not* dreamers," Toya contested, her fingers separating slowly, sliding across Betina's palm, straining to preserve the fragile link for as long as she could. "And I *do* see things the way they really are. Betina and I are *Freundinnen. Beste Freundinnen*, and you, Tilly Reinhart, are just jealous!"

Toya pushed Tilly, sending her sister sprawling backward. She grabbed Betina's hand again and pulled her as fast as she could run down the riverbank, away from Tilly's envy of their friendship, away from their parents' dispute, away from the truth that might part her and Betina forever come morning.

Like a thief of dreams, night rushed by and robbed Toya of sleep. Too soon it would be dawn, and she would leave behind the only home she'd ever known. She stirred uneasily on the pallet of blankets in the floor, wishing Papa had not already sold their beds.

A scattering of pebbles hit the chalet's outside wall. Toya listened more closely. Was the wind becoming stronger? Would it prevent them from sailing tomorrow? Would she never see Betina again? Squeezing her eyes shut, she prayed for the storm of all storms upon Nassau and the River Lahn.

"Toya, wake up!" a hushed voice cried. Pebbles hit the wall again.

"Is that Betina?" Tilly yawned, opened one eye, and glanced toward the window. She snuggled deeper in the covers the sisters shared and mumbled into her pillow, "Tell her to come back when the sun comes up."

Elation filled Toya as she recognized Betina's voice, countered by the knowledge that the wind would not buy her more time. "She must have run away," Toya whispered, plotting a dozen places to stow away her friend on the ship. But when she peered out into graying edges of dawn, Toya's hope plummeted.

"No, let me go, Papa!" Betina struggled in her father's arms. "I want to go with Toya! I want to go to America!"

"You must say *auf Wiedersehen, Liebling*." Tears fell from Herr Bram's eyes as he spoke the harsh words, refusing to free his wriggling daughter. "A hard truth, *ja,* but one you . . . we must all face."

Afraid if she moved away from the window for even an instant Herr Bram would turn and take Betina with him, Toya held up the hand that had clutched her friend's so tightly. "No matter how far away I go, Betina!" she yelled.

Thrusting her hand up, Betina spread her fingers as if she stood only inches away from Toya and their palms could touch. "No matter where," she echoed.

As the Brams turned and left, the warmth of her twin's palm rested upon Toya's shoulder.

"Now that she is gone, you and I can be more than sisters." Delight at this new turn of events filled Tilly's tone with enthusiasm. "Now *we* can be best friends."

1

New Genesis, Texas
March 1849

"Come on, Betina. I want to repair the waterwheel so I can meet Opa down at the river." Toya pulled her dark-haired friend toward the stone well several yards behind the Reinhart house. Dawn wind whipped at Toya's long linsey-woolsey skirt and pulled strands of her strawberry-blond hair away from Toya's waist-length braid. She gripped the bucket and extra rope she'd brought along in case they were forced to replace those at the well.

Twenty-year-old Betina Bram's long-legged gait could easily match her petite friend's shorter strides, but she had not fully wakened and did not particularly care to go fishing with Toya and her elderly friend. "Go on without me. We will repair the wheel later."

"*Nein.* You have not seen my aunts without their morning coffee, but you know how *they* repair things. We shall mend the wheel. But we must hurry. I told Opa we would join him this morning to learn how he whistles the fish to the shore. He says it works only before dawn."

"*You* want to learn such, Toya. Not I. I dislike fish—handling fish, smelling fish, eating fish!" Betina's nose wrinkled, displaying a patch of freckles across its bridge.

Toya slowed down for her sleepy friend. Betina was like a pot of coffee. It took time to make her brew, whether with anger or excitement. But when she did, the warmth of her convictions affected all who loved her.

"Remember, I must settle down soon and become a good *Frau*," Toya reminded her friend, "and you want him to use his powers to find my mother's handerkerchief. Let us have an adventure this day!"

"How can the old man find what I have not for three years?" Skepticism deepened the chocolate-brown of Betina's eyes as she focused on Toya. "You are worried about your upcoming marriage to Peter, *ja*?"

"Worried? *Nein* . . . but there is much to finish before I stand with him at the altar. And don't scoff at Opa's gifts. Many of our people believe he has been touched by the hands of heaven. He knows things . . . predicts things."

"As you believe."

Betina's practical nature always left Toya having to persuade her friend into sharing her own belief in things not easily explained. But Toya had witnessed the old man's gift, and knew if anyone could find the missing treasure, Opa could. At least when Toya talked, Betina listened and did not mock her because she believed.

Betina changed the subject. "Let us speak of Peter. He is a *gut* man . . . well-respected in the community. He is wealthy and handsome too."

"He's gone all the time." Toya bit her bottom lip in thought, focusing her emerald gaze on the well, not wanting Betina to see the tears filling her eyes. She might think the sadness sprang from missing Peter.

"He will be back soon with the new immigrants. Your aunt says the wedding preparations are already under way."

"Aunt Fred sews day and night on my dress." Toya sighed. "I take all work offered so that I might hire someone to do this for her, but she won't accept the help. She strains her eyes, and they already do not see well. I need a miracle." She sighed. "Or at least better wages."

The two friends shared a silence that needed no words. For many hours they had discussed and planned ways Toya might become self-sufficient. Toya decided she could not accept any more of the benefits the *Verein* allotted the Reinharts because of her engagement to the town councilman. Peter Stoltz insisted on sharing his portion with them because he would move into their home one day and help care for Toya's widowed aunts. But what if something happened on his frequent journeys to the fatherland to bring back a new wave of immigrants? She must find a way to provide for her aunts without his help.

Betina finally broke the silence. "Is it true Peter wants to marry the week he returns?"

"His last letter says so, though I don't understand the rush. I have not yet agreed."

"You plan not to honor your pledge?"

Dual emotions—surprise and something else Toya could not read—darted across the freckled face.

Both women knew the promise Toya and Peter made to her twin would not allow such a possibility.

"*Nein*, just delay it . . . a bit longer," Toya finally confided. Not wanting to spoil the day by dwelling on eventualities, she swiftly changed the subject. "Just as you are delaying us now. Ready to help me draw water?"

"If I must," Betina grumbled, but a wink followed to hearten her friend. "Spending the night at your home has its price, I see."

The two of them laughed, knowing where one led, the other usually followed. Just when they reached the well, they discovered the circle of rawhide that normally held the gourds looked frayed and beyond repair. A test of the sodden rope on which the makeshift dippers were tied proved it too heavy to rotate.

Betina surveyed the damage. "This does not look like such an easy task."

"True"—Toya held up the extra bucket and rope—"but we've come prepared. As my papa always said, 'A ready hand accomplishes its duty.'"

Betina bowed her head in reference to Toya's departed parent, but the respect for the man quickly evaporated into a giggle. "Herr Reinhart always did indulge his confidence in you...."

"Opa, where are you?" Conrad Wagner called, hurrying down the cedar-covered slope. Its descent was steeper than most of the surrounding hill country bordering the Comal River. He should have never indulged his grandfather's request to be left back at the house while Rad went about his chores.

Work in his peach orchard and bee farm kept his towering physique one of the strongest in the community, but Rad's breath came in hot, ragged gasps. He didn't know how much longer he would be able to work his farm and keep watch over Opa. He'd lost two hours already that morning trying to find his wayward grandfather. His gaze scoured the Texas countryside. Opa was nowhere in sight.

Pebbles crunched beneath Rad's boots as he skidded to a stumbling halt. The land leveled into a meadow, paralleling the crystal-clear river that fed the German settlements of New Genesis, New Braunfels, and Comaltown. He'd looked everywhere else he could think of, except Opa's favorite fishing haunt. If the old man wasn't there, Rad would be forced to ring the church bell to gather a search party.

Day was well under way, the pink of sunrise glowing to brilliant blue. Though only mid-March, spring had thawed the remnants of winter, filling the air with the fragrant scent of blooming mesquite and peach blossoms. Greening mesquite shoots signaled the peach crop would be safe from a false spring and that frost would not return again this season.

Fear gripped Rad, tainting his mouth with an acrid taste. He removed his hat and wiped a forearm across the perspiration beading his hairline. A sun-streaked strand of gold fell into his eyes, a reminder that he needed to see Herff, the barber, before week's end. If he could corral Opa long enough to manage a haircut . . .

Rad cupped his hands over his mouth and shouted, "Opa, if you are out there, give a yell."

He waited, listened, strained to hear anything to direct him. A slight breeze rustled the treetops. Was that a laugh? He hurried toward the riverbank. The lapping gurgle of the spring-swollen water struck terror in his heart. Opa's recent memory losses made the old man take chances that daunted younger men. What if his grandfather dared to cross the river alone?

"Ash Wagner, sing out!" Rad raced downstream, using his grandfather's given name instead of the endearment usually offered his beloved elder. Cattails and buffalo grass hid the river's edge from view. Rad ran closer. "I am worried about you, Opa, and cannot find you. Answer me!"

Three years of living in the new country had urged him to use the English spoken by the Texican Americans. When it became too difficult to express his feelings, Rad lapsed into his native tongue. His shout became a sharply spoken order.

"Quiet, babblemouth, or you'll frighten my friend."

The unexpected command caused Rad's heart to tighten in response, as if someone gripped it in a stranglehold. He almost stumbled over his grandfather before spotting him in the high grass only steps away from the bank. The slender man sat on his knees, gently shooing a three-legged frog toward the water.

As he exhaled, the breath caught in his throat. Rad examined his grandparent from white hair to the muddied tips of his boots. Other than the fact that he'd chosen to wear too large a bib and tucker, the standard garb preferred by the older gentlemen of New Genesis, Opa looked none the worse for his active morning.

Not so himself, Rad decided. It would take a good hour for his blood to quit pumping this fast. His clothes were so soaked from the strain of his search, he could wring them out and widen the river's edge by two inches.

He knelt beside his grandfather and wrapped an arm around Opa's shrunken shoulders. "I have been worried about you, Grandfather. Why did you not tell me where you were going?"

Opa glanced up. Though sixty-seven years old, the man's eyes were still as blue as the sky above the Alps on the brightest summer day—a shade passed down to Rad. Rationality shone in his grandfather's gaze now. Opa could be persuaded to return home.

"I did not tell you, Grandson, because I was not going far. And now you have found me. As you can see, I am busy with a friend." Puzzlement furrowed Opa's brow. His voice grew stern. "Are your chores lagging, Conrad? The peaches may have decided to come early, but the bees will not be so cooperative unless you tend them well."

"You are right, Opa. They will fuss, and I need your help this morning. It seems one of them wants to wander off on his own. He will not fly with the swarm and comes back too exhausted to do anything but lie outside the door of the hive and complain."

The white hair bobbed as the old man's head bent to study the frog's progress. "It is spring, boy. A time for tempting fate and finding one's own way. Be patient with this wayward bee. Let him sow his oats. He will find the best pollen because he is not afraid to look where others won't. Let him fly untethered now. He will achieve his destiny in his own good time."

Opa gently waved his hand behind the frog. The frog leapt inches forward, then several more. "See there! No need to pound the ground or shake the grass. Gentle persuasion is enough to urge the frog to be a frog."

"But would it not be easier to pick him up and take him to the water?" Rad rose from bended knee.

"Easier for you." Opa looked up at him. "But that missing front leg will not keep my friend from wanting to cross the distance on his own."

Rad understood his grandfather spoke of more than frogs and bees. His gaze did not meet the piercing blue of Opa's eyes. "That is true, Grandfather, but is it not good that he has a wise friend to help him to the shore? One who will make certain he is not harmed?"

The frog hopped into the water, its legs gyrating to propel itself into the current.

Opa stood, dusting his hands upon his bib and tucker. "You may be right, Conrad. A companion just might be the answer to our growing dilemma. Of course, it should not be a grandson who has his own life to live and chores to finish. A *bachelor* grandson, at that." He waved goodbye to the frog. "See, there is still much river to enjoy with only three legs. He may have to swim in circles, but at least he joins the stream."

"Your wisdom is definitely your own, Opa." Rad laughed, acknowledging one of his grandfather's many gifts. The old man could utter something so profound, Rad and the people of the community spent weeks discussing its truth. Yet, in the same breath, Opa's impish humor would flare, causing them to question his good sense.

Opa sighed loudly, almost deliberately. "I wonder if there is a three-legged lady frog somewhere?"

Rad thumbed up his hat. "We are not going to talk about that, Grandfather. I've told you—"

"And I have told you that we came to America to give our family the right to freedom. We have that freedom now, and we own land to leave as a legacy. But we have no family to give these precious things to." Opa's voice boomed over the countryside. "I am an old man. Supplying the family is your obligation. Let the next generation of Wagners take root in America, I say."

Arguing would get them nowhere. They had traveled this path of disagreement many times since arriving in New Genesis. Needing to walk off some of the tension building inside him, Rad suggested they head back to town. Perhaps a change of subject would smooth Opa's ruffled feathers. "Gertrude still needs milking, Grandfather. Her mood will be as sour as her milk if I do not relieve her soon."

"Then I will walk with you, but do not let your mood sour as well."

"Do you see a frown?" Rad suspected his grandfather knew him far too well.

"That is not the face of a happy man." Opa fell in step beside him. "Do not be such a sly fox. All I ask is that you choose a bride and give me great-grandchildren to bounce upon my knee while it can still bounce."

"Opa, you're as powerful as that beer you brew. It is your memory that needs strengthening." The words exited Rad's mouth without thought. The moment they were out, he wished he could take them back. He and his grandfather had talked about many things, but they always managed to skirt the issue of his declining mental capabilities.

Rad immediately changed the subject. "I've already told you, I will not choose a bride. The one I want is already taken."

"Unhappy is the bee that searches only one field for his pollen." Opa rattled off one of the many pieces of advice he offered to whoever would listen.

"But successful is the bee who searches the fields to find the one special blossom that will yield the perfect pollen.

How much sweeter the honey that comes from such patience," Rad countered.

Opa laughed and nodded in approval. "Who made you such a wise man, Conrad Wagner?"

"A very smart old relative of mine."

"This smart old relative is someone you love?"

Rad nodded. "Dearly."

"Do you trust him?"

"Where is this leading, Opa?"

"If you love and trust this relative and consider him wise, then I should think you would consider his advice worth following."

"What advice have you given that I have not taken?" Rad helped Opa up the steep incline, surprised that his elder reached the top of the hill with little effort.

"Let me remember. The first time was when I told you not to pull your swaddling off when you were outside near an ant bed. The second was to make certain you wipe the crumbs you drop in front of the cookie crock you pillaged. Then there was—"

"I meant this decade, Opa." His grandfather may have not lost long-ago memories—only recent ones.

"I *advise* you to hire me a companion—someone to stay with me while you work." Opa's reply was more command than suggestion.

Rad began to walk, lengthening his strides as if they could carry him away from the confrontation he felt brewing. Frustration swelled inside him and vented itself in a single word, "No."

"We have the money. You need the time. You cannot keep chasing me every time you think I do not have my full wits. Now, quit walking and talk to me."

Stomping to a halt, Rad attempted to keep the dual emotions, half resentment, half frustration, from his tone. "Opa, *I* will take care of you. You are *my* responsibility."

"Pride will snip your roots, boy. Of course you can take

care of me. But it would be easier if you had someone to help you. I would be happier if I had someone to listen to me rattle. You are not the most talkative *Deutscher* I have known."

Rad smiled despite his irritation. "No, I'm not, but then, no one enjoys conversation better than you, Opa. I'm not sure there is anyone here in Texas—maybe even in all the American states—who can match you. Speak to *me*, Grandfather. I will talk back to you as much as possible."

"Such words, such words, you flattery cat," Opa challenged. "I don't want you talking *back* to me. I need someone to talk *to* me. To tell me where my best patch of mint grows when I forget. What you need is time to get things done. I can give that to you if you don't have to run all over the countryside, worried about me."

"But, Opa—"

The old man raised one palm, commanding Rad's silence. "Enough. So shall it be."

His grandfather had used the biblical phrase all his life to signal the end of a discussion and the unalterable choice he made. Rad began to brood.

"I will see this done now," Opa reiterated.

"But what about Gertrude?" Perhaps he could delay the choosing of a companion until his grandfather forgot about wanting one.

"The milking can wait. Clabber has its worth." Opa's shoulders suddenly slumped, and one eye peeked at Rad, the pitiful expression etching the elderly man's face almost comical. "Of course, you do not have to go along, Grandson. Perhaps I will find my way, perhaps I will not."

"You are a stubborn old kettle." Rad gave in to his grandfather's wishes, deciding he would save time by taking him to town rather than arguing. When Ash Wagner made up his mind about something, Rad knew there would be no changing it. All his life the beloved elder had to bow low with hat in hand before a greedy and eccentric Prussian monarch. He'd vowed that in America no one would tell him what he could and could not do.

New Genesis lay two miles away. A full winter's worth of pent-up energy had unleashed itself upon the natural grasses. For every fragile root basking in the coming spring, weeds threatened to block the sunlight. Delicate pink petals floated upon the air currents.

"The blossoms...they are already falling." Opa reached out to catch one in his palm. "The peaches have set. This is good."

"They'll be double or—if we're lucky—triple in size within weeks." Anticipation of the fruit's early arrival eased the memory of the poor crop suffered the previous year by all the German settlements in Texas. "Now we can have something more than corn and sugarcane to eat. I hear they are even planting wheat in New Braunfels."

"Peaches grow strong in Texas," Opa reminded Rad. "The Society has kept records since 'twenty-six. The corn fails, but peaches rarely flounder. This is what you know, this is what you do."

Soon rooftops came into sight. Pride filled Rad as they approached the community stretching out on the plain before him. Gently rising hills formed a boundary on the south. All the streets crossed at right angles. Most of the houses were made of log or stone. A fence enclosed each one, a tradition inherent to Rad's ancestry and established here in the new country as well.

Gold rushers passing through to California often complimented the people of New Genesis about the beauty of the hamlet and its frame houses in such rugged territory. Chalets in the fatherland might have been more colorfully painted, but the cedars surrounding the Comal and Guadalupe rivers offered timber that knew no equal in Germany. The borders along the homes' rooflines and shutters curled and looped as if the wood had taken such shape naturally.

Rad's gaze searched for only one, the freshly painted three-story home rising stately above all others. With the sweat of his brow and the strength of his back, he had felled every cedar in its walls. Opa had planted each flower and shrub that graced its fenced lawn.

America kept its promise to the Wagners and gave them a home worth keeping. They would have been happy with only that parcel of land, but the Society had granted them the farmland outside of town as well. Farmland on which to grow peaches and raise bees. Life in New Genesis, Texas, America, held many promises for him and Opa.

Though barely three years old, New Genesis boasted ready-made clothing shops, dispensed saddles and harnesses, cotton and silk goods. Stores sold implements and all manner of food and sundries. As one of the last stops before heading into uncharted territory between Texas and California, New Genesis provided plenty of opportunities to work. A man could easily find employment. Rad jokingly called them jobs for "er" men—carpenters, shoemakers, tailors, butchers, bakers, and others.

Still, Rad enjoyed growing his own "er" titles—peach farmer and beekeeper. Nothing seemed as satisfying as working with his hands to make food enjoyed by his compatriots.

Someone waved from the porch of the apothecary. Rad waved back. The man motioned them toward him.

Opa shielded the sun from his eyes. "Who are you waving at?"

"Gunnar Williams. It seems he wants us to stop and speak to him."

"He wants to know if his mare will foal this season. I have told him twice it will not be so. Still, he asks me. Why ask my advice if he does not listen?"

"Some people want to believe only what they wish for, Grandfather."

"This is true."

As they approached the apothecary, the ruddy-cheeked man stepped off the porch and rushed to Opa. His dark hair and black eyes looked more Russian than German, but Rad supposed the rotund man's features were from his mother's heritage rather than his German father's.

"Ash, it is so good to see you this morning. I wonder if I might ask you—"

Opa placed a hand upon the man's shoulder and shook his head sadly. "Gunnar, you are spitting against the wind. I have checked your Brunhilda's droppings. There will be no foal this spring. I shall prepare a potion. Add some portulaca. Perhaps next year she will be better suited."

"Thank you, Ash." Gunnar half bowed before Opa.

The old man refused such gratitude. "No man bows to another in America. This is our new motherland. We are to help our neighbors. I will help you."

Embarrassment stained Gunnar's cheeks. "I appreciate your help, good *Freund*, but if I might express another concern? My wife, Lucia, she has lost her mother's embroidered handkerchief. She cannot find it and is near hysterical from grief. It is all she has left—a gift her father gave her mother on their wedding day. I cannot soothe her. Can you help me, please?"

Rad stood behind Opa and shook his head, silently asking Gunnar not to encourage his grandparent to use the "gift" granted him more by the community than by the Almighty. The townspeople relied on Opa for *Handauflegung*, the laying on of hands. Rad had enough experience with his grandfather not to scoff at that particular talent. But expecting him to believe his Opa could find lost items, or predict the weather or the future was asking too much of anyone. Only Betina Bram didn't scorn Rad for his skepticism.

"Give our blessings to Lucia, Gunnar. But I'm afraid Opa and I must—"

"Tell her to seek comfort in the Book of Psalms," Opa interrupted. "She will find peace there."

"She would rather find the handkerchief." Gunnar ran a hand through his hair, his face carved into a mask of concern.

"She will, if she will look in Psalms. That's where Lucia left it so she would not lose the treasure," Opa insisted. "Again you ask. Again you do not believe."

Gunnar sped away. Rad watched Opa's expression and couldn't quite tell if this was another of his grandfather's embellished tales or truth. "Opa, is it really there?"

"I made you believe it was, did I not?"

"Well, anything is possible," Rad admitted. "But—"

"Gunnar needed to believe it is not lost. If they can believe, then they will find it. Now, let us go to the Reinharts."

"The widows?" A sense of foreboding prickled the hair at the back of Rad's neck. "Which one will you ask to be your companion . . . Albertine or Fredericka?"

"I was thinking more of their niece."

2

"We must hurry, Betina. Daylight has broken. I don't know how much longer Opa will wait for us." Toya wound the rawhide around her waist twice and tied it to the bucket.

Betina's eyes rounded as she puzzled over her friend's strange actions. "What are you doing?"

"As Opa says, we're given choices so we might do more. If the waterwheel cannot turn, then I'll try another way."

"Such a mind you have, Toya Reinhart. And a stubborn one at that. Why not ask someone's help? Like Herr Ludwig's . . . or I'm sure Conrad Wagner would lend a hand."

Never Conrad. Toya shook her head adamantly, quickly dismissing that possibility. His sheer appearance would present a danger more imminent to Toya than any she might find at the well. Just thinking about him made her skin heat. As far as asking anyone else to help, there was no need. "I am capable of this simple task, aren't I?"

Betina watched as Toya tied the rope to the yardarm, then around her waist, then finally about her wrist. "Nothing I can say will stop you from proving it to me, I can see. What is your plan?"

"I'll anchor the rope so it won't slip out of my hands. Now grab the bucket and tie the other end of the rope to it."

"This is not good, Toya," Betina warned. "What if—"

"You fret too much, *Kumpan*. Now, will you help or not?"

"All right." Betina sighed, resigned to this new adventure Toya was bent on having. Still, what were friends for but to laugh over mistakes made together? "I do not have a good feeling about this. Remember the last time you said we could handle anything we set our minds to? I ended up with chicken feathers and molasses in my hair for weeks!"

"This is different. It's only a bucket and a rope."

"And you, my friend, are too daring for your own good."

"Complain *after* I've failed . . . then I will feel justly disgraced."

"I waste my words again." Betina did as instructed and knotted the rope around the bucket handle . . . twice. As she worked, the day Toya left Germany flashed through her mind. Food was scarce and the sugar in the cookies a prized delicacy. Toya had selflessly given Betina what might have been one of her own family's few meals for the voyage to America. From that day since, through feathers and fun, she'd given Toya her undivided loyalty.

"Ready?" Toya checked the knot securing the rope to her waist, then the two Betina had fashioned.

Betina shook her head. "But when has that ever stopped you?" Toya was never easily deterred. She would sacrifice her own happiness and welfare for others—even a foolish pledge made to her twin—if Betina couldn't find a way to stop her. Now her friend's desire to stall the wedding confirmed Betina's greatest fear—Toya would forfeit the rest of her life to a man she didn't love. Yet Betina realized she, of all people, had no right to interfere. Not after what she had done.

Toya grinned. "You worry too much."

"And you too little."

As Toya lowered the bucket over the well's rim, her gaze suddenly focused on a point in the distance. "Someone is coming. Perhaps you will have your help after all. Can you tell who it is?"

Betina glanced to make certain her friend was handling her task easily. Toya bent at the waist over the well's rim. Assured, Betina walked a few yards away, then shielded the sun from her eyes. "It is too far. Just two men—one small, one large."

"Help, Betina! I'm falling!" Toya shrieked.

Startled, Betina swung around. Toya had lost the precarious balance on her tiptoes, pulled down by the weight of the full bucket.

"The rope is twisted around my wrist!" Toya screamed. Her body slid forward.

Betina rushed to the well, grabbing Toya at the hips and locking her legs around Toya's. The momentum continued despite their efforts.

Toya braced her hands against the stone walls. Her palms skidded across one stone, two ... then caught.

"Hold still, Toya. Do not move. Do not even breathe." Betina whispered words of encouragement to her friend, wishing for once she were the stronger of the two women. "Now, inch backward if you can. One hand at a time. *Ja ... ja ...* just like that. Slowly ... slo—"

"Nooo!" Toya's cry echoed off the stone as her hands slipped on the slimy surface. One leg slid from Betina's brace, then the other.

Grabbing for handfuls of skirt, Betina willed the material not to rip. Both their bodies trembled now with sheer effort.

Suddenly, Betina remembered. The two men. Could they hear her?

"Help!" Betina shouted. "Please help us! Toya is in tr—trou—*Schwierigkeiten*!"

"Don't let me fall." Toya's voice sounded uncustomarily timid. "I promise if you hang on, I'll never do anything like this again."

"If you go, we both go," Betina assured her, then tried to ease the moment. "I intend to see you keep that promise."

Terror flooded Toya as she prayed. If only someone would hear . . . Perspiration dampened her hands, forcing Toya to dig her fingertips into the uneven surface of rock. Her arms and shoulders quivered. Her dress began to rip at the waist.

"Pull backward, Toya!" Betina cried, her fingers grabbing more skirt. "Help me help you!"

Toya exhaled a long breath, afraid even that might upset her balance. "I am such a rattlehead. I never listen." *Poor Aunt Fred and Aunt Albert. To lose us both.* Grief for her twin, Tilly, sprang to mind as Toya squeezed her eyes shut, bracing herself against impact. She pictured the broken waterwheel hanging uselessly from the well's overhead brace. Could it offer a solution to her predicament? "Can you loosen your hold long enough to—"

"No!" Betina cried. "I can do no such thing."

"—grab the rope?" Dizziness overtook Toya, a kaleidoscope of stars sparking in front of her eyes. She blinked. "Perhaps it will hold my weight."

"Or finish breaking. Whatever you do, Toya Reinhart, do not move. Do not plan! Do not dare do anything but listen to me." Impending doom resounded from Betina's voice. "Oh, where is Peter when we need him! Help us, someone. Please, help us!"

Moments ticked by. Toya's head felt as if it were getting lighter. The rope cut deeply into her wrist.

"Toya, are you all right? Toya? Answer me, *Kumpan*! Oh, thank *Gott,* Conrad. Opa. How glad I am to see you!"

The sound of relief in Betina's tone sent hope surging through Toya. Conrad! Of all who might come to her rescue . . . dear, beloved Conrad would be the one!

"Move, Betina," Conrad commanded. "Let me brace my legs around her. Opa, you get on the left side. Betina, you grab the rope so the weight will quit cutting into her wrist."

"No, we will lose her if we change places," Betina insisted. "Just—"

"You must trust me not to let that happen."

"Do as he says, Betina." Toya tried to sound braver than she felt. "It is the only way."

The transfer took place, sending petticoats cascading over Toya's head. Two iron bands seized her waist, pulling hard. Toya jerked backward, her arms flailing at her skirt as she tried to see. Suddenly, Conrad's chest pressed warmly . . . securely . . . against her back.

"*Danke,* Conrad! *Danke schön!*" Betina offered a string of German praises.

Conrad waited for Betina to catch her breath. "Will you fetch her aunts?"

"*Ja, ja.*" Betina nodded, then took off toward the house.

"Opa, will you . . . ? Now, where did he go?" After a second to scan the direction the old man had taken, Rad's voice filled with relief, "One step ahead of Betina, it seems."

Toya slumped backward, fighting to control the quaking of her body. Her head rested in the crook of Conrad's neck as she lingered against the haven of his broad shoulders. For just a moment . . . this one moment . . . she would seek the comfort of his strength.

Embarrassment flared across her skin as she realized her thoughts now focused on how well his body fit hers instead of thanking him for saving her life! Suddenly, Conrad gently nudged her around and pulled the length of her body against his. His heart beat strong and sure, urging hers to match its rhythm.

"Calm yourself, Toya. I am here."

His whispered words of concern brushed warmly against the top of her head, sending a shiver of sensations down the length of Toya's body. She leaned into him, gripping the front of his chambray shirt and allowing a closeness she'd given no other but him in three years. For the first time in a long while, she felt protected and small.

"Your hair smells of sunshine," he whispered.

She closed her eyes and drank in his own curious scent, a fruity blend of peaches, honey and the earth—the scent that had captivated her since an unforgettable kiss that even years of grieving for her sister had not diminished.

"Conrad . . ." Toya exhaled the name that had filled her dreams every night since that fateful kiss.

"I am here, *Liebling*." The endearment exited in a husky rumble as if it were a never-ending oath.

"Conrad Wagner, you good man," Aunt Fredericka announced as she, Albertine, and Betina rushed from the house. "What we now owe you we can never repay."

Toya forced her eyes open, taking in the sight of temptation standing before her. "G-good morning," she stammered.

"*Guten Morgen, Fraulein.*" Rad Wagner's face lit with a grin that could stretch from Galveston to New Genesis.

Fire spread through Toya in the wake of Rad's blue gaze. His examination went from the top of her head to her shoes. He had seen beneath her petticoats—held her in places no man had ever touched. All that mattered now was that the near spill had left her strawberry-blond curls disheveled and her dress torn. Thank heavens she had twisted the bulk of her waist-length hair into a braid, or it might have looked like a mat of straw.

"Your eyes are lovelier each time I see them," he whispered so the others wouldn't hear. "As green as the mint along the river."

Perhaps if he concentrated on her eyes he would forget other things he had seen. "Don't, Rad," she whispered, torn between the desire he stirred within her and the promise she and Peter had made to Tilly. Though her heart thrilled at Rad's compliment, everyone knew she had given her word to marry another. She must continue to deny the attraction that had grown between her and Rad since their first meeting.

The women rushed forward. Her aunts patted her to see if she was, indeed, safe from the near disaster. Betina attempted to straighten Toya's hair, running her fingers through the tangles.

Grateful for a chance to compose herself, Toya deliberately laughed to set them all at ease. "I am fine. A bit ragged and scuffed, but I'll live to draw water another day." The scrapes did not hurt her half as much as having to ignore Rad's gentle touch. "In fact, it was rather exciting."

Rad reached down to pick up his hat, dusted it on his pant leg, then set it atop his head. "An excitement I would not care to repeat. But you are safe now."

His gaze swept over her once again, insinuating a sense of caring that almost proved her undoing. The promise made to Tilly came back to haunt Toya. A promise Toya meant to keep.

"You have bloodied your dress, dear heart." Alarm widened Aunt Fred's eyes to gray saucers. She leaned forward and squinted. "Let me see what you have done to yourself."

Toya gently swatted away Fredericka's hand as it tugged at her skirt hem.

"Not now, Fredericka!" Aunt Albert straightened her slim shoulders, patting the braids of salt and pepper hair that covered each ear. Her hazel eyes glowed with pleasure. "We have *visitors*."

"You would not have to look so closely, stubborn one, if you would drink that chamomile and mint I bring you each morning," Opa Wagner announced as he rejoined them.

"Ash, you old beer brine." Fred's gray eyes squinted at him. "Why do you pay another visit this fine morning? You've already been here once."

"I am here to seek a companion."

Betina's hands clapped joyfully. "He comes to pay court."

"Finally." Albertine glared at her sister, her chin lifting in silent challenge. The man had captured both widows' hearts from the moment the trio had met. "We thought you would never identify which of us you prefer."

"There you go again, Albertine, using those high-meadow words." Fredericka brushed braids of gold over her shoulders, making her look more youthful than her fifty years. "If Opa did decide on one of us, he wouldn't be standing there with hat in hand ... would you?" Anticipation rocked her forward and back. "I think he will choose the younger of us."

Betina and Toya shared a look, then chuckled. But Toya noticed Rad did not seem at all amused by his grandfather's predicament.

"You are only a *year* younger, Sister," Albertine reminded Fredericka. "Do not chop the cedar for my coffin yet."

Opa winked at the chubbier of the two. "Both of you ladies would make any man proud to call you wife. But Fred is right. I will announce my choice in my own way."

He grinned at Fred. "I would offer you my finest stein, and let you enjoy its lager. Then I would grab you in my arms and give you such a kiss, you would spend the rest of spring sizzling like the wurst you make on my birthday.''

A fit of girlish giggles shook Fredericka's well-rounded frame. Toya thought her aunt never looked so young and pleased.

Betina moved to stand beside Albertine, offering her silent support.

"And me?" Albertine tried to conceal her envy, but failed. "How would you let me know?"

"You?" The slender man tipped his hat. "Why, I would come calling, Albert. I would wear my best bib and tucker, pick you a bouquet of wildflowers so large, the fragrance would drift clear to Fredericksburg, and spend the night hours dancing in the moonlight."

"Ohh, Opa. You are such a beguiler." Pleasure transformed Albertine's face, smoothing the wrinkles that aged her slim features.

"So which will it be?" Toya and Betina asked in unison.

One aunt would need consoling; the other, anchoring from the headiness Opa brewed as expertly as his *Bier*. Toya stared at the elderly gentleman. The people of New Genesis treasured Ash Wagner. As the oldest survivor of their voyage from the fatherland, his wisdom and knowledge of tradition would always be the community's greatest resource.

Betina tested the name possibilities. "Albertine Wagner, Fredericka Wagner. Both have a fine sound to them."

"He wants you." Rad's soft-spoken reply held an edge as he leveled his stare at Toya.

"Toya?" The aunts' surprise became vocal.

"So it begins," Betina whispered, and slowly separated herself from the others.

Concern enveloped Toya when Betina crossed her arms as if for protection. Why did Betina feel threatened?

"She is too young for you, Opa. *Mein Gott,* Toya is only

twenty!" Fredericka looked at him as if he'd grown six arms.

"Four years younger than your grandson," Albertine scolded. The wrinkles furrowed her face as she frowned in disapproval. "A mere babe."

"A woman," Rad countered, forgetting that all could hear the desire layering his tone.

Passion flared inside Toya, drawing her concern away from her best friend and making her more aware of the effect of Rad's every word. If only Peter could stir her like this.

The town councilman was always off doing his duty for the community. Perhaps she'd just been away from him too long. He'd been in Nassau since September to fetch the new wave of immigrants. She couldn't even remember the color of his eyes.

"My ladies, all is not what it seems." Opa plopped his hat back on his head, looking exceptionally delighted. "An old cook likes to add a bit of spice now and then... to give flavor to his days."

"Opa, you are incorrigible," Rad scolded.

"You are too, Conrad Wagner, for teasing them like that." Toya found her irritation at Rad a welcome respite. Perhaps anger would calm the riot of sensations his closeness created.

Eyes the color of a field of bluebonnets focused on her. Toya longed to walk the meadows of Rad's mind to see what thoughts of her blossomed within.

"He truly wants *you* as his companion. To help him when"—Rad struggled for words—"when I am in the orchard and cannot assist him."

Toya was surprised by his confession that he could not provide his grandfather's every need. Rad's fierce pride was well known among the community. Yet he willingly surrendered it to protect his grandfather. She had always admired Rad for the frugal ways and hard work that made him succeed in the new world where others had not. Her respect for him deepened. Opa's well-being was, clearly, foremost in his heart.

"Someone to reach where these old bones cannot," Opa added. "Someone to test her chili recipe against mine. I will pay you well."

Someone to help him when he loses his way or can't remember. Toya realized what the elderly man refused to say and what Conrad wouldn't. Though she owed Ash for the thousand kindnesses he had extended her aunts, the thought of being in Rad's company day in and day out seemed too risky. What if she couldn't resist the desire he evoked within her?

"I told him Albertine or Fredericka would be a better choice." Rad's features remained stone.

"You did, did you now?" Toya crossed her arms. Aggravation chilled the warmth of Rad's earlier declaration despite the fact that she had just mentally voiced her own assessment of the situation. "We are *all* quite capable."

Opa walked over and gently tilted Albertine's chin. "Do not look so downtrodden, Albert. You would not have me truly choose between you, would you? I select the rose to assure a visit from each honeybee."

"But what of wedding preparations?" Albertine's fists rested against her slim hips as her gaze leveled on Toya. "Didn't Peter's letter say he planned to return in early April? You have three weeks at best."

The wedding! Albertine's favor for the town councilman would not let the preparations go untended. Toya glanced at Rad and could hardly bear the pain of watching him walk away. He moved over to the well and began to repair the broken waterwheel. He still suffered from her refusal of his proposal in favor of marrying Peter Stoltz. Her heart felt as if someone had dropped a weight inside it. Did Rad know how deeply it hurt to have to reject him now as it did on that agonizing day years ago?

Still, it had been the right thing to do. Toya and Peter had promised before Tilly went off into the hills and was lost to them forever that they would fulfill the arranged marriage the twins' father had demanded between Peter and one of his daughters.

"There might not be a wedding," Ash announced. "Especially if word gets around that Rad saw her petticoats."

"Opa!" Rad swung around to face his grandfather. "All of you here know that was merely to keep her from falling. There was no other way."

"Still, there may be talk." Fredericka nodded. "Some will call you hero, others will not."

They were right, Toya realized. In a small town, word got around far too easily . . . even sometimes when seemingly everyone kept quiet. She owed Rad her life. A fact she'd forgotten in the midst of trying to deny her feelings for him. If she refused to help, everyone would think she was afraid to be in his company . . . afraid to be seen with him. If she agreed to help, they would believe she did so out of gratitude for his saving her life.

"This makes no sense," Rad insisted. "Toya is needed here with her aunts. Frau Fredericka's eyesight is—"

"Getting better," Fredericka argued. "And Sister's ailment seems to be less troublesome when Opa comes calling. He needs Toya more than we do, and this will give us reason to visit more often, *ja,* Sister?"

Albertine nodded vigorously. "Indeed it will, young Conrad."

Faced with her aunts' approval and Opa's request, Toya could not graciously decline. "Then I accept, Herr Wagner," she announced, vowing to find ways to be harsh to Rad so he would gladly find someone else to make him happy. She couldn't bear watching him live alone without someone to work alongside him, without children to share his goodness, without someone to love him as he should be loved.

Toya instantly shed the images of another woman holding Rad's babies in her arms. "I will become your companion, Ash. At least for the spring and summer."

"But Herr Stoltz—" Betina objected.

"Will understand that I have a duty to serve the community just as he does," Toya interrupted. "If he can spend months away with his own work, then surely he can wait a few more while I assist Opa."

"That's the spirit," Aunt Fred complimented, wrapping an ample arm around Toya's shoulders. "Make him wait. It is good for the soul and stirs a man's blood."

"Aunt Fred!" Heat fused Toya's cheeks as she noticed the effect of her aunt's words on Rad Wagner. His hands paused at the task of repairing the waterwheel. His back straightened into an immovable wall of granite, and his feet braced apart as if he prepared for a blow. "Peter is not that k-kind of . . ." she stammered. "He does not think of me in that . . . well, he just doesn't."

"A man in love does many things his mind will refuse but his heart commands." Opa smiled at each of the women he courted.

"Perhaps I shall join you and Opa," Betina suggested, her brown gaze shifting from Toya to Rad. "After I close the shop each day."

Rad's strong shoulders and arms flexed as he rotated the now-repaired waterwheel. "That is a good plan, Betina. Opa would appreciate your company . . . as well as Toya's."

While grateful for Betina's offer, conflicting emotions raced through Toya like a runaway team. Betina's presence would provide a buffer to the attraction between Toya and Rad, but it might also place strain upon her and Toya's friendship. Rad and Betina had been spending a great deal of time together lately, causing speculation that the two might be courting each other.

A possibility Toya was uncertain she could embrace.

"There." Rad stepped away from the well, wiping the dust from his hands. "It is finished."

"No, the work has just begun...." Opa offered a wink.

As Opa and Aunt Fred shared a burst of laughter, Rad, Toya, Betina, and Aunt Albert looked on in puzzlement.

3

Toya ran a hand over her dress to ease any remaining wrinkles. There had been no time to iron the garment.

Betina stood behind her friend and shared a glance in the mirror. "The calico matches your eyes. The choice, it is good. He will admire your beauty."

"Opa is interested in the way I cook, not in my elegance." Though she avoided the truth, Toya silently chided herself for her vanity. She should be trying to discourage Rad, not attempting to look her best for him.

He seemed impatient to be on his way and now stood leaning against the fence with his arms crossed over his chest. While Betina thanked Fred and Albert for allowing her to spend the night, Toya grabbed the basket sitting on the rocker beside the door. Rad frowned at the bags of spice bulging over the basket's sides.

"We are only a few streets away. There will be enough food for three or four. You need bring no meal."

"These are my seasonings for chili. I thought Opa, Betina, and I could spend the afternoon cooking a batch for both families."

Excitement spurred Opa's steps as he hurried to see the contents. "My kettle is yours, Toya. Perhaps your secret herb will add flavor to its texture."

"And perhaps you will share the many secrets your kettle has known with a willing and adoring apprentice." Toya and the elderly gentleman were fierce competitors in their effort to be known as the best chili cook in all of Texas—an honor widely respected by all.

Betina laughed. "Two cooks in one cauldron. I am not sure this is a wise decision I have made . . . to share these evenings with the both of you."

"Opa. Gertrude will be sour as old dough," Rad insisted, opening the gate to leave. "We must go now, or she will not share with us this day or any other."

"*Ja, ja,* Grandson." Opa doffed his hat to the aunts and bid each good-bye. "Come see me tonight, ladies. The moon will be full. Let us put it to good use . . . *ja*?"

Toya and Betina hurried down the porch steps to follow the men. They caught Opa with easy strides but trailed Rad by a great length. "Is this Gertrude someone I have not met?" Toya asked her friends. "A sister . . . a cousin?" Another possibility made her stare at Rad's retreating form and wish that the idea had not occurred to her. "A friend?"

"She is the new milker brought up from Austin." Amusement filled Betina's tone.

Opa grinned. "Your curiosity is udderly unnecessary."

"You clever cat." She winked and returned his teasing. "I understood . . . *purrfectly.*"

Toya took a deep breath and filled her lungs with the warm, moist air of the early Texas spring. As they made their way down the lane shaded by live oaks and cedar, she scanned the rich farmland and green fields surrounding the hamlet and thought New Genesis one of the prettiest towns in all of the Republic. Rows of homes and various businesses lined the streets with progress hard won by the town's settlers.

Rad halted and waited for them to catch up. He pointed to a huge hole in the street. "Watch your step, Opa... ladies."

The old man shooed his grandson away. "Mind your orchard, Conrad. The *Frauleins* shall keep me from stumbling."

"See that you mind them." Rad walked on ahead.

"I plan to. Good fortune shines upon us this day." Opa smiled at the women. "I am honored, ladies. Do not think my grandson's face is always so pinched. When he does not get his way, he puckers like a prune. Soon he will see this is all for the best. He carries too much on his shoulders. They are big, *ja,* but even big can bend beneath the Texas wind." Opa veered to the right.

"Where are we going?" Toya pointed in the direction Rad had taken. "Shouldn't we follow your grandson?"

"Oh, Ash, Ash Wagner, is that you I see?" A woman with red hair spied him from the mercantile three doors away. "I have to discuss something with you. And *now*!"

Opa's gait became a lope. "*Nein.* Steer me away from that tattle-mouthed waggle-bottom. She is nothing but an old buzzard looking for new kill."

Betina giggled. "She does tend to gossip."

"Ash! Ash Wagner! Where are you going? Can you not see me?" the woman hailed.

"How could I not see her?" Opa whispered. "Her broad shadow could block the noon sun."

"Perhaps Fraulein Pyrtle needs to tell you something important." Toya ran to keep up with the older man's pace. She glanced back and noticed the red-haired woman stamping after them like an enraged bull.

"Ash Wagner! Toya Reinhart! Betina Bram! Are you all deaf? Do not walk so fast. I cannot catch you! Conrad, stop your grandfather, please! I must speak to him."

Opa halted, making the women sidestep to keep from running over him. Toya stumbled and fell into the dirt.

Betina reached out to help her. Merchants hawking their wares in front of their businesses rushed toward the women.

Opa's mouth twisted to one side as he whispered, "I am sorry, but the woman is like a pesky flea that keeps biting. If she cannot bite quick enough, then she arms herself with someone who can." A glance at Rad's long strides clarified the woman's ally. "Even if my legs sprouted spokes, I could not outrun my grandson." His lopsided grin broadened. "Though I try at times."

"See what Lineva wants," Rad insisted as he caught up with them. "She will hound you until you do."

Many in the community were equally curious to discover why the woman demanded Opa's time. The smithy let loose his bellows, wiped the soot on his apron, and headed over to join the ever-growing crowd of onlookers.

Betina gathered the basket's spilled contents. "Lucky that you had these spices tied in kerchiefs, or you would have to replace them."

Rad bent to help Betina. When their hands accidentally touched, she blushed, deepening the dusky rose of her cheeks. Betina's dark curls and brown eyes made her a rare beauty among the fair-haired community. Irritation, and another emotion Toya refused to acknowledge, inspired her to complete the task. "Here, let me help. Should you not see to your Gertrude?"

"By all means, let us be on our way," Opa insisted. "You have much to do, Grandson."

Lineva Pyrtle adjusted her shirtwaist as she attempted to calm her breathing. She straightened the fancy feathered bonnet perched atop her red curls. "Wellll . . . I must say, you all were in quite a hurry."

"I have been all morning." Rad's gaze slanted to his grandfather. "And now it seems my grandfather has caught my fever."

Toya fidgeted, knowing her rescue had caused him the delay. Rad Wagner was known for his dedication to his

A TASTE OF HONEY 37

orchard and bees. By now he must be an hour or more off schedule.

Opa used his grandson's impatience to his advantage. "As much as I would love to stop and blub—I mean *chat,* Lineva, I, too, have chores that must be done."

"We are all quite busy, Fraulein Pyrtle," Toya insisted. Had Opa done something to deserve Lineva's scorn? Toya's gaze met Opa's. To his credit, he did not turn away, but the continuous quirk that lifted one corner of his lips, and the twinkle in his eye, hinted he was blameworthy of something.

"Well then, I shall be brief." Lineva's dark eyes focused on the elder Wagner. "Did you leave that hymnal on the rocker outside my doorway this morning?"

Speculation rippled through the crowd, fueled by snickers and clucks of disapproval. Everyone in New Genesis knew Lineva refused to use a hymnal when they sang during church services or the singing festivals held by the local German settlements. The woman never got the words right. Gentle reminders had been met with the fierce declaration that she knew every word by heart! A voice as strong and out of alignment as Lineva Pyrtle's had become quite an annoyance to a community that prided itself on harmony.

Had Opa taken fate into his own hand and done what no other townsman dared? Toya wondered. Was this his way of making Lineva understand she needed to refresh her memory of the words if New Genesis ever hoped to score first place in the *Sängerfests*? Some of the community loved Opa for his eccentricity, while others thought him one button loose. There would be no walking the middle road on this issue.

"Me?" Opa's mouth rounded in shocked denial. "I was down at the river... fishing... er... frogging, *ja,* Conrad?"

"That is where I found him."

"All morning?" Lineva flashed Conrad a look so cold, it would send Satan to fetch an overcoat.

Toya glanced from grandson to grandfather and suspected that while Rad would not lie for Opa, he might not have told the entire truth.

"I saw him at the Reinharts' long before dawn!" roared the smithy. His stout arms and brawny shoulder span defied anyone to oppose his claim. "He took Fredericka her morning dosage."

"He visited the Weiss family not long after that, I am certain." The baker pointed to the house on the knoll. "He gave cookies to the Meinaur children. I saw them swap a glass of milk for the treats."

"All of that is true," Opa admitted. "And I was there when Rad saved Toya from drowning."

Every eye focused on Toya. Murmurs echoed over the street.

"Opa," Betina muttered. "You were not to tell any—"

"It was nothing." Toya waved off their concern, not allowing Betina to finish the admonishment. "The rope slipped. I fell. Herr Wagner caught me. That is all . . . nothing more, nothing less."

"Just how did he do this? Surely, he was not in the well below you. How could he catch you?" Lineva spiced the curiosity stirring the crowd.

"Pulled her up by her pantaloons," Opa boasted.

Lineva gasped, looking at Toya as if she were dressed in scarlet and showing her ankles. "He saw beneath your petticoats? What scandal!"

One of Opa's eyes closed as he glared at Lineva. "None frillier than those that hang on your line, Lineva."

For the first time since the crowd gathered, Lineva was speechless.

"Come, Opa. We leave Fraulein Pyrtle to her pondering." Rad's glare defied every rebuff. "Toya's skirts hanging about her head while she fell is no offense. If Lineva had been in the same predicament, I would have pulled her up by her thighs as well."

"He touched her thighs!" Lineva closed her eyes as if Toya stood naked in front of her. "And he called her *Toya*."

Rad gripped his grandfather's arm. "We have better things to do than listen to this narrow-mindedness. Should I have let Toya drown for propriety's sake?"

"A marriage should commence!" Lineva's bonnet bobbed with the lift of her chin.

The baker added his agreement. Townspeople who gathered around them murmured opinions of what should be done about the compromising situation.

"Nothing happened." Toya looked at Betina for support. Strangely, her friend remained quiet, not defending Toya. But Toya had no time to mull over Betina's lack of response. Lineva was like a dog nipping at her heels with reproach.

"Then why are you with them?" Lineva persisted. "Have you forgotten you are to be married to Herr Stoltz? He would not approve of your being in the Wagners' company."

"I am to marry Peter." Toya's gaze locked with the belligerent woman's. "But I may choose whom I will and will not befriend. For your information, I am to be Opa's companion while Conrad deals with his peach crop. That, Fraulein Pyrtle, will require me to accompany them a great deal."

"Do your aunts approve?" someone asked.

"It is good Toya can help Conrad in his hour of need." Betina placed a hand upon her best friend's shoulder, finally offering her allegiance. "*Ja*, the widows gave their blessings."

"Quite questionable to work for one man who wishes to marry her while accepting the allotment of yet another to whom she is pledged," the banker interjected.

A division of alliances parted the crowd as if Moses had waved his staff.

"This is not for us to judge." The minister frowned at the growing dissension among the townspeople.

"Enough!" Rad's demand silenced even the loudest among them. "Toya has agreed to work side by side with my grandfather. Betina will also help when the business at her dress shop allows her extra time. That is all that needs to be remembered here. Worry your own troubles. I shall take care of mine."

"But will Fraulein Reinhart remember her pledge to Peter Stoltz?" Lineva's fists rested against her expansive hips. "Will he believe this is only a show of gratitude?"

"Do not concern yourself over this matter, Lineva." Rad deliberately moved alongside Toya. "Peter is a reasonable man. Toya will see the pledge is kept."

As will you. Toya noted the grim determination setting Rad's jaw. There was nothing Rad Wagner allowed to go unfinished. That would include seeing she kept her word to the councilman . . . even if it broke both their hearts.

The knowledge tasted caustic in her mouth and, for a moment she wished Rad would kiss her to take away the stain of bitterness. To chase away the clouds forming in the sky overhead and return the sunshine. To make her forget that she'd pledged her body to one man, when her soul belonged to another.

4

"Looks like I'm to have woman trouble this day." Rad eyed the cow's swishing pendulum of a tail. Morning grew old, and Gertie was in no mood to be sociable. Her bawling warned she would not take kindly to his ill humor. "Easy, Gertie. Easy now, girl. Perhaps you will calm yourself and help me decide what I'm to do about"—he glanced through the stable doors—"*her*."

Toya attentively followed Opa as he proudly showed her his herb garden.

Whom was he fooling? Since the moment he first saw her he knew there was something special about Toya. Wondrous green eyes that laughed, opinions that challenged, and a will that dared to live life fully.

He'd watched her for years, discovering that though she was kind and gentle, Toya was also proud and inquisitive about the world around her. Few could sway her mind. She had views about life and her place within it, often voicing them without considering the repercussions. The stunning beauty played and teased but did so within the bounds of their strict German edicts. She rarely completed any project—an idleness foreign to Rad—yet she never failed to lend a hand to begin one.

Even her way of walking defied convention, taunting a man. She was all woman, his Toya, with an inexhaustible curiosity and an unwavering sense of loyalty.

His Toya? She would never be his now. If only he hadn't kissed her. Held her in his arms. For it was then that Rad realized he had been wishing for her, wanting her, waiting for her all his life. And now he knew the true depth of his loss. If only she hadn't promised to marry Peter.

One of Opa's proverbs diverted Rad's musings. *Busy hands occupy the mind.* Gratefully, Rad set himself to work to keep his thoughts away from Toya and what could never be. He apologized to the guernsey for the delay, grabbing the milk bucket and stool from the shelf.

A quick survey assured him the leather and metal harnesses hung in the tack room at the rear of the stable, shined or oiled as needed. Laying hens clucked and cooed, the fat biddies happy with their choice nesting perches. Though the pitchfork still balanced in the haystack where Rad left it, he had finished the mucking of the stable and henhouse before discovering Opa's disappearance. Everything else in the outbuilding behind their chalet remained orderly. Decay would never find a foothold there.

After placing the stool next to Gertie's flank, Rad rubbed his palms together briskly to warm them. He sat, leaned his left cheek against Gertrude's warm belly, then gently grabbed two of the cow's bulging teats. A soft moo greeted his practiced efforts as dual streams of fresh warm milk swish-swished into the bucket.

A soft roll of thunder echoed over the prairie, bringing with it a slight breeze that blew into the barn. The fragrance of wet grass and earth permeated the air, making the hay in the loft smell even sweeter.

As Rad concentrated on relieving Gertrude, the rhythm of the rain lulled him. Despite his efforts to keep his mind away from Toya, he could not. For when he allowed himself to be distracted, she inevitably filled his every thought.

She had chosen wisely, he realized. Peter Stoltz seemed the perfect man for her. He was the son of a well-respected family, dedicated to the welfare of the townspeople . . . and handsome and charming. The press of Gertie's soft belly against Rad's cheek reminded him that his own features were rougher than thistle, and he had as much charm as a badger.

Trouble was, Rad liked Peter. Peter Stoltz was a loyal son to his father, a man who earned his own way and helped the community he lived in. A gentleman with a code of honor that would never cause his loved ones disgrace. There didn't seem anything wrong with Toya's husband-to-be.

Peter just wasn't right for Toya. She needed someone to remain by her side, not wander all over the world. She needed someone to safeguard her when she became too daring, to prevent her curiosity from overshadowing good judgment, to show her that love could be a lot more than simply a promise kept.

Gertrude turned her head and stared at Rad. "Mooo. . . ."

"I hear you." He accepted her criticism as if the guernsey had access to his thoughts. "And, *ja*, I think I am the man she needs. I would love her and understand her. I would let her flit about as she chooses, but when she needs a steadying hand, I would offer that too. Just as I did at the well."

The rhythm of Rad's hands increased, trying to work through the tension that now gripped him. Until that morning when Toya leaned back into his arms and he felt the firebolt of longing that swept through them both, he had not known his sense of honor could falter. Until then he had never known his desire for her could not be mastered by the strength of his resolve. And until then he had never once doubted that he would help Toya keep her pledge to Peter.

He wanted to be the man to stoke her passions and watch her soul glow in his arms.

The fine hair on the back of his neck rose and prickled. Someone watched. Rad glanced at the open door and saw that Toya, Opa, and Betina must have gone inside the main house to get out of the rain. Gertrude mooed again.

"You are right, Gertie. As Opa says, I'm being addle-brained. Is it only wishful thinking when I sense she watches me?"

"Who's watching you?" a voice asked from the doorway.

Even before his eyes lifted to focus on the emerald depth of her gaze, he knew Toya had heard the words meant for no one. An orange-striped feline chose that moment to uncurl from its morning nap atop the hay. Meowing loudly, it stretched, then began to rub its length against Rad's leg, arching its back in a request to be petted.

"Uhh . . . Monarch, my cat. She is always watching me," he evaded. "Waiting for me to leave Gertie or the milk pail unattended. She expects the guernsey to nurse her if I am not alert."

"Need help?" Toya stepped closer. "Betina and Opa are cooking up something for lunch. They sent me out here to see if there was enough milk collected to take them back a pail."

Rad stared at her, then swiftly focused on the business at hand. The image of Toya's rain-soaked curves molded itself into his memory. "I am almost finished."

"Surely that will do. It's nearly full."

Her voice grew closer, and he could feel her body heat behind him. A shiver swept through Rad. "*Nein*, I must fill it completely."

"But you'll catch cold," she insisted. "The rain has made it chilly in here. See, you're trembling."

Cold was the last thing he felt with her standing so near. A wildfire the size of Texas blazed through him, initiating the shiver of attraction he could not conceal.

"If you're too stubborn to listen to good sense, at least let me help you." Toya bent beside him and reached for a teat.

"Be gentle or she'll balk. Here, let me take away the chill before you touch her." He guided Toya's hands to his face and warmed them with his breath.

Green eyes stared apologetically, then lit with a spark of adventure. "I've never done this before. We buy our milk from Opa, you know."

"I know," he whispered as if it were a great secret they shared. Rad always made certain the Reinharts received the thickest cream and the sweetest milk of the day. How young she looked now, all wide-eyed and excited at the prospect of learning something new. A longing to kiss her full lips consumed him.

"Will it hurt?"

Nein, *it will be the purest pleasure,* his heart answered silently. Then he realized she meant something entirely different. Why was it that every time he shared Toya's company, he became a dreamer instead of a doer? "Will what hurt?"

"Pulling on her like that. You do that quite well, and it seems... I mean, she must enjoy your hands on..." Toya's cheeks blushed a becoming shade of rose. "I do not wish to hurt her."

Rad laughed, needing the merriment to relieve his building tension. "You won't, *Liebling.* I will show you how. Easy, Gertie, easy, girl. Our friend Toya wants to comfort you this fine morning." He nodded at Toya. "Now, come sit in front of me. *Nein,* face the same direction I am. *Ja,* like that."

Her back settled against him, pressing against his chest, molding her form to his until he thought he would die from the sheer heaven of it all. The scent of her hair wafted through his senses, reminding him of wildflowers and soap. "W-when you feel comfortable with what you are doing, I will move away and let you milk her on your own."

She half turned, causing her lips to brush against his cheek. "Now what?"

Now what, indeed. *Concentrate, man, or you will embarrass yourself.* "Put your hands where mine are."

"Like this?" She continued to look at him with inquisitive eyes.

He swallowed back a lump of desire that rose from his core and threatened to knot in his throat. "You must pay close attention to where your hands touch if you want Gertie to enjoy the strokes. Never look away, but study your caress . . . er . . . touch. She will appreciate your attentiveness."

"I'm sure." Toya sighed. Her lashes lowered to half-mast, then instantly widened. "I mean, I'm sure she likes being handled gently."

Rad smiled, pleased with himself despite the knowledge he was leading them down a path neither had the right to tread. So, it wasn't his imagination after all. Toya was just as affected by his closeness as he was hers. What would it hurt to have this one moment to savor for the long, lonely nights to come?

"I want you to gently tug one teat, then the other, softly squeezing as you do. *Ja*, that's the way." Their hands worked in unison. "Just like that. First one, then the other. One, then the other. Again. Again. And again." His lips brushed the back of her ear. "You learn quickly, *Liebling*. See how well you please her. Use a slow, steady rhythm. Soft and gentle. Slow and steady. Caress, tug."

The milk added height to the liquid in the half-filled bucket. Rad could feel Toya's shoulders working, could see that she had the task well in hand, yet he was reluctant to move away as promised. At this moment, with their bodies touching, he was convinced they were meant to be together, convinced that she rightfully belonged to him and he to her, certain it was something even deeper than desire.

He sensed it when he looked at her, felt it when he touched her, tasted it the only time he'd ever kissed her. It was so sweet and thrilling, he knew that time itself had ordained their love.

Suddenly, the swishing stopped and Toya began to laugh. Rad's attention darted to the stream of white liquid shooting across the room to splatter against the cat's tongue licking wildly to clean her orange-striped cheeks.

"Meowwch!"

Rad couldn't determine whether Monarch's announcement, or Toya in his arms, was pleasure or pain. "Stop that, you scamp!" he playfully whispered in her ear. "You will spoil her."

Toya stared at him with such affection that her gaze shimmered with emerald fire. "As you spoil Gertrude?"

He stared down at her, a strength of purpose seizing his every sinew. "Oh, hell!" he murmured.

"Rad—" she started to say.

His mouth touched hers, smothering her whisper. He asked no permission, gave her no chance for the least bit of hesitance. His lips molded over hers, claiming them completely, offering the fire of his passion... and demanding it in return. A rush of yearning stole both breath and reason from him.

Her fingers curled on his chest. Her lips parted in open invitation. His tongue delved into the sweet, secret recesses of her mouth—hungering, tasting, savoring. Raw, exhilarating sensations wound through him like damnation's serpent tempting him with the forbidden.

The fever inside him raged—hot, pulsing, alive. The closer he drew her against him, the more he knew the fever threatened to consume them both. This was an adventure she could deny herself no more than he could ever denounce loving her.

His lips parted from Toya's, felt the absence of her sweet heat, then demanded her kiss one more time. Reason ravaged him, reminding Rad of all he was, all he would ever be without her—a man bound by honor to see that the woman he loved kept hers. She should not be there with him. She would be scandalized, shunned.

She was pledged to someone else.

"Rad . . ."

His name was barely a whisper on the breeze, yet he heard it. He suddenly emitted a soft oath, thrusting her from him. He bolted to his feet, marched away, then finally leaned against the door, staring out into the misty rain.

"Damn your promise, Toya!" Rad spun around to glare at her. "Take that bucket to Opa, and if you need any more, send Betina out to fetch it."

Wordlessly, she grabbed the pail and started past him. But he grasped her arm, making her halt. "If you want to learn to milk, then wait until your future husband can show you. And make certain, Toya, make very certain, he can kiss you better than I did."

5

Opa's kitchen glistened despite the various kettles and confections cooking under its roof. The sweet fragrance of cinnamon, wild clematis, and clover mingled with the heat of the stove, making Toya aware that the old gentleman had stirred up her favorite of his recipes. Normally, her mouth watered just thinking of Ash Wagner's prizewinning sweets, but at present her mind refused to conjure anything but the memory of Rad's kiss. The taste of him lingered on her lips, saturating her senses.

And what a kiss! Ten times more bone-melting than the one that still filled her dreams three years after they'd shared it. A thousand times more soul-searing than any Peter had ever given her! Yes, when Peter returned, she would make very certain he kissed her better than Rad did . . . so she could forget.

A delicious feast of sliced ham, scrambled eggs, golden-brown biscuits two inches thick and gleaming with butter, and the treasured cinnamon treats filled Opa's gaily decorated platters. He'd even gone to the trouble of spreading lace over the table.

Like most cooks, Toya understood his desire to set a beautiful table, but she didn't want him to consider her company. She worked for him. She needed to make his life easier, not tax his efforts. When Betina left, she would gently remind him of such.

Toya hoped he wouldn't be disappointed by her lack of appetite this morning. It seemed she wasn't hungry for anything at the moment—anything but kissing Rad again.

Better to set her mind on less troublesome avenues.

"I've brought the milk, Herr Wagner." Toya set the pail upon the counter and moved alongside him as he stirred something on the stove. "Hmmm, that smells wonderful. Stew?"

"*Danke,* and *ja.*" Opa added a sprinkle of chopped onion and sage. "For later. It will simmer all day while we work."

"Where is Betina?" Toya glanced past the doorway leading deeper into the chalet.

"When I told her we would be doing some spring washing this morning, she offered to strip the beds. I said *nein,* but, like my Conrad, she feels she should earn her breakfast. Now we must fetch them both so the food will not grow cold."

Opa studied the stew for a moment, a frown creasing his brow. Toya followed his gaze as he scanned the row of spice jars that filled the rack next to the flour tin. His fingers reached for one spice, hesitated, then touched another. Finally, Opa delved inside his bib and tucker, withdrawing a chain that held a tiny gold key. His shoulders seemed to sag ever so slightly as he pulled the key from around his neck and slid it into a small locked box standing adjacent to the spice rack. Just as he started to turn the key, the wrinkles of his face molded themselves into a grin, a grin clearly familiar to that amicable face.

In a flash he replaced the key and grabbed one of the spices Toya didn't recognize. Not realizing that she had been holding her breath, she exhaled a pent-up sigh.

The old man glanced at her, then turned so that she could not see the exact amount he poured into his spoon. As he stirred the ingredient into the bubbling stew, Opa winked at her. "A secret to share later."

When he cannot remember. A tinge of sadness filled her, but she was glad that for then, he would not have to consult his recipe box. Today he would preserve his wisdom. But tomorrow would come all too soon. His legacy, his ways, should not be forgotten. If there was anything she could do . . .

"Rad worries too much that I will forget."

Alpine-blue eyes met her gaze, their clarity so sharp, Toya wondered if they could read her thoughts.

You worry too much that I will forget, his eyes seemed to say.

"Yet *he* forgets to eat if I do not remind him. Ahh"— the old man shrugged—"but he would not be Conrad if he did not carry my weight upon his shoulders."

You should not take such a weight on yours either, wünderkind, his expression warned.

"I'll call Betina to breakfast if you'll tell Rad," Toya offered, heading toward the doorway before he could protest. Under no uncertain terms would she venture out into the barn again. Not after Rad's warning that she send someone else to replenish the milk supply. At least, that was her mind's reasoning. Toya's heart knew differently. The farther she stayed away from Rad, the less her soul would crave the taste of him.

"Betina?" She headed down a hall that separated the kitchen from the remainder of the house. Toya fiddled with the calico-colored ribbon that secured the botton of her braid. It was wet and needed to dry so it wouldn't mildew. She untied it and was pleased the damp braid remained intact. Perhaps later she could borrow a brush and repair the damage the rain had done. But then, would Opa have a brush? Focusing on her assignment for the moment, she called out again, "Betina, where are you?"

Receiving no answer, Toya glanced at the stairway leading to the higher levels. The bedrooms were probably upstairs, since most homes in their community offered a parlor and study on the ground level. In case Rad had altered the traditional arrangement, Toya searched each of the lower rooms. She discovered that he'd added a large room that held no furniture whatsoever. No shelves filled its walls. It was as if the room were in waiting.

Finding no one on the ground level, she headed upstairs. Her hand glided over the cedar railing as she climbed, trailing the ribbon along its glossy length and enjoying the smooth texture beneath her fingertips. A thick Aubusson carpet added comfort to her ascent, and colorful tapestries graced the walls. The spartan furnishings bore the fine craftsmanship known among their people and would last for generations to come. The Wagners might be only simple beekeepers and peach farmers, but their choice of trappings bore the mark of aristocracy.

"Betina, it's time for breakfast." She reached the landing and peered into the first available doorway. No one was there. "Betina?" she repeated, moving on to the next room. "Are you up here?"

Upon inspection, she discovered Opa's room. Surely it must belong to the old gentleman. Various smells pervaded her senses as she glanced at the small bed that took up only one corner of the room. The coverings already had been stripped, and the tick mattress lay bare. The size of the sleeping arrangements hinted that this was the least of Opa's concerns. Finding room for countless jars of every size and shape seemed to require the most consideration. Jars filled the window ledge and every shelf of a huge baker's rack that graced the wall closest to the windows.

Toya smiled, remembering her own cluttered room back at her aunts' house. The kitchen might be the proper place for such herbs and spices, but only in a cook's private haven could the real experimenting be done.

She exhaled a long sigh. She supposed when she married she would have to accumulate her treasures in a less intimate storage area. Just as she must resign herself to honoring her pledge to marry Peter.

Why had she made such a foolish promise to Tilly?

Because she was your sister, Toya reminded herself again, shaping the ribbon into a bow, *and you could not deny her dying wish. Because she reminded you that the arrangement between Father and Peter must be honored.* The ribbon suddenly knotted. *Because you were afraid you could not count on yourself... like you could always count on Tilly and Father and... Peter.* Toya attempted to untie the knot but managed only to tighten it further.

Aunt Fredericka and Aunt Albertine had eagerly lent her solace, but Toya felt that they should lean on *her* in their latter years. She refused to become a burden to them. For all these reasons she'd accepted Peter's proposal. But not one of these logical, seemingly necessary and good-hearted reasons eased the sense of loss she felt in Rad's presence.

Unwilling to let her mood darken any further, Toya shut the door to Opa's sanctuary. She checked the remaining rooms on this level. No Betina.

"Be-ti-na? Are you deaf?" Toya called, then remembered that Lineva Pyrtle spoke the same words of her earlier. Toya deliberately summoned her the second time, mimicking the townswoman's nasal twang. "Miss Bram, can you not hear me?"

Chuckling, she realized that Rad must certainly have built the house to buffer sound. Logs made of cedar that grew thickly along the Comal River had been stripped, sanded, and painted, then interlocked and mortared together to form a solid barrier against unpredictable Texas weather. It had demanded great patience to build such a fine house— great patience and a will of iron. Respect renewed itself within Toya. With each day she knew Rad, she discovered something more about him to admire.

Finally, she reached the landing of the third floor, and her awe of Rad's home increased. Most of the chalets in New Genesis were only two stories, but the Wagners' boasted three. She'd always wondered why Rad felt the need for such a large home. With all the bedrooms on the second floor and the various rooms downstairs, this home offered plenty of comfortable surroundings for a large family.

Images of towheaded children filled her mind. Mentally, she assigned each a room she had visited. Opa would take that beautiful room downstairs that had not been used. That way, when he couldn't manage the stairs, he would be close to the kitchen he so loved. The boys with Rad's blue eyes and square jaw would occupy the east side of the second landing. The girls would take the west. Girls with his smile and their mother's . . .

The images faded. She didn't want to imagine their mother. *Couldn't* envision her. For every time she tried, Toya pictured curly-haired darlings who looked much like herself and Rad.

To her amazement, she discovered the highest tier of the Wagner home contained only one door. One room for such a wealth of space? Toya paused outside the entrance and lightly knocked. "Betina, are you in there?"

"*Ja.* Come in. I am almost finished."

Toya opened the door and started to step inside. But her mouth gaped and she paused, unable to believe what she saw.

The room went on forever, apparently wrapping itself around the entire chalet. The ceiling slanted to form the pitch of the roof, giving the feeling of an extended loft. A huge four-poster bed that would have taken a team of draft horses to tote filled most of the near end of the room. It looked as if Goliath himself slept there. Leather-cushioned chairs and a mahogany armoire invoked the feeling of strength and masculinity. Definitely a man's room.

Rad's?

Impulse drove her onward. Impulse and the need to see what she would never share with the man she cared for so deeply.

Forest-green curtains framed a massive window that opened the entire east side of the house to view. Atop the window frame, dried peach blossoms, wild grapes, and greenery formed a natural valance. How did he manage time to freshen the design? Or had he discovered a way to keep the fruit from spoiling?

In front of the picturesque window stood an easel that held a canvas. A painter's cloak, dotted with colors, lay over a chair that sat adjacent to a table housing various hues of paint and a jar of honey. Betina was nowhere near the bed, but, rather, stared intently at the canvas.

"I think you should see this." Betina motioned Toya forward.

Toya's curiosity overruled the feeling of disquiet that enveloped her as she moved to satisfy her friend's demand. She sensed that the canvas held some sort of revelation. "See what?"

Ignoring the fluttering of her heart, Toya halted beside her friend and focused on what held Betina's attention so completely.

It was then that she smelled him. Peaches and honey. The musky scent of a man who worked in sunshine. Rad. This was, indeed, his bedroom. Like Opa's, Rad's private sanctuary. And it contained a portrait of *her*!

The calico ribbon fell from her fingertips as Toya stared at the painting and blinked, disbelieving that anyone could have captured her so completely on canvas. Though every nuance within her expression and body language declared her adventurous nature, he'd somehow managed to capture the haunting look of her eyes. A reality she confided to no one but Betina.

This was not the fledgling attempt of a would-be artist, but the painstaking deliberation of a master intent upon searching his subject's soul. Was Rad the artist?

"You did not know this of him?" Betina lifted the painter's cape from the back of the chair.

And you did? A surprising emotion swept through Toya like a chilling wind, but she instantly cloaked herself with the warmth of friendship she and Betina had shared for so long, shedding the sting of envy. Betina had every right to spend time with Rad. After all, her hand in marriage had not been promised to anyone, and Rad could court anyone he chose.

Betina handed the garment to Toya. "See, it even smells like him. It seems Conrad is a man of"—she nodded toward the canvas—"many interests."

The tips of Toya's fingers traced the fawn-colored nankeen as she held up the cape to her nose. Despite the paint, she could discern the scent of its owner as if he actually stood in their presence.

She quickly returned the smock to its place, feeling as if she'd intruded not only upon Rad's refuge, but upon his private feelings as well. She had no right. Yet, she felt suddenly and ultimately as if she belonged there in the room that emanated Rad's strengths. In the room filled with the beauty his soul sought to express, where images of their children conjured themselves so vividly in her mind.

Oh, Rad, if only... Longing cut through Toya like a well-aimed saber, piercing her with regret. She could not look at the painting any longer... nor the love that had etched its powerful appeal.

The sunlight shining in the window enticed her, urging her to face the cold light of day and its realities. A movement outside caught her attention.

She stared toward the stand of trees that shaded the barn.

Toya caught her breath as a man's indistinguishable form moved toward the trees. He suddenly stopped and shaded his eyes as if looking for something.

The fine hair on the back of her neck stood on end. Was it Rad? Had he spotted her? She couldn't tell from this distance.

Backing away from the window, she hurried to the bed. "Let us strip this and go down to breakfast. Opa's biscuits will be cold, and his—"

The door burst open. Toya spun around, her eyes widening in surprise first, then embarrassment. Rad! The man below couldn't have been he.

"I—w-we were just gathering the linen," she puffed, hurriedly collecting the quilted cover and sheets. Halfway around the bed she stopped. "Betina told Opa she would strip the linens before break—"

In cougarlike strides Rad reached Toya and jerked the quilt from her hands, demanding her full attention. His gaze swept the room, then chilled her with its icy regard.

"Where is Opa?" Rad's tone offered no tolerance for hesitation.

Before Toya could respond, his attention averted to Betina and the fact that she stood before his painting. For a moment Toya thought the man would lose his control completely at their intrusion of his privacy. His jaw stiffened. His legs bolstered themselves as if bracing against an enemy. But his eyes, his bluebonnet-colored eyes, focused on Toya, searching, examining, blazing through her every thought.

"So you have seen," he whispered.

She tried to look away. To close off the look of raw hunger in his eyes that asked for understanding. For acceptance. For an eternity of passion.

"Perhaps Opa has gone to the barn." Betina glanced from Toya to Rad, then back at Toya. "I will go now and see."

"*Nein,* I will search for him. He hired me to be his compan—" Toya's protest died as guilt consumed her. It was her duty to watch him. To see that Opa did not wander off. A duty she failed miserably. And all she did was stand there, like a moon calf, staring at Rad's lips.

Why had she allowed Rad's earlier warning to send someone else out to the barn keep her from thinking clearly? She should never have asked Opa to fetch him. She'd seen Opa's moment of forgetfulness with the spice. Why hadn't she paid attention? Panic seized her. "I do not think we will find him in the barn, Tina. I saw him disappear through the trees a few minutes ago. I thought he was Conrad."

"I told you this would never work." Rad moved ahead of her to the door, turning to glare at her. "Caring for a Wagner demands a lot more than you apparently want to offer. Go home, Toya. Go back home, where you can't hurt anyone but yourself. Opa and I will do just fine without you. *Ja,* just fine."

6

By noon Toya was sick with worry about Opa. They had searched everywhere—in the barn, the herb garden, the Wagner chalet, Aunt Fred and Aunt Albert's, some of his brewing comrades, the chalet again, his fishing hole—all to no avail. The only thing she could be certain of was that he had ridden away on his favorite horse. A swaybacked nag who'd seen better days. Not the most reassuring travel arrangements he could have chosen.

Rad's seething silence threatened to unnerve Toya. If only he would yell at her, tell her she was incompetent, anything but stare off into the distance with that look in his eyes. The man loved his grandfather dearly, but a hint of desperation colored his gaze to a deeper shade of concern.

All agreed to meet back at the barn to coordinate their efforts if the search of New Genesis proved fruitless. Resting and watering their horses took precious time, but it became necessary.

"I will ride out to the orchard and see if he's there." Rad filled his canteen from the rain barrel placed near the barn door. "If I do not return in two hours, ring the bell.

Explain to the others what has happened. Tell Karl Lindstrom to put whatever rations the men need on my account. We will comb all of the Republic if necessary."

Remorse consumed Toya. If only she had been paying attention and not sent him out alone. But she couldn't even keep focused long enough to watch him for an hour. No, she had shirked her responsibility, then taken the easier assignment of fetching Betina. All because she couldn't control her emotions in Rad's presence. *Let him be safe*, she prayed, *and I will never leave his side again as long as I'm on duty.* "I am truly sor—"

"I will find him."

Rad's declaration held the stone-carved pledge of commitment. She knew he would stop at nothing to locate his grandfather. No amount of time or distance would keep him from his fulfilling the deed. No shirking of *his* responsibility would even be considered. Rad was not a man who left anything undone or consigned a duty to anyone else—no matter what the difficulty.

"Let me go with you." She remounted, steeling herself against any objection he might voice—even in silence.

"I ride faster alone." Rad wrapped the canteen around the saddle horn, then mounted in one fluid movement. Settling deeply into the saddle, he reined the sorrel half quarter.

"Wait, Conrad!" Betina shielded her eyes from the sun that silhouetted his muscular frame. "She's right. If you find Opa and he's . . . hurt, you can stay with him until she rides for help. This is good sense, *ja*?"

"*Ja*, you speak wisdom." Rad thumbed his slouch hat in a respectful good-bye, then his gaze averted to Toya. He studied her from braid to slipper. "Ride fast, not foolish."

Before she could answer, he spurred his mount into a gallop. Toya's words were lost in the sound of his leaving. "I will not lose my way."

"See that you don't," Betina warned, staring up at her,

one fist resting against her hip, the other continuing to shield the sun from her eyes. "He worries too much of Opa; he does not need to concern himself with rescuing you."

Though her friend meant only to help, annoyance swept through Toya like a hot breeze. It was their habit to speak frankly to each other, but since when did Betina know what Conrad needed? Since Tina and Rad had been visiting each other every Sunday for the past few months? "I know the way to his orchard." Concern, guilt, and a surge of jealousy sharpened Toya's tone. "I ride by it every *Sunday*." There, she'd said it. Betina was smart enough to understand what she implied.

"So you do." Betina didn't acknowledge Toya's challenge. Both fists curled against her hips. "But I also know if you think taking a different route would get you there before Conrad and help you find Opa, you would challenge the unknown just to soothe Rad's silence."

"You know me too well, Tina." Despite her desire to remain irritated at her friend, Toya reprimanded herself. Betina only wanted to warn her to be careful. She would have given the same warning to Betina if the situation were reversed.

And what wrong *did* Betina commit helping in Rad's orchard? Why *shouldn't* the two of them spend the day talking? Why *couldn't* they court each other?

Because Toya wanted to be the one who shared his days talking of nothing and everything. Because Toya didn't think she could endure watching them court. And she definitely did not want to admit to Betina that once again she was right. Yet, that's all she could do and not lie. "That is exactly what I planned to do."

"Just this once"—Betina grabbed Toya's canteen, filled it, then lifted it toward her—"do not try anything new. This is an emergency, not an adventure. This is a time for clear-headed thinking, not curiosity. *Ja?*"

Toya accepted the canteen, realizing for the first time that her hair had dried and come unbraided. Where had she . . . ? The ribbon! She'd dropped it in Rad's room! How would she ever get it back? "Why must you always be so sensible?"

Betina smiled indulgently. "Because, *Freunde*, you are always so inquisitive. Good intentions start your race, but curiosity often keeps you from crossing the finish line. Now, go find Opa and while you're doing so, see if you can help Conrad find a better humor."

"*Ach!* This is a fine bale of hay!" Opa jostled up and down on the Percheron's back as the massive horse headed for home. "An ungrateful hunk of American horseflesh you are, Donner! Slow down. You will bounce out all my blood before we get there."

Opa rattled off a string of German commands as he attempted to sway the animal's tenacity. But Donner persisted, as did the blood oozing from the nasty gash on Opa's right foot. The fall from the tree had ruined a good pair of Hessian boots that were less than a year old!

If he didn't know better, Opa would wager his grandson had trained the beast to return home after a few hours. Either that or the oat eater knew going home meant getting a fresh bucket of feed. He suspected the Percheron's gait was more self-serving than rescuing.

"Slow there, horse. I said slow! Do you not understand the *englisch*?"

All he could do was hold tight to the reins. The *Streithammel* would soon learn to quit being so quarrelsome and mind his master, or he would no longer find the *Bier* in his trough once a week. That is, if they made it home with any sense left unjarred.

Donner suddenly eased into a trot. Satisfaction lifted the old man's chin until he realized the traitorous horse had not decided to heed his demands but caught wind of Conrad cresting the hill ahead of them. "Oh, now you listen, rattlebuck. Think he will make *Bier* for you?"

Donner snorted, his ears twitching.

"Quit your braying. Sometimes you are such a mule. A real friend wouldn't race home just to satisfy his gluttony. A real friend would measure his gait and soothe his master's creaking bones and joints . . . like his master eases his favorite steed's joints with a taste of schnapps. A *real* friend wouldn't gallop for home when his owner's lifeblood pumps out with every bounce. You and my grandson must have a conspiracy against me." He winced, half in resignation, half in pain. "Again, you will not be the only one tethered."

Rad reined alongside Opa and matched his mount's stride with Donner's gait.

"Hello there, Grandson!" Opa looked up as if he'd been napping and just woken. "What keeps you this fine morning? There are crops to plant. The peaches are setting."

"Breakfast, Grandfather. Breakfast keeps me." He studied Opa closely and wondered if he had fallen asleep in the saddle. So many times lately, he could fall asleep even in the middle of a sentence. "Have you forgot— Are you not hungry?"

Glancing up at the sun, Opa wiped beads of sweat from his brow. "It's long past breakfast. Time for lunch. You should have brought it with you."

Rad noticed that pain rimmed Opa's eyes and his coloring had paled despite the heat of the day. Probably, just too much sun. Had to get him out of the heat. "Yes, Opa, I should have. But I thought if you didn't mind, we would eat and take a nap. I'm a bit tired from the morning's work, I'm afraid. You would not mind if we rest . . . for just a little while?"

Alpine-blue eyes looked upon him with concern. "Remember, boy, every harvest has a fallow season. Just because there is no movement does not mean the seed does not thrive."

The old man's shoulders sagged slightly, making Rad aware that Opa's strength waned. He needed to get him home in a hurry. A closer look sent thoughts racing through Rad's head. He would have to take up another inch or two of Opa's bib and tucker. It seemed the more Rad sewed, the thinner Opa became. How much weight had his beloved grandparent lost in the past year alone—twenty, thirty pounds? Perhaps Toya would take the sewing task off his hands. At least it would give her and Opa an activity that might occupy him enough to keep him in the house for a while. Surely, she could manage that!

"I think I will rest too." Opa yawned. "The orchard looks healthy. It will take both of us—maybe Miss Reinhart will help—to glean its yield."

Rad secretly hoped Opa had forgotten his arrangement with Toya so he could send her home and tell her that her services were no longer needed. He would leave the sewing until he returned from the fields each night. Mending one tucker an evening would soon complete the chore. But Rad knew Toya's leaving was no real answer. Just that morning's activity alone proved he desperately needed someone to help him safeguard his grandfather. Twice in one day, yet!

The orchard and bees demanded too much time to give up half days of work. The next two to three weeks were critical with the care of the peaches. If only Opa hadn't chosen Toya. She could be exasperating in her carelessness, and too tempting for her own good. No, Toya only compounded Rad's growing dilemma.

They had already crested the hill and descended the other side when Toya found them. Her expression froze. A moment passed before Rad realized that she was staring at Opa. He hurried to reassure her. "He was on his way back when I found him. No harm done."

"He is not well." She dismounted in lightning speed and rushed to the other side of Opa's horse.

"What is it?" Rad grabbed Donner's reins and halted the animal. He maneuvered his horse around the Percheron and realized what he had failed to see earlier. Opa's boot bore the length of a deep gash and was stained crimson.

Though white with pain, Opa's expression betokened more anger than hurt.

"Fell out of the tree while I was checking the peaches. Landed on my foot. Got tangled in the branches and the roots. It does not feel broken but, *ja*, I will hobble for a while."

Rad took charge. "Toya, ride to the house and fill a big pan with cool water. Then heat another panful. You'll find the bandages in the box underneath Opa's bed. That's on the second fl—"

"I know which one is his," she interrupted.

And mine, Rad reminded himself. She had invaded his private quarters and left her essence in his room to haunt him even more than she already did. She had seen the portrait and not spoken a single word.

Rad steeled himself against the hurt he'd suffered when she'd kept silent about his portrait of her. But what did he expect her to say? What could she have said that would make any difference? There was no time for wishful thinking.

They must get Opa home and stop the blood loss.

Rad eased Opa down onto the mattress until the old man balanced on its edge. Toya knelt to take off the damaged boot. Opa's foot had swollen so much already that it was difficult to remove the boot. Rad cut it away with a large knife.

Gingerly, she felt the injured foot. "I think there may be a bone broken."

Opa bit his lips to hold back the pain that even her gentlest touch brought. "*Nein.* I have seen worse." He refused to be nursemaided.

"Shall I fetch someone?" Her gaze sought Rad's.

"Who better to heal me than me?" Opa wiggled his toes to show that the foot, though swollen and cut, still had its mobility. "I'll soak it for a while, then one of you can bind it up. If I don't try to trim the trees anytime soon, I will live to walk again."

He took a deep breath, then exhaled. "My only regret is that I will be slow to help with the chores. I have always pulled my share and now may prove only a hindrance."

"Do not concern yourself, Opa." Rad bathed the foot with the water Toya had set on the table next to his grandfather's bed. "The chores . . . all of them . . . will get done. Your job is just to rest now and recuperate."

"But there is so much to do—"

"And I will do it." Rad's tone brooked no argument.

"No, *we'll* do it." Toya took the cloth from Rad and rinsed it out so he could use it again. "I can handle his chores. Surely anything he can do, I can—"

"*Wunderbar!*" Opa lay back on his pillow. "We can begin the sowing tomorrow. Rad will plow. I can seed. You can fertilize."

Fertilize? *Wunderbar.* Toya blinked, wishing she had not been so impulsive in offering a helping hand. But she owed it to Opa. He wouldn't have gotten hurt if she'd been paying attention. And she had vowed to stay at his side as long as she remained his employee. That meant wherever the wanderer went. "I thought you might need to stay close to the house for a few days, Herr Wagner. We could do the household and barn chores."

"Like the milking?"

Though Opa asked the question in innocence, it echoed with challenge. Toya's gaze locked with Rad's. Heat fused her cheeks as the memory of that intimate first lesson warned that she would never do the chore again without remembering his searing kiss. "Yes, even the milking."

Opa shook his head. "No, I will help where I am needed most. That is at my grandson's side. In the orchard and at the hives."

She would be thrown into Rad's company for hours at a time, working with him side by side and spending considerable time in the orchard near him. Envy of Betina came back to mock Toya. Hadn't she wanted this very thing? Yet, hadn't she feared just the same?

Rad wrapped Opa's foot with clean bandages. "Rest this afternoon and get a good night's sleep, Miss Reinhart. Tomorrow's chores begin two hours before dawn."

Two hours before dawn? She glanced at Opa for confirmation. The old man looked extremely pleased with himself and nodded.

"From dawn to midnight for a while. I have planting to do and some of it can be done only after twilight." He winked at her. "It makes the corn sweeter."

Suspicion swept through Toya. Like many of their people, Opa often farmed at night, believing the moon tides affected the earth's fertility. But the old man had more than planting on his mind. Just what seed did he intend to sow?

7

Pungent smells of newly turned earth drifted across the partially plowed field. Leather and metal harnesses jingled as Rad commandeered the two huge draft horses towing a plow through the dark, reddish-brown soil. He hauled back on the reins, stopping to squint into the fading Texas sun. The day grew old.

Every muscle called out for rest. His arms ached from tugging on the long leather reins and forcing the hulking creatures to bend their brawn to the plow. Yet the earth was rich and alive. He would plow two more rows before dark.

The horses tossed their heads in protest, their ears twitching and tails busily swishing bothersome insects. "Just two more, then I will let you rest," Rad encouraged the team, though his own muscles twinged in rebellion.

He glanced back at Opa and Toya, thrilled with the sight of them working alongside each other. Toya scooped cow chips from the buckboard and placed them into the plowed furrow, swatting at the incessant flies. Opa took seed from the sack of grain tied around his neck and shoulders, then stabbed the ground with a long stick. Poke. Drop. Poke. Drop.

Toya completed the procedure normally left to the seeder. She stomped the dirt to cover the manure and seeds, saving Opa the effort. His grandfather's foot held up better than Rad expected. The old man may be losing his memory, but his health, otherwise, was stalwart. The fertilizing and seeding were back-wrenching tasks that smelled mightily, but both Opa and Toya had braved the chore without complaint.

A glance at Toya revealed cheeks and nose that glowed a bright pink despite the wide brim of her bonnet. Rad had lain awake most of the night, envisioning seeing her near, anticipating the day to be spent with her, showing Toya his land and all he was willing to accomplish . . . had accomplished. Yet he dreaded the day just as greatly, for Opa's keeper would do nothing but distract him from his purpose. And all to no avail. For she would soon become Peter Stoltz's distraction, not his. Rad had almost started the plowing that morning without going by to offer her a ride, but he would not treat her so ungentlemanly. And Opa's needs overruled his own insecurities.

Just as he'd imagined, Toya never seemed more beautiful than then. Tossed by the wind, wisps of her hair had loosened from their single braid to frame her face in strawberry-blond curls. Nothing looked more appealing than a woman with wild hair and sun-freckled cheeks.

"Are we stopping now?" Hope filled Toya's expression. Her voice cut through the still air. "We have supper to cook and a few other chores to finish before I go home."

The rosy glow of the setting sun turned the horizon from brilliant blue to dusky rose, then to gold. Rad looked past Toya's beauty and saw what he should have noticed hours before. Her shoulders sagged. One hand rubbed the back of her hips to ease aching muscles. Exhaustion shadowed her eyes. Dirt streaked her sunburned cheeks.

He glanced at the field and weighed the possibility of leaving the two additional rows unplowed. *A harvest is only as bountiful as the seed planted.* His grandfather's words raced to remind Rad of his own longstanding creed—do today all that is possible so tomorrow will tender new opportunity.

Still, he could wake an hour earlier in the morning. The time would allow him to complete the field as he'd planned so he could concentrate more time on the orchard and beeyard.

"Supper sounds good, Grandfather." He unharnessed the team and signaled for Opa to stop seeding. "Do you feel like cooking, or shall I?"

Opa shook his head. Untying the grain sack, he laid it on the buckboard away from the tarpaulin that divided the manure pile from tools. "Fraulein Reinhart has worked hard today, Grandson. We best feed her something passable if we want her to help again, *ja*?"

Rad's shoulders flexed as he shirked off his own exhaustion. Deep dimples bracketed his smile. "Are you saying I do not share your knack for cooking?"

"Do roosters crow?" Opa cut his gaze toward Toya.

"Only for someone too stubborn to get up before dawn," she countered, sharing in the light banter that suddenly eased the strain of their grueling work, "and *stay* up."

Rad laughed, realizing that she was not one to rise with the roosters. Yet Toya had willingly lent a hand that morning anyway. She'd honored her word, and his admiration for her grew. Rad spread out his hands and spun halfway around. "The earth is full of promise, *Liebling*. What better reason to start the day. What more could we ask for?"

"Less smell." Opa wiggled his nose elaborately.

The trio laughed.

"The flies don't seem to mind," Toya quipped, her green

eyes suddenly surveying the field. "But I haven't seen a single bee all day."

"Like me, they prefer wildflowers to manure." Opa's comical expression sent his grandson and Toya into chuckles.

"Gather your implements," Rad finally instructed as he sobered. He began to unharness the plow, then hitched the two draft horses to the wagon being pulled by the third Percheron.

Soon everyone had settled atop the driver's box, putting Toya in the middle despite her protest to the contrary. Though she said Opa should be shielded on either side due to his injury, the old gentleman assured her that he preferred to sit on the edge. No slash of the foot would make him a coddled baby!

Rad hung the lantern on the hook nailed to the front of wagon so it would light their way home. He leaned behind Toya and shot his grandfather a warning look that said *I know what you are scheming, old man. A sly fox you are not.* But Opa's slim shoulders just shrugged. His eyes rounded in mock innocence as if he had no clue to Rad's meaning. Rad shook his head, unable to hide the grin that curved his lips. An impish slash of white teeth filled Opa's face in response.

"Today has been a good day." Opa spread one arm wide to encompass all the world around them. "And tomorrow will—"

"Come too early." Toya erupted into a yawn. Her palm rushed to cup her mouth. "Excuse me."

A slight breeze rose, stirring the tree leaves and causing her to sigh with the cooling pleasure it offered as the animals shifted into motion. The sigh swept over Rad's spine, making him fight off his own exhaustion. But his was not the fatigue of labor. All day long he had battled the need to touch her, to brush back the wisps of hair from her face, to taste again the moistness of her lips.

Now he ached to wrap his arm around her and pull her closer, to nestle her against him and rest her head upon his shoulder. Her sigh conjured so many images, so many needs, so many desires, Rad was pleased he'd decided to end the plowing. The sooner he took Toya home, the less he would be tempted to kiss that sigh from her lips.

"You know, Grandson"—Opa reached behind Toya and tapped Rad on the shoulder—"it is a full moon, and I would like Fred and Albert to pay me a visit. After all, I did invite them last night and had to cancel."

"Why not wait until you are completely well?" *What else did his grandfather plan?* "Toya explained to her aunts that you hurt your foot."

"True. But it has held up well today. How can I deprive my friends good company when they look forward to it so much? And how better to heal my sole than make my heart happy?"

Toya gently elbowed the old man. "You cut the *top* of your foot, not the bottom of it."

"Quick as a quail you are, Toya Reinhart." Opa chuckled. "I doubt my grandson even noticed."

"I noticed." Rad flicked the leather straps elaborately, urging the horses home. "But I try to keep his witticisms reined as much as he will allow. Otherwise," he scolded gently, "he'll continue them all night."

"This old man could teach you a few things about enjoying the night." Opa winked, arching one brow.

"Grandfather!" Rad couldn't believe the feisty old farmer had uttered such a thing . . . and in front of Toya no less! The full moon livened up more than the night, it seemed.

"A happy heart *is* a body's best medicine." Opa's tone echoed with teasing and admonition. "I am sure Fred and Albertine will sit with me if I become too tired to walk . . . or do anything else that strikes my fancy."

Though he never uttered the words, Opa's silent command rang through Rad's thoughts. *So shall it be done!*

Fortunately, darkness settled over the Texas hill country, hiding Toya's expression from Rad. And his from her! What he would not give to share his Opa's audacity at times, to throw caution and her pledge to the four winds . . . to make love to her beneath the full moon.

Crickets serenaded the moonlight. The soft buzz of katydids joined the evening chorus, interrupted occasionally by a frog's throaty bass. Wildflowers winnowed in the breeze, scenting the air with a sweetness that momentarily relieved the odor of their remaining cargo. But it was the magic of Toya's nearness that cast its spell upon him. Enchanting him. Conjuring images he'd dreamed of every night since they'd met.

Of Toya . . . standing beside him at the altar, vowing to love him forever.

Of Toya . . . laughing at something their children did and sharing a look of pride meant for his eyes only.

Of Toya . . . gray-haired and plump, sitting in the rocker next to his, too old to do much more than hold his hand, yet still too much in love to let it go.

Rad slapped reins against the wide brown backs, sending the big draft horses into a trot. He had to do something. Think of something. Find some way to withstand the allure of the woman sitting next to him so he could help her honor her pledge. But how?

Normally a man who found numerous answers to problems, Rad found himself at a loss now. His heart refused to consider anything his head suggested. Perhaps Betina could . . . *ja!* Betina! Betina was the answer.

Hurry, he told the horses, take me home or the night's charm may master us all.

8

Moonlight bathed the Wagners' barnyard in an iridescent glow. Nowhere in all the world did the sky seem so expansive, so close that Toya could almost reach out and grab a handful of stars. Many a night she'd chosen to sleep under the heavens, guessing the constellations and laughing when one of the twinkling stars winked back at her as if in conspiracy. But tonight the earth and its wonders drew her speculation. How in God's world would she ever survive the sensual spring shadows in Rad's company?

The day had proven difficult enough for her, watching the flex of his muscles as he plowed, listening to the low, melodious songs he sang to soothe the horses' labor, catching his watchful gaze at Opa to make certain the old man had not taxed himself too much, then sensing that same regard targeted at her.

The yearning she caught simmering in his eyes, then cooling itself behind his rigid self-control haunted Toya even then. Despite her efforts to keep busy and forget the response his look ignited within her, temptation continued to pulse through every inch of her body.

Like heat waves from the sun, her blood warmed and raced as the memory of Rad's kiss radiated through her. It was as if he stood behind her, whispering soft, caressing words along the slope of her shoulders, up the back of her neck, halting only a breath away from her earlobe.

She trembled, rubbing her palms against her arms as if he had touched her and she could coat herself with his embrace. If only her aunts had refused Opa's invitation!

Several well-placed lanterns stationed along the stone fence added light. A slight breeze swayed the treetops and set shadows into motion beyond the wall.

Hunger pangs grumbled discontentedly within her. Grateful for the distraction, Toya focused her attention on Opa and his cook fires.

Mesquite-smoked beef sizzled in a skillet over one of the open-flamed fires he built to prepare supper. A thick broth flavored with sage, thyme, and rosemary bubbled in a kettle beside the skillet. Nothing smelled better than a meal cooked outdoors in a breeze-cooled Texas night. And no one in the Republic cooked it better than Ash Wagner.

For as far as she could see and beyond, the countryside teemed with anticipation, as if the night waited to reveal a great secret. *How serious I am,* Toya scolded herself. *Always looking for something to . . . to what?* Surprise her? Being there should be wonder enough. "Mmm, Opa, it is a fine pan you fry tonight." Toya's mouth watered as she approached the old gentleman bending over to stir his kettles.

"*Danke.* And it's splendid you are looking, *Fraulein.* As pretty as your aunts. Are you feeling more rested now?"

"*Ja.*" Toya rolled her shoulders to rid herself of lingering exhaustion. She couldn't believe that she actually stayed with the task of fertilizing all day, but she had. If she could endure *that*, no telling what else she might accomplish. Being in Rad's company offered certain advantages. At least she made a greater effort to complete projects when he was near. That would help in whatever other employment she sought to become financially independent.

"I appreciated having a chance to clean up before we started supper." She glanced at the trio in the herb garden. "I know it was a lot of trouble for Rad to take me home, then come back for us again. We could have walked over. It's not that far."

"Nein." Opa stared at his grandson, who strolled through the garden with Toya's aunts, pointing here and there to things that might interest them. "The night may prove longer than we anticipated, and Fredericka is not seeing well enough to walk. Here, taste this and see if it needs anything more." He offered her a spoonful of thick liquid.

Affection welled within Toya as she sipped the stew. The old man doted on her aunts and worried about each of their ailments.

She suspected that some of those afflictions were exaggerated to guarantee Opa's visitations. He often courted both women, but Toya couldn't determine which of the two he preferred. Then again, she sometimes hoped she would never know. One of their hearts would be broken for certain. That she could not endure.

All she had left were Betina and her beloved aunts. Though related only by marriage, each aunt had become a surrogate mother to her. And both had decided Opa would make a fine second husband.

The reminder of why she'd accepted Opa's employment in the first place helped rid Toya of her uneasiness about being there. As long as she kept focused on her aunts' needs and her pledge to Peter, dealing with her attraction to Rad should be less demanding.

When she realized Opa awaited an answer, she announced, *"Wunderbar!* It is one of the finest stews I've ever eaten." Yet she owed him the truth—cook to cook. "But, myself, I would prefer a bit more thyme."

Opa grinned. "A true chef you are. Never let a stew go half boiled. No matter how seasoned the cook."

"Testing me, are you?" Toya laughed at the old kettle.

Unable to contain a chuckle, he shrugged. "A bit of bite now and then adds to the experience. A good cook is always on the watch for a fresh ingredient."

"I've been called impulsive, too curious, even fresh, but never a fresh ingredient." Toya slanted her eyes coyly at him. "*Danke.* I think."

"Albertine is looking especially pretty tonight, do you not agree?"

Toya followed his gaze to her oldest aunt and realized that Opa had not gotten to spend time with either of the women since their arrival. "May I stir for you awhile? I would like to test the texture."

Opa patted her cheek. "A sweet thing you are, Toya Reinhart, but you should practice your guile a bit more." He untied the apron he'd wrapped around his fresh bib and tucker. "*Ja,* I would like to welcome my visitors before I start my serious conjuring."

"So that is what you're boiling in the other pots?"

"Cleaning the herbs, I am." He stirred another of the pots and lifted a green vine from inside the brew. "It is a good thing to plant in the light of a full moon. Everything is more fertile at night—the soil, the seed . . ." He pointed at his grandson, who approached arm in arm with their newest visitor—Betina. "Even the planters themselves. See how well he looks with Fraulein Bram?"

Toya focused her attention on the stew, stirring industriously. She felt unsettled at the sight of Betina's dark-haired beauty standing so close to Rad's handsome brawn, making it difficult to retain her previous good humor. She had no right to be jealous. No right to disapprove. No right to wish Betina were not so beautiful. She should be glad two of the people she cared most for had found companionship with each other. "They make a handsome couple. Have they been courting long?"

Opa began to count his fingers. One. Two. He stopped at four. Four Sundays? Toya understood now why Betina had not joined her for her Sunday picnic lately. She'd assumed her friend's dress shop and life had become so demanding, Betina didn't have the time to visit as frequently.

Settlers heading west to the California gold fields arrived weekly and appreciated her best friend's skill with the needle. Many not only paid her to mend but ordered new garments to last them during the arduous journey cross country. Betina was never without work for long. Come to think of it, Betina's visitations had fallen off a lot longer than four weeks.

"Four months now." Opa rubbed his chin in thought. "Perhaps five."

"Five *months*!" Astonishment hollowed a sinking feeling in the pit of her stomach. Much could happen between a man and a woman in four months. Her own father and mother had fallen in love in two weeks and remained married until their death. What might have been possible suddenly seemed very likely. "They must be serious about each other."

"They do talk. I have never seen my grandson speak so often. He is usually quiet as stone."

What did they talk about? she wondered, battling a question more disturbing than a budding romance between Rad and Betina. Why hadn't Betina told her about the courting? Weren't best friends supposed to tell each other everything?

When had she started keeping secrets from Toya? And why?

Toya encouraged Opa to join her aunts. "I know two other someones who would love you to spend time with them."

"I will not leave you alone. It can wait."

She shooed him like a pesky fly. "Go on. I am not alone.

I have many thoughts to occupy me. Peter will be home soon." A wedding to arrange, she reminded herself.

"Peter it is, then." Disappointment engraved itself in Opa's expression.

Or perhaps it was just her imagination. Did he dislike Peter? He'd never said as much. If only there were something to detest about the councilman, how easy it would have been to deny Tilly's request. "I received a letter today. He should be returning from Nassau shortly with the next group of immigrants. He hoped to arrive soon enough to show them the bluebonnets in bloom."

"Peter should be cautious of the time he takes." Inquisitive blue eyes stared at Toya as Opa reached out to cup her cheek. "The bluebonnets have spent too long a winter waiting for spring, my dear. When burgeoning with such readiness, a blossom can no more wait to flourish than a bee can resist sating himself in its tempting nectar. Spring is here. The bluebonnet, she needs to be admired now. So she can thrive."

Toya could not speak, for the old man had seen into the very depths of her longing. Yet she'd given her word, no matter how foolishly offered. She forced herself to smile as Betina and Rad approached. "Perhaps the blossom will be more resilient than anyone presumes."

"She has spoken very little since she arrived. All she does is stir those pots while everyone else enjoys the night. What harm is there in talking?" Rad bent down, grabbed a pebble, then let it skip across the stream's moonlit surface. Ripples eddied in its wake.

Betina rose from her sitting position on the blanket Rad had spread for them by the bank. She dusted the hem of her skirt, then gathered a handful of rocks. "Such questions from a man who could make a mute seem talkative. Toya's eyes speak her heart, Conrad. Have you not seen the way she's looked at us all night? She must be dying inside, seeing us together."

"Why? We're just friends." He skipped another stone. "Do friends not sit and talk about their troubles and their dreams?"

Betina laughed, following his lead, but her stone sank like an anchor. "Of course. But I suspect she would prefer you had a friend of a less feminine persuasion, though she will never admit as much. She probably plots our wedding as we speak."

Rad stared at the object of his brooding mood and wondered if it was truly possible. Could she be jealous of his and Betina's friendship?

Thinking over the time spent with the dressmaker, he supposed to others it could look as if they were courting. In truth, he'd enjoyed sharing picnics and walks, listening to Betina talk about herself, her dreams, but particularly about Toya. From these talks he'd gleaned hundreds of facts about the woman he loved.

At first he felt guilty, thinking he used Betina. Then one day he apologized to her, wanting her to know he sincerely valued their friendship. Betina laughed and said she hadn't told him anything she didn't *want* him to know. A grin blazed across his face then, as it did now, when he realized the dressmaker was nobody's fool and that Toya might, indeed, be envious of her friend. He quickly masked the smile so Betina would not make fun of his moon face as she had the day of his apology.

Of course, Betina's claim was preposterous. Toya had seen the painting in his room, seen the love he could no more deny than he could stop breathing. His gaze searched the shadows for his beloved. As if he could reach out and touch her from this distance, his heart called to her. How he ached to know what she felt when she saw his adoration on canvas. What thoughts had crossed her mind as she stood in his bedroom and he watched her watching him?

How could she believe that any other woman would ever capture his soul?

Toya stopped her stirring, turning in the direction of the stream that ran along his property. Rad's breath caught in his throat. His heart thumped like rampant drums against his chest bone, his stance widening to bolster him against the forceful blow of her beauty when she faced him. It was as if she sensed him staring. Heard him call to her. Knew that he needed her.

For one eternal moment Rad did nothing but look and cherish the sight of her. *I know you, Toya. Not just the sound of your laugh when you watch Fredericka outdrink the men at the Sängerfest, or the color of your eyes as they shed tears for Opa's forgotten memories. I know that you love to sleep outside and dance in the moonlight when no one watches. I know that you tidy your sister's grave every Sunday and talk to her as if she were really buried there. I know that you will never break your word to Tilly no matter how much you do not love Stoltz. These things I know, Toya Reinhart, and I love you for each one of them.*

His hand reached into the pocket of his trousers, and he touched the treasure he'd found earlier in his room. *I wish this were you.* He willed his thoughts to erase the distance that separated Toya from him. *How I long to touch you. To comfort you. To show you how deeply I love you.*

"Look, she sees us." Betina waved. Toya seemed to hesitate, then waved in return. She spun around and grabbed a spoon, busying herself once again with the kettles.

"She avoids me because of her pledge." Rad's hand jerked from his pocket and grabbed another pebble, skipping it across the stream. Force propelled the rock to land on the other bank. "Which I admire, mind you. She gave her word and must keep it. But I thought we could be good friends, like you and I. Friends talk, don't they?"

Betina grabbed his hand and halted the rock-throwing.

"Conrad. Stop this. You are only whipping a tired horse. How much more do you need to know? Haven't I told you everything about her... her best color, her favorite food, where she prefers to spend time relaxing? Countless things I have confided. Still, you want to know more."

"Everything would be too little." He squeezed Betina's hand and linked it within his elbow. "But you are wise. I only pour salt into an open wound when sugar would be more healing." He encouraged her to match his strides. "Let's go find Opa and the others."

"I thought I saw him with the Reinhart widows not long ago."

"I'm afraid the three of them could get into considerable mischief in that length of time. My grandfather makes fine use of a night such as this."

Betina laughed and glanced back at her friend. "You should be so bold."

Where has everyone gone? Toya wondered, tired of stirring and watching the herbs. An hour had passed since Opa left with her aunts to go for a walk. Duty urged her to find him. Her aunts would not leave him alone, so there was no need to worry about him getting lost in the dark. But they also tended to argue over which of them would have his attention at any given moment. The lengthy absence of the trio warned that some kind of devilment was afoot.

Minutes later her suspicions proved well founded. She met Aunt Albertine dancing along the bank of the stream as if she were a wood nymph, her hem in hand, twirling first one way, then another. Her normally neat salt and pepper chignon stood slightly askew at the top of her head.

"Aunt Albertine?" Toya couldn't believe what she saw. Her oldest aunt's posture was usually as rigid as her principles. She looked like a young child frolicking in the grass.

"Hmm?" Albertine swayed right then left. "Doesn't the night sound lovely, child?"

Toya laughed. If you could call the buzz of katydids, croaking frogs, and crickets lovely. "*Ja,* lovely." When Albertine halted, Toya stared into her aunt's eyes, searching for some sense of the woman's strange mood. "You are feeling well tonight, Aunt Albert?"

"Particularly well." She sighed.

"And Opa is well too, I presume?"

Hazel eyes, illuminated by the moon, lit with laughter. "He feels very well, *danke.*"

The huskiness in her aunt's tone made Toya blush. "Aunt Albert!"

"Ah, sweeting"—Albertine hugged Toya to her slim shoulders—"there is nothing so rejuvenating as a spring kiss from a seasoned bee charmer."

Toya laughed and returned the hug. "Where will I find this dashing little pollinator?"

After a giggle that sounded like the tinkling of tiny bells, Albertine pointed behind her. "With Fredericka and Betina. He had them both in a heated discussion about why flowers should be planted on the west side of the yard." Admiration filled her tone. "It makes sense if you think about it. The stone wall on the east would block the rising sun during the day, giving them less light to grow. And he says that the fuller the moon, the more effective the moon tides are on the seed. Did you know that the number of petals and leaves per plant is based entirely on how full the moon is when the plant is—"

Toya gripped her aunt's arms. "Aunt Albertine, can you share this with me in a little while? It all sounds fascinating." She started to say "Opa-ish" because the old man loved to compare local Indian lore with the teachings in the old country. "But I need to bring Opa closer to the yard. He might tire and Aunt Fredericka is not well enough to see her way back. If he tries to lead them, they both may wander off and hurt themselves."

"Not to worry. Betina is with them."

"Where is Rad?" The words escaped Toya before she realized she'd spoken the question that filled her thoughts. Why had they decided to part company? "I thought Betina was with Conrad."

"The young man is such a brooder. Opa said he needed to conduct a 'finding' incantation for Betina's lost kerchief, and she must be present for it to work properly. Rad mumbled something about Opa's conjuring taking a good portion of the night. Rad had something he needed to care of and said he would go back to the yard. We assumed he was with you. You know that he does not approve of his grandfather's *Handauflegung*. But I do, especially when he lays his hands on—"

"Aunt Albert!" Toya gently scolded her aunt's rowdiness but was thrilled that Albertine and Fredericka enjoyed Opa as much as the old man loved flirting with them.

"I meant to say, on those who believe." Albertine wagged a finger at her niece. "Now perhaps you should go find Conrad and tell him we need to return home soon. I will find the others and escort them back to supper. The stew is surely ready by now."

"Aunt Albertine?"

"*Ja*, sweeting?"

"You do look quite beautiful tonight."

"I *feel* quite beautiful." She tapped Toya's nose with her fingertip. "But spring awards beauty of many kinds to anyone who's willing to risk her heart. Are you a gambler, Toya?"

"In all things but one, Aunt. I do not gamble with my word." Grateful for the night shadows, Toya headed back down the path she'd taken earlier, wondering if her vow would falter under the weight of her aunt's close scrutiny.

9

She sensed Rad watching her, but Toya said nothing. Bee work required patience, skill, and concentration, especially at night, when the bees could be most irritated. She didn't want to distract him. A rich, resonant roar emanated from the hives. Thousands of insects' wings transformed the nectar they'd gathered all day and scented the night with the fragrance of warm honey.

"Is something wrong?" Rad fanned the smoke that contented the horde. "I will be finished here in a moment, then we can talk."

Subdued excitement exited in throaty, almost kittenish purrs from the colonies, but Toya knew the slightest discordant tone might set them off.

"Nothing is amiss," she whispered, moving out of the shadows and into the moonlight so he had a clear view of her. To Toya's amazement, Rad didn't use gloves or a bee man's shroud to protect his hands and face. A bee sting could kill a chicken instantly, make a horse suffer intensely, close off a human's ability to breathe in a matter of minutes.

"Are you certain?" Rad didn't sound convinced.

"*Ja.*"

"Please. Do not leave," Rad implored. "We have yet to talk . . . about your plans for tomorrow with Opa."

The plea in his voice kept her from retreating. She should have searched for the others while Aunt Albert found Rad. But her heart seemed to have a will of its own, urging Toya to seek time alone with him. Yet each time she did, she came away singed like a moth drawn too close to the flame.

"All right, then, but my aunts have grown weary. After they eat, we need to go home. We could walk, but Aunt Fredericka would have a difficult time seeing the way."

"There is no need for that."

Rad said something to the bees she could not hear, then finally moved toward her. As he approached, Toya sighed heavily, expelling the tension growing within her.

"You are tired."

Since it had not been a question, she didn't respond.

He offered his arm.

"I can see well," she declined. *Touch me,* her flesh cried out. *Don't,* reason warned. "I will not lose my footing." *Just my heart,* Toya's soul mourned.

"Then please allow me to walk with you. I enjoy your company."

Toya attempted to collect her shattered emotions. He was her host, after all. To refuse would be rude. "*Danke.* I enjoy yours too."

They strolled past the back of the barn, where Rad kept his beeyard, and moved toward the bank, where he ladled up two bowls of the stew she had stirred all evening.

Toya frowned as he handed her a bowl and gently took her arm, steering her toward the house. "Where are we going?"

"I have a surprise for you. Something I want to show you before the others return."

"But it's after midnight."

"You are not afraid to be alone with me, are you, *Liebling*?"

"You talk nonsense." Toya lifted her chin, then wished she hadn't. The movement gave her a clear view of his face. Moonlight brightened his handsome features, adding golden flecks to the shadowed blue of his eyes and emphasizing the challenging lift to his lips. "And quit calling me that. I can never be your darling."

"Shall we?"

Temptation echoed from those two words, seducing Toya. Baiting her with the one lure she could not resist—satisfying her curiosity. "What did you want to show me?"

"If I told you, it would not be a surprise."

He escorted her inside the Wagner home, past the kitchen, stopping outside the door of the unfurnished room she'd looked into earlier.

"An empty room?" She stared at him in wonder. "Have you decided to prepare it for Opa?" Possibilities rose in her mind. "It would be much easier for him to be closer to the kitchen as he grows more infirm."

Perhaps Rad wanted her opinion on how many shelves to build to hold Opa's countless spices, or how best to arrange the remainder of his grandfather's furnishings. Or what color Opa might prefer the walls. What a wonderful surprise! From the skill she'd seen exhibited in Rad's artistry and the tasteful decor of his own bedroom, he didn't need to confer with her about his gift for Opa.

"The surprise is not for my grandfather." Opening the door to show her the room, Rad stepped aside to let her enter.

Toya's mouth gaped as she stared at the transformation. A lace-covered table set in the middle of the room, glowing with candelight. A soup server and a pair of crystal goblets stood on either side of a fresh bouquet of wildflowers, complimented by china plates and silver utensils ready to serve dinner for two. A light breeze billowed the curtains at the open window, offering a welcome coolness. Linen napkins completed the entire effect that seemed soothing, enticing, intimate.

"Neither of us has eaten." He took their soup bowls and placed them at each setting. Gently, he scooted out one chair for her. "I thought you might join me before you left."

"I am not hungry." *For food.* She realized where her thoughts led and dared not look at him until her cheeks cooled their blush.

"Something to drink, then. To relax you. Opa would be sorely distressed if you refused to try his juice of the grapes. He picked them himself along the Comal. They grow wild near his fishing hole. He and Fredericka share a great deal of joy during their midnight grape stomps."

"So that's why her feet were so discolored." Toya laughed. "And I thought her circulation was bad."

To refuse would be impolite. He'd gone to so much trouble. Imagine, plowing all day, transporting her and her aunts to and from home, brushing down the horses, seeing to the bees. All that, and he still found time to assure *her* enjoyment.

Under different circumstances Toya would have been endeared by his attentiveness. But Rad's kindness inflicted a wound to her resolve. It was difficult to ignore the power of his presence when the two of them were so alone. To elude the enticement in his eyes . . . to resist the lure of his lips when she knew how he tasted . . .

You can do this. Toya nodded her consent and allowed him to seat her. She watched in astonishment as he removed a towel from over the porcelain soup server sitting next to the wildflowers and revealed a bottle that looked so icy, it was as if frost still colored the glass. "It looks cold."

"It is. An artesian spring feeds the creek about a quarter-mile upstream. It freezes anything in a day. But I wanted only to chill this, so it didn't take long. I placed it there after I took you home to refresh yourself. I went back for it after Opa asked me to find some useful way to excuse myself." Rad chuckled.

He's not the only Wagner making use of such a beautiful night. Rad had planned this hours in advance. She watched him pour. Her thumb gently traced one of the ornate petals rising to form the goblet's vessel. How easy it was to enjoy such a man. How difficult to remember she shouldn't. "You couldn't know that I would agree to join you."

When he ceased pouring the liquid, Rad added quietly, "I hoped."

"Why did you really bring me here?" She almost touched his fingers, halting only a nail tip away from caressing their long, sculptured lengths.

"I wanted to be alone with you."

His hand retreated to pour his own drink. The sound of wine filling Rad's goblet echoed with the honesty of his reply. Their gazes met, his probing, searching, seeking something from her she found increasingly difficult to deny. In the candlelit blue of his eyes, she saw the intoxicating lure of equally restrained passion banked behind rigid control. Why, his hand was trembling!

Knowing that his resolution wavered proved almost unbearable to Toya. She exhaled a sigh so deep, it flickered the candlelight. Shadows danced along the wall as the flames fought to regain their strength. It was then she noticed the sketchings in one corner of the room. She turned to view what had been drawn on the wall and wondered why Rad chose to draw a mural rather than decorate the wall as he had others in the house.

With sudden realization, Toya noted the drawing depicted a man and woman sitting on a stool, milking a cow. She blinked, certain that her imagination played tricks upon her eyes. But when she looked again, the scene remained in all its vivid detail. The closeness of their bodies as she nestled against him. The image of Monarch, the striped tabby, licking milk from its whiskers. Though the man's face was cast in shadows, an expression of anticipation had been captured on the woman's face. The anticipation of a kiss?

Sensations warred within Toya at once. A certain thrill that he treasured the incident enough to draw it. Anger that he dared put it on display for all to see. Confusion that she was both pleased and upset by his open demonstration of affection. Rad might be a man of few words, but his sketchings spoke volumes.

The artwork made it more difficult to withstand the power of his passion. They both needed the cold voice of reason to cool the heat of their fervor for each other. She needed to leave the room at once, to quell the dangerous longing he aroused within her, to remind him of his role as host to all and beau to Betina.

"B-Betina will wonder why I have kept you from her so long."

He set his goblet down, leaned across the table, and gently grasped her hands. "Shall I stop spending time with her?"

Did he think her jealous? Toya dared to meet his gaze. "What you do with your time is no concern of mine."

He laughed. "I like it when you really look at me. She's right, you know. Betina says you speak with your eyes what your tongue will not. I shall pay more attention when you're quiet."

"Please don't. It makes things more difficult."

"What does?" His question exited in a husky whisper. "What things?"

"Paying attention to me. Painting me." She knew he had no doubt she referred to the painting in his bedroom and not the one drawn there. "This candlelit dinner. You make it troublesome to fulfill the job Opa has hired me to do. He expects me to remain by his side, but how can I when—"

"You are here with me?" Rad sat back and eyed her speculatively. "Why do you imagine that is, *Liebling*?"

A heartbeat passed as she carefully considered the answer. "I . . ." The half lie tasted bitter. She swallowed hard and started again. "I knew that Opa was safe and where he wanted to be . . . with my aunts. And you went to so much trouble, I did not want to appear ungrateful—"

"Ungrateful! For what?"

"For your saving my life at the well. And for Opa's kindness to my aunts. For your standing up to Lineva Pyrtle and the other townspeople regarding my honor. I should like to think that you did so because I could be of real help to the two of you . . . as one friend to another."

She studied his face to see the impact of the term "friend." His expression hardened liked clay baked in a kiln. His fingers unthreaded themselves from hers. Rad stared for some time at the sketches, then drank his wine to the last drop.

"If that is all you require from me, Toya"—his eyes stared over the rim of his goblet, piercing her with the sharpness of their glint—"then so be it. But be very sure of what you want."

What I want? God knows, it's you I want, Rad. But it is Peter to whom I've pledged myself. Hot tears flooded her eyes. She blinked away the emotion threatening to spill down her cheeks. With deliberate exaggeration she rubbed her eyes. "The w-wax is smoking too much. Sometimes my eyes start to itch and burn when I stay out in the fields too—"

"The others are returning." Rad motioned to the sound of laughter drifting on the breeze that blew through the open window. He stood, staring out into the night. "It looks like they have the same idea we did. They're returning with their soup bowls." Rad gathered the goblets and partially used wine bottle. "There is still enough time to straighten up here."

The distraction gave Toya a moment to gather her shattered sentiments and bury them beneath the facade of loving Peter.

"It seems neither of us is very hungry. Are you ready to go?"

"You're angry."

A moment passed before he responded. Finally, when his eyes focused on hers, the glint had eased into a surprising gentleness. "I am not angry. How could I be when all you've done is chosen to keep your word? I am disappointed in myself for trying to tempt you. It is unlike me—to be so impetuous."

Toya smiled, endeared by Rad's honesty. How could a man seem even stronger when admitting a weakness? "I fear I may arouse ... er ... influence you to be so impulsive."

"*Ja, Liebling.* You do. But only because I want to do such things."

Suddenly, his arms went around her, shifting her body close to his. Unfathomable desire fired the smoky blue of Rad's eyes, refusing to be banked any longer by his strict moral edicts. The look was so raw and full of need that Toya could not meet his gaze and remain standing. It took her breath away, stole all resistance to the rush of feelings she'd tried desperately to dispel all day.

Toya closed her eyes, afraid that she might melt in his arms. His fingers spread against the back of her head, cradling her.

"Look at me, Toya."

She swallowed, shaking her head. *If I look at you, I will forget all that holds us apart. I will forget all that can never be. I will remember only how you make me feel when your lips touch mine.*

Her eyes opened despite her willing them to remain shut. "*Nein,*" she sighed.

His mouth met hers in a featherlike kiss before he whispered against her lips, "Know that it is I who kisses you now. Remember the feel of *my* arms holding you this night."

His mouth slanted over hers in a hot, wild kiss that held nothing back. Raw desire rocked Toya to the tips of her toes, forcing her to slide her fingers through the thick burnished gold of his hair and press him closer. Tantalizing tremors coursed through her body as Rad's tongue thrust and parried in a sensual duel with her own, eliciting a husky moan from the bee charmer's lips.

Toya abandoned all conscious thought and any objection that would deny his touch. Their bodies began to shift, as if searching for just the right fit to each other's contours. Rad began to move against her hips. A whimper of pleasure escaped her as fire ignited in her abdomen, blazing a trail of white-hot yearning to the core of her being. Her tongue fiercely explored the rough velvet of his mouth.

A craving consumed her as his eyes turned indigo blue—the color of moonlit bluebonnets. She wanted to know what would darken them further, yearned to watch every shade of passion devour their depths.

With all her being she realized she wanted him to make love to her. Needed him to. Could no more stop him now than if he were a wildfire and she a single drop of water.

She took his hand and gently guided it to the swell of her breast. He touched in reverence, testing its weight upon his palm, drawing lazy circles as if to erase the fabric that covered the hardening peak. It strained for a more intimate touch. His head bent to kiss first one treasured pinnacle, then the other, lathing them with the hungry nip of his teeth and tongue.

She gently pressed his temples, encouraging him upward to soothe the craving he had left wanting. The startling heat of his tongue traced a path up her neck and across her jaw to taunt the sensitive skin at the tip of her earlobe.

Words, whisper-soft, brushed hotly against her ear. The fine hair on the back of her neck stood on end.

"I want you, Toya." Every muscle in his body tensed as Rad breathed raggedly and groaned, "But . . . not . . . like . . . this."

Love me! Her thoughts screamed against the assault of his words. Yet she didn't dare utter the plea. Not when his words shattered the magic their bodies created—stones thrown against a looking glass. Shards of broken illusions pierced her with sorrow.

His blond head came up slowly, his eyes demanding that she look at him. It took everything in Toya's willpower not to curl up into a ball.

"I don't want to be your *friend*, Toya. It will never be enough to be just your friend. If I cannot become your husband, your lover, the shelter of your soul, then I prefer to be nothing to you. Do you hear me? *Nothing.* For I want nothing less than your love."

When Toya finally found enough resolution to speak, he stopped her with a lift of his hand.

"I will help you keep your promise to Peter. Never again will I attempt to ravish you. I give you my word."

No, don't. Not your solemn word. Do not give voice to what we both will regret. His pronouncement should have made her happy, should have eased her concern about humiliating Peter. All Rad's vow did was tear away a chunk of her heart. Toya felt certain it would never again be mended.

A knock sounded on the door, jarring her senses. She cried out and spun around, trying desperately to gather her wits and extinguish the fire that still raged inside her.

"Toya? Rad? Are you in there?" Opa called from the other side. The door opened slightly. He peeked at them from around the edge. "The Reinharts and Fraulein Bram said they'd better eat and be on their way. Church comes early this day."

She hoped her cheeks were not as red as they felt. Toya faced him and the fact that she'd almost done the one thing Conrad Wagner would never forgive her for. If she'd made love to him, she could never marry Peter. If she didn't marry Peter, it would become another obligation she had not completed. The one thing Rad valued above all else was finishing what one promised to do.

And finish she must, no matter how much it hurt her to do so. No matter that she could never love Peter now. Not after the way Rad had made her feel tonight. She only fooled herself in believing she could grow to love the councilman as her sister wanted, as their father had hoped. As she had pledged to do.

Nein. Making love to Rad was the worst mistake she had ever almost made. Thank heavens he found the good sense to think for both of them. She should be grateful to him. Yet all she wanted to do was rail against Rad and the unfairness of loving him. "Tell them I am ready to leave when they are."

The old man eyed the pair speculatively. "Are the two of you finished with whatever you were doing?"

Toya winced at the hope generated in Opa's features. She flipped her braid behind her shoulders and straightened her back with purpose. The only way to keep sane until Peter's return was to make certain she refrained from being alone with Rad as much as possible. To guarantee any happiness for a future with her husband-to-be, she must see that the councilman inspired all the yearning Rad had ignited within her tonight. Never again must she let down her guard.

"I assure you," she answered Opa with new resolve. "We are quite finished."

10

Toya sat through church services grieving the loss of what she and Rad might have shared. Night had come and gone with little sleep, for the feel of Rad's arms had haunted her long past the first streaks of dawn. She'd half-heartedly packed her weekly picnic to be taken to Tilly's grave, still not particularly hungry. She'd lost her appetite last night and didn't have one that morning. She must eat something or she would make herself ill. Perhaps that's what she needed to do to get over this overwhelming sense of loss she felt—eat. Or, at least, cook. Cooking always relaxed her.

Trouble was, how could she rid herself of the memory of that soul-scorching kiss? She could bake from now to Armageddon and never generate enough heat to challenge the fire Rad created inside her. The adventurer in Toya wanted him to step out of the pew, sweep her up into his arms, and carry her away to some private haven he'd created for them and make mad, passionate love to her. The thought of such a possibility flushed her skin with heated memories of his touch.

Toya fanned herself with a kerchief, trying to steady the hymnal held in her other hand.

Betina leaned over and whispered in Toya's right ear. "It is almost at an end, and it looks like rain. The picnic will be fun and cool. I am glad you asked me to join you."

Often Rad worked in his orchard while Toya visited her sister's grave nearby. But they usually ignored each other ... or at least pretended to. Perhaps he would join them today, and the picnic would give him and Betina more time together. Nodding, Toya offered a smile.

Playing matchmaker to the pair might be the best thing that ever happened. If they married, then Rad would have the children he yearned for, and Betina, she would have a good man to love her, to care for her, to share her sorrows and joys with. Images of the wonderful life Betina would enjoy as Rad's wife sent currents of envy coursing through Toya. She sent up a prayer. *Give me strength, Lord. I am weak, but my spirit is willing. Truly, it is.*

"Ready to go?" Betina nudged Toya with an elbow, urging her to exit the pew.

Toya replaced the hymnal, waiting for the congregation to move. When she finally stepped into the aisle, she accidentally bumped a strong chest as she vied for room. "Sorry, I was—" She glanced up, apology dying in her throat.

"I am in no rush, *Liebling*. Please go ahead." Rad motioned that they should pass in front of him.

Toya ignored him but was still very much aware of his quiet strength behind her. She could almost feel his body heat. Perhaps inviting him to join them was not such a good idea. Perhaps matchmaking was best done from afar.

"Where are you ladies headed?"

She elbowed Betina, but the dressmaker refused to take the hint.

"Owww. To a picnic, if I make it there in one piece. The congregation is a little unruly this morning."

"A visit to your sister's grave?" Rad stared at Toya, who in turn glared at her best friend.

"She visits Tilly every Sunday." Betina turned around and backed her way up the aisle. "She said your grandfather had plans with Gunnar Williams. It seems his wife has also misplaced her kerchief. There must be an epidemic of forgetfulness among those of us with kerchiefs." She winced. "I meant no offense to—"

"My grandfather would be the first to laugh." Rad smiled to ease her discomfort.

"W-what I meant to say was if you intend to work in your orchard, you might save us a walk. It smells like rain in a few hours. Ouch!" She started to hop and scowled back at Toya.

Toya pretended stepping on her friend's foot had been an accident.

Betina persisted. "She would have more time to visit if you took us."

Wait till I get you alone, Toya mouthed silently, deliberately moving to one side so Rad would be directly behind her and could not see her displeasure with Betina. A picnic amid the wildflowers on Toya's and Tilly's land seemed the idyllic place for Betina to pursue her intentions with Rad. But watching them openly court became less of an enjoyable prospect the farther they proceeded out of the church.

"I've been wanting to discuss your land for some time now, Fraulein Reinhart." He pressed a firm hand against her shoulder, offering a slight squeeze of encouragement despite the formality he used in front of other townspeople. "This will give me an opportunity to check my peaches to see how far afield my bees are swarming. It might also allow us the opportunity to discuss some plans I have in mind."

"Good, then you will join us for lunch." Betina winked. "Our Toya has made one of her special potato bacon cakes.

I believe that is your favorite, is it not, Conrad?"

"But you said it was—" Toya realized her friend had long manipulated the day by requesting the potato cake. She'd been led to believe the dish was Betina's latest favorite, when in truth the schemer wanted to please Rad. Betina must really be infatuated with him to go to such lengths. Well, Betina had better hope that Rad liked plump women, because Toya intended to make certain her dear friend ate a fair share of the scrumptious, hip-expanding pastry.

"*Ja,* join us," Toya relented. "You should see our Betina eat. She will probably devour two, maybe three pieces all by herself."

Brown eyes rounded. Toya blinked at her friend's panic and offered her a silent warning, *You started it. This is one thing I intend to finish.*

"I do not care that we just got started." Toya pointed at the brown mass emerging from the tree line. "I think we should leave."

A booming, organlike note rose and swelled over the field of wildflowers as the swarm of bees foraged for the next cluster of pollen.

"Just be still, and they will cause you no harm." Rad pointed to newly blooming pear-shaped petals. "The clover is yielding. The flow is on. They really love snow asters too. Well, anything white, I suppose. Look there, they're just having fun . . . enjoying spring."

Toya watched several insects contort, doing aerial flips and spins as they sang with subdued excitement. The bees rolled, flying on their backs at times, contorting as they gave off a powerful scent that gusted with the breeze.

"Smell it?" Rad whispered to the two women, who seemed mesmerized by the horde's antics. "That's a signal they have found a refuge. They emit that fragrance to beckon the others to a treasure field."

"But this is *my* meadow." Toya sat perfectly still, afraid to move for fear of drawing unwanted attention. Bees might be fascinating to study, but they were armed with little barbs, malignant with pain. She didn't want to fight them off every time she visited Tilly's grave. "And I prefer they frolic elsewhere."

"That is what I want to talk to you about, *Liebling. Nein,* hold still. You have become a rest stop."

Toya's heart raced to keep time with the black and yellow striped insect's challenging, high-pitched shriek as it landed on her forearm and slowly waddled up her elbow. Ze-eee-eep! Ze-eee-eep! The bee panted heavily, giving little hops like a wounded duck, its abdomen swelled three times greater than its head.

Toya was afraid to speak. Afraid to breathe. Afraid she would start trembling, and the murdering devil would grow irritated.

Betina leaned toward Toya, careful to move slowly. "It can smell fear."

"Such an insightful scholar you are." Toya willed the creature to fly far, far away and take his comrades with him.

Rad laughed and set the trespasser's wings to humming.

"Shhh! Now look what you've done." Panic seized Toya. "Oh, God. Is it so big because it's going to have more of them?"

"*Nein.* It carries the gathered pollen. I will be surprised if the greedy little bandit is able to reach the hives."

"Go home, bug," Toya pleaded with the creature.

"You can move." Rad stood from his sitting position on the picnic blanket. "Just do not move quickly."

"Easy for you to say." Toya would sit there all day without moving another muscle if necessary. "You did say they prefer to return to their hives at night?"

"*Ja.* But they will leave soon. From the looks of them, they have foraged a few hundred miles. See how that flower bends there? Do you see the bee clinging to the downturned edge? Yes, that one. Watch it roll in the pollen."

"It's practically bathing in the dust." Betina giggled. "Lusty little dervish."

"Back away, Betina," Rad warned. "See the newcomer. A wasp. The pirating devil can hurt you."

"Ugh. Stop him." Toya watched in horror as the wasp, indeed, approached with swaggering bravado. The sinister buccaneer strolled along the same leaf as the bee, waited until the intended target quit rolling and noticed the danger. The wasp lurched, bit its victim in half, then dashed away with the poor creature's loaded abdomen.

With its dying breath the bee sounded an alarm. A cloud suddenly formed above the meadow, hovering, forming and reforming until it became almost solid. The swarm rose in the air, rolling like mist over the grass. It surged sideways, then spiraled like a thunderhead building to malign the sky.

"Remain still, both of you. Betina, I've shown you what to do before. Toya, I'll protect your back." Rad moved behind Toya. "Pray that they decide to go home instead of launching an attack."

"I want those things away from my land," Toya demanded shakily between gritted teeth.

"I'll see that I keep them in their hives on Sunday when you visit."

Rad's hands began to rub the tension from her shoulders.

"You can do that?" Toya watched the swarm make two more evolutions, then migrate toward Rad's orchard. "*Lieber Gott!* I thought that thieving marauder would cause the death of us all."

Betina released a pent-up breath. "*Ja,* me too."

"I cannot control where they seek the nectar." Rad's fingertips delved into the hair at Toya's temples, gently rubbing away the tension. "I can decide *when* they come and go. Still, I offer another solution. Why not sell me your land?"

A TASTE OF HONEY

Toya shirked from his touch and walked over to her sister's grave. Betina followed closely behind. Of all the things Toya hadn't wanted to hear from Rad, his offering to buy her land was the last.

"I had hoped you would let me buy your property. Your bluebonnets will be blooming in days. My bees prefer to feast on them and satisfy themselves on clover and aster only until the bluebonnets arrive."

Toya traced the words carved on Tilly's tombstone. BELOVED SISTER. VANISHED FROM THIS LIFE TOO SOON. Though her anger was directed toward the bees, Toya felt betrayed by his request. She'd thought all this time he had not asked anyone else to marry him because he'd wanted only her.

The memory of that day came vividly into focus. The Society made it clear a married man would be alloted twice the land a bachelor received. She'd not taken Rad's proposal seriously at first, believing he wanted her land only because it lay next to his.

But he had not asked another to take her place after her refusal, quelling Toya's suspicions that he offered the proposal only to increase his holdings in America. She'd secretly thrilled that he truly wanted *her* as his wife. Now she could see that his intentions all along were to gain the land. This piece of land. What better timing to initiate those plans than when she needed better employment?

"What does it matter which flower they plunder?" she argued, unable to keep the obstinacy from her tone. "Why *my* bluebonnets?"

"Because honey made from various flowers tastes differently." Betina revealed the close attention she'd paid to the beekeeper during their shared meetings. "Rad says some of the other colonists in Fredericksburg and Austin have done several studies regarding the matter. If the bees feed on hawthorne, then the honey tastes like nuts. If lime trees, then there will be a mint taste to it."

Delight filled Rad's face at the dressmaker's knowledge on the subject. "Today's honey will probably taste like cinnamon. Sweet clover tends to vary, but usually it becomes cinnamony. With a field so close to home, the bees will not tire themselves so easily. As you saw from the way they dropped onto the petals, they must have foraged for miles, possibly hundreds. If less time can be spent gathering pollen, more can be used in creating the honey. The closer the flower field, the more contented the bee."

It took every ounce of Toya's determination to remember that she wanted Rad and Betina to share more than knowledge of each other's work.

"If they use bluebonnet pollen"—Betina's tongue darted out to lick her lips—"the honey will taste like aged wine. You know how our countrymen relish anything that tastes of spirits."

"Best of all, it strengthens the heart and can heal a wound quickly." Rad's grin became a wicked slash. "And it will clean out any blockage."

Betina laughed. "Why, Conrad, is it a sense of humor you have grown? You are normally such a cabbage-face."

Every friendship had its limits! To ward off having to listen to any further joys about conscientious bees or Betina's discovery of Rad's more admirable traits, Toya raised a palm to halt them. "Even if your honey provided age-slowing qualities, I would not want it made anywhere near me."

"Then sell the land."

"Nein." Toya pointed to her sister's tombstone. "As long as that remains, I will always keep this place."

"She's not really there," Rad reminded Toya gently.

"Where would you have me move it?" Tears began to form as guilt festered in her heart once again. "I never found her, did I? I was too busy worrying about my own—" Toya's palms cupped her eyes to shield her tears from view.

"Stop it! You could not have known she would ignore our demands." Rad reached to gently tug Toya's fingers away. "You did not lead her into the hills to die."

Toya stared up at him, felt Betina's comforting hands wrapped around her shoulders to lend support. Taking a deep, calming breath to fortify herself against the grief that still gripped her after all these years, Toya met his gaze squarely. "I knew she was not well. The snakebite was only part of the reason she talked such nonsense. Tilly wasn't happy for a long time before that. Maybe the snake venom did something to her. Poisoned her ability to think. Drove her to—"

"Tilly wanted to go." Betina's hands returned to her sides. "She wanted to get away from . . . from all that saddened her."

Toya backed away from her friend, needing the space to build a wall between her and the truth Betina spoke. "From me?"

A look passed between the others that Toya found annoying, even puzzling. She felt left out. Abandoned. By Peter. By Rad and Betina these past five months. By Tilly. "Is there something I don't know? Something I haven't been told?"

"N-nothing." Betina stared off into the distance. "You know as much as us."

Why did Betina have such difficulty looking at her when she said that? The realization that Betina harbored secrets from her for any reason raked against the foundation of their lifelong friendship.

Had Betina known something all this time and chosen to keep it secret? Tilly and Betina seldom got along, each vying for Toya's time. The attention had been flattering when younger, but as Toya grew older, the pair's countless arguments grew frustrating. The accusation that she spent more time with Betina than she did her own sister became a sore point between the twins. One that never healed. Tilly never quite forgave Toya for having such a deep, abiding friendship. She had gone to her grave without resolving the dispute.

"I remember being crazed with grief." Anguish laced Toya's tone. "I remember that she had been snake-bitten and talked out of her head for days. I also remember that she was growing stronger. Talking more sense. That's the only reason I left Tilly alone that night." That, and the fact that Rad had proposed and kissed her.

Toya looked at Rad for understanding. Compassion filled his eyes.

"She wanted to go up into the hills and die, the way the Indians do. But she had come through the worst of it and was getting better." Rad's words soothed, inspiring reason where only emotion raged. "Remember, your father thought her well enough to continue plans for her and Peter's wedding. No one could have known she would disappear. Everyone would have simply thought she ran off had not Betina found the note Tilly left for you."

Toya swung around, searching Betina's face. Is that what bothered her friend? Had she known Tilly's plans and was sworn to secrecy? "You knew, did you not, Betina? You knew and yet you didn't tell me."

"There are some things even I have not shared with you, but knowing Tilly meant to kill herself was not one of them." Honesty rounded her brown eyes. "As much as Tilly and I disliked each other, I would never have allowed her to kill herself. You must believe that, Toya."

"I want to believe you." Toya crossed her arms, warding off the increasing sense of betrayal she felt. "I need to."

Rad pulled a handful of flowers and placed them on Tilly's grave. "Your sister's passing was a terrible tragedy, but you must go on. She wanted you to. Just like she asked you to take her place as Peter's bride. She wanted you to continue your father's plans. Herr Reinhart knew if Peter married one of you twins, he would see that both of you were taken care of and would lack for nothing. The same with your aunts. And he's proven himself worthy of your father's trust, hasn't he?"

Ja, her mind screamed. Peter was this. Peter was that. Peter was everything to everybody but nothing of what she truly wanted. "Father would be pleased with him."

"Herr Reinhart meant for you to do something with your life and this land. Tilly wanted you to fulfill his wish if she couldn't. Why not sell to someone who will value what your father and sister foresaw?" Rad brushed away wilted peach blooms that had blown across the grave. "If you prefer to keep the headstone here, you can still visit on Sundays. I'll keep the bees in their hives so you can picnic unafraid."

Toya sorely needed the money to be financially independent from Peter. But she could not gain from what a neighbor should offer freely to another. "I will loan you the use of my field."

"*Nein.* I will own it."

"Do not set that stubborn jaw against me." Toya's tilted to match his in obstinance. Full of pride he was. Stubborn German pride. "Every immigrant wants to own a piece of America. That includes myself."

"Then I shall rent it. A Wagner will never accept charity."

"It was not charity I offered, but the use of pollen. You are just being *starrköpfig* . . . as a mule. I would make this offer to anyone."

"I am not anyone! I am Conrad Augustus Wagner. And I do not want to be just anyone. Do not say such a thing to me ever again."

His vexation startled her. She would have shouted back at him, but the sound of wounded pride echoing in his tone silenced her retort and tugged at her heart. He wanted to be more *to her*. This outburst stemmed from her refusal to acknowledge the love he held for her. "I shall gauge my words more carefully," she offered softly, naming a possible rental fee. "Does that sound fair?"

"Done. But only if I add a jar of honey each week for your aunt. Fredericka enjoys it so, and it will help her joints."

He held out one massive hand, and she shook it to seal their bargain. The warmth of his callused palm encompassed hers, blending the beat of their pulses. The bargain felt so right. So fitting. She had not simply acted on impulse, but actually saw the sense of it all. Being near Conrad did have its advantages—he was teaching her to think before she acted. "It is a good bargain we make, Conrad Wagner. You are a persuasive man."

Betina grabbed the basket and wineglasses. "He'll be a wet man if you two do not help me gather these picnic things."

Toya slid her fingers from his, aware that she allowed the touch to linger longer than propriety required. Turning away, she wished the words would come that might convince Rad he would forever mean more to her than such words expressed. That she would never consider him as just anyone. She would remember him as the man whose kiss melted away her every thought but of him.

Rad Wagner had become the only man she would ever love, and her own words had doomed her to an eternity without him. How in all that was holy could she ever face Peter and he not see the anguish written on her face? How could she ever give herself to Peter in the marriage bed and he not sense that she loved another?

Toya hurried back to the wagon, needing distance to separate her from the others. She refused to let them see her come to grips with her despair. As she stared forlornly into the horizon, her heart felt heavy as the clouds sagging with rain. If only the torrent would hurry, would pour so heavily, no one might guess that her face was streaked with tears.

But no amount of rain could relieve the tempest of emotions swirling through Toya's sorrow-swollen soul.

And no marriage bed shared with Peter would ever make her forget the rapture of Rad's touch.

11

The rain drove everyone indoors. At first Rad worked in the barn while Toya and Opa experimented with recipes in the chalet. Betina visited when the dress shop closed, sharing part of her time with Toya and the remainder with Rad.

When the two friends finally had a chance to talk, Betina denied any infatuation with Rad, insisting all they discussed was how to make wise business decisions. Just as Toya served as Opa's apprentice, Betina claimed she did with Rad.

Halfway through the week, the rain stopped, but they needed a few days drying time before work could begin again in the fields or the orchard. Today, the bees took to flight—a sign that the weather had stablized.

Toya, Opa, and her aunts spent most of the morning helping Rad in the orchard. Many hands were needed to check the countless trees after the rainfall. Rain saved him from having to irrigate but also created an ideal environment for mildew and brown rot spores on the budding peaches. If the mildew had taken root, then the trees would have to be thinned. The sooner he could rid the orchard of the threat, the less likely the entire crop would fail. And this was too important a crop after the long dry spell of the past two years that yielded few vegetables and almost no fruit. Anticipation for one of Opa's mouthwatering cobblers kept the workers diligent.

Toya walked behind Rad now, checking the undersides of the fruit and gathering those that had fallen on the ground into the gunnysack tied around her neck. A sanguine hue and the sweet, lingering scent of withered peaches blanketed the earth.

"How many have you lost to the downpour?" She studied the rows and rows of trees and realized the branches seemed to contain thousands of peaches.

"Do not concern yourself, *Liebling*." He reached up and plucked an amber-colored fruit to show her a perfect specimen. "The rain was a natural thinning of those too frail to withstand what is to come. This, you see, is from an older branch. Peaches from the trees which have been here for years will ripen days earlier than the younger ones. The fruit will be juicier and sweeter. And the color will be more yellow than pink. The more amber the shade, the finer the peach."

"That's what I tell my ladies here." Opa winked at Toya's aunts. "The older the cook, the better the boil."

Fredericka giggled. Albertine blushed and Rad harrumphed. "*Ja,* well, that is good, Grandfather. Now, would you and the Reinharts like to work at that end of the orchard while Toya and I—"

"First we stop for lunch." Opa unthreaded the gunnysack from his neck. "Such a taskmaster you are. The sun is nigh past noon, and we still have not rewarded these fine ladies for gracing us with their company. I have made a surprise for each of you." He helped them take off their gunnysacks. "A thistlecake for you, Albertine."

"And for me?" Curiosity lit Fredericka's eyes.

"A stein of *Bier*."

"Just one?"

All of them laughed, knowing that Fredericka Reinhart was incapable of drinking just one stein of Opa's *Bier*. Toya's aunt had won the blue ribbon for drinking more than any other imbiber at the annual Independence Day *Sängerfest* for two years running.

"It is too hot to eat much." Toya wiped the perspiration from her brow. "I think I'll have just a peach if that's all right with Rad."

"I will do the same." Rad moved branches aside to choose the perfect fruit.

"You and young Conrad enjoy yourself. The ladies and I are going to wander off to the wagon and enjoy the meal I brought." Opa flashed the younger pair a smile and yawned loudly, deliberately. "We might need to rest awhile before we return. I like to nap under the canopy of the trees."

"Do not worry about us. We'll rest, then be along shortly." Albertine met Toya's gaze.

The older woman stressed the *us*, but her look assured Toya she would see that Opa didn't wander afield or be gone long enough to be concerned.

Rad waited until the others headed up the rows toward the wagon before he handed Toya a peach and took one for himself. "Walk with me to the creek, and we'll wash them."

She nodded, following him down several rows until they reached the tributary of the Comal River that fed most of the farms in New Genesis. She glanced up just in time to see a tail slip beneath the top of his collar. "What was that?"

"What was—*Lieber Gott*!" Rad's shoulders shook fiercely as he tried to shed whatever creature had crawled into his shirt. Frantically, he jerked the chambray from inside his trousers, but the wiggling trespasser persisted, making its way down Rad's spine.

"It will get in your trousers!" Toya squealed. The hair on the back of her neck stood on end as she imagined tiny legs crawling down his back. "Oooh, Rad, stop it. Don't let it—"

He ripped his shirt apart at the buttons, tore it away from his shoulders, and threw it on the ground. A green lizard six inches long scurried away into the vetches and clover that had been planted to nourish the orchard's soil.

Toya giggled. "Is that one of Opa's rituals for a good crop—the lizard dance?"

"D-do not . . . encourage him or"—Rad's breath finally slowed allowing him to laugh too—"he will add it to the others. All it will do is raise more lizards, I am guessing."

"You dropped one of the peaches. Want me to pick another?" Toya offered.

"*Nein.* I am not that hungry."

"You can share mine." She gently tossed him the one she held. "I want only half."

"Then I shall show you how to eat a peach in the right manner. It takes a certain knack, you know."

"How would I ever guess? Everything you do takes a knack." While she liked to perform many tasks at once, Rad drove Toya to distraction with his single-mindedness. The man refused to start another chore before finishing every aspect of the one he presently worked on. She, on the other hand, thought if something took precedence over another, then it was the most important responsibility to fulfill—at the moment. *Ja,* he definitely had a knack, and she no sense of priority.

His aim toward perfection was the only thing that bothered Toya about Rad. Her ego suffered extravagantly when, compared to his, her work habits seemed slothful. She had yet to find one thing he could not do efficiently, or at least figure out how to do it well . . . or the one thing that she could do better.

Every merit a man could possibly have—gentleness, patience, the ability to work hard and diligently . . . the list was endless—made her feel positively inadequate by comparison. Worse, this continual admiration of him wreaked havoc on her efforts to shed the strong attraction she felt toward Rad.

"Was that a compliment or criticism?" A quirk lifted Rad's lips. "Too earnest you look, *Liebling*."

"A compliment. You do everything well . . . even lizard dancing." Toya tried not to stare at his magnificent bare torso, but failed miserably. Sunshine shone upon every work-hardened sinew, defining the rugged, expansive chest. Her throat suddenly dried, and she couldn't swallow.

With a sleek, powerful stride, Rad dipped the peach in the creek's cooling water, then offered it to her. "Here, take a bite."

Toya's mouth watered in anticipation, but her hunger had long grown past the peach. Her eyes hooded themselves. "So said Lucifer as he tempted Eve."

His fingertip instinctively searched for the gushy side of the fruit. "Sink your teeth into the flesh."

She indulged herself. Juice trickled from her mouth to dangle on her chin as a thousand magical senses gushed in her mouth, her throat, the nether regions of her desire. Chewing the savory treasure became a primal act of pure, succulent, lustful appreciation of the flavor. She sighed in deep contentment.

"I have never been envious of a peach until now."

Her gaze met his, locked. "No peach has ever tasted this good before. Here, try it."

"*Danke*, I will." His lips lowered to hers.

"Rad—" His name became a whisper upon her lips even as her hands pressed against that glorious chest. Like a tinderbox awaiting a spark, her desire for Rad flared, burning away any precaution.

Beneath her palms she could feel the beat of his heart. For a moment Toya lost herself in the thrill of touching him. Countless times this past week, she crushed the desire to reach out and caress the ripple of his muscles as Rad brushed down the horses, lifted pieces of furniture to dust and polish, or painted vibrant strokes when he thought no one watched. Countless times she strained to hear his words, loving the realm of Rad's intelligence and his thoughtfulness toward Opa and her aunts. Toya deliberately did not eavesdrop on Rad's and Betina's conversations. Countless times she told herself he would one day belong to her best friend, if *she* would just step out of the way and give them a chance.

But it was *her* lips that generated the heat growing beneath her touch, *her* kiss that sent a quiver through Rad's work-hardened physique, *her* fingertips tracing a trail up his chest to wrap themselves around his neck.

"Rad?"

"Hmm?"

How could a single syllable sound so seductive? "How does it taste?"

"*You* taste wonderful, *Liebling*."

If she died and went to heaven then, she would forever remember the hot, breathy baritone that whispered against her ear, then nuzzled something unintelligible against the hollow of her neck.

"Why me, Rad?" She wanted to make sense of what was happening to them. Why couldn't she resist this man no matter how much she tried?

"Because I knew from the moment I saw you that you were the one."

Oh, what a wonderful thing to say. The man may not speak much, but when he did, he said the right things.

"Of course, you looked like someone else I'd just met."

He chuckled. "So I may have been mistaken."

She tweaked a few of his chest hairs, making him squirm. "I *am* a twin, rattlehead. Now, be serious, I want to know. Why me?" She had to know. To understand. To hold it to her during the lonely days to come as Peter's wife.

Toya took the slightest step backward, unconsciously allowing her palms to caress his ribs and trace the slope of skin from chest to waist. Everywhere she touched, his flesh rippled in response.

Rad stood there, frowning, yet allowing her to explore.

She sensed he waited, wondered. Why *did* she play this game of holding him at bay, then touching him as if he belonged to her? If he ever dared ask, Toya could not offer him an answer that made any sense. What would she say . . . my hands speak when my heart cannot . . . my lips dare what my brain disavows?

"What did you think when you saw me?"

Though he strove to sound as if he were teasing, Toya heard the hope in Rad's tone. She remembered the first time she'd seen him nearly stumble into town. He cradled a woman in his arms. Five children followed him like a gander leading goslings. The woman wore threadbare clothing and had suffered greatly on the journey from Galveston to New Genesis.

It rained for months, and there had been no transportation for the newly arrived Germans. The immigrants had walked from the coast and became ill. Many died along the roadside. Only a handful survived. Rad had seen to it that Frau Hertz and her brood were among those survivors, carrying her during the day and seeing to her children's needs at night.

Ja, Rad Wagner made quite an impression that first day. "I thought you were a man who sacrificed your own needs for others."

She remembered him gently laying the woman down,

then sliding his cap from his head in slow motion, the look of wonder upon his handsome features as his eyes met Toya's for the first time. Her heart had raced at such heroism, at such politeness, before wondering if he was married to the woman. She'd felt ashamed for wishing it not so, but equally pleased when she discovered that he was a bachelor.

"And has your view of me changed?" he asked softly.

"You are as strong as this America you love. As reliable as a harness jingle. You will never change."

"Reliable, huh? I am not sure that is such a good quality when trying to entice someone who prefers excitement, variety, and her fair share of adventure."

"Reliability is a fine merit, but you have others."

"What others?"

"You are a strong man, Rad," she whispered, halting her hands' slide down to wherever they intended to delve. They seemed to have a will of their own.

"The land has made me strong. From breaking the stone for building the fence. From chopping logs for the house."

Her hands measured the breadth of his shoulders. Where her touch lingered, heat flourished in its wake and left a noticeable pulse beat.

"If you continue this way much longer, I will not promise I can control the strength . . . of my desire for you, *Liebling*."

Her fingers threaded themselves into his hair, giving his flesh time to cool, yet unwilling to relinquish touching him completely. "Your hair is the color of goldenrod along the riverbank."

"A German's hair I have," he reminded her unnecessarily.

"And your eyes, they are filled with a dozen shades of blue. The blue of Lake of Lucerne. The blue of the Texas sky when it births a rainbow. The color of bluebonnets in full bloom." *If you look at me like that, you'll have to kiss me again.*

She found his temple, laid a palm against his cheek, and followed the line of his mouth with a fingertip. "These are fine lips. Full and moist and lush with the flavor of peaches."

Toya knew exactly what she was doing. And she knew, too, that it was unfair. This would only lead to frustration. But she could not resist tasting him as he had her.

Rad's grip was like iron as he backed her against the nearest tree and pressed her against its trunk. The kiss that followed warned that he was done with her games.

When his tongue touched hers, a deep pulsing ignited in her lower regions and raced to every nerve ending in her body. Before she realized what she was doing, Toya turned to allow him to fill his palm with her breast while his other hand cupped the back of her head.

His lips tore away from hers as he pleaded hoarsely, "I have wanted you too long."

Her nipples hardened in anticipation. "No . . . wait."

"No more waiting, Toya. You want me. I see it in your eyes. Taste it in your kiss." His hand slid open the first button of her blouse, the second. "See"—his lips lowered to taste the budding pinnacle of her breast—"you can no more deny it than I can forget you will belong to another. But I am no rock, Toya. Flesh covers these bones. A heart beats in this chest. Reason flees from my thoughts when I hold you. Tell me you want this to be, and I can forget the wrong of this. I will find some way to make it right with Peter when he returns."

"Rad! Toya! Come quickly!" Opa raced toward them with Fredericka waddling closely behind. "We have a visitor!"

Toya heard Rad's sharp, indrawn breath and quickly rebuttoned her blouse. He moved back with an audible groan and marched a few steps away. She thought she even heard his teeth grind.

"Who is it, Opa?" Rad ran a hand through his hair. "The way my luck is holding, it can only be Peter."

Fredericka stopped alongside Toya, huffing and puffing as she attempted to regain her breath. "If only . . . that were so. T-there would be more . . . of us . . . to help." Tears sprang into her eyes as she started jabbering in German.

Toya reached out to calm her aunt. "Slow down, sweet. I cannot understand you."

"The children." Opa wrapped an arm around Fredericka. "You know how Fred loves the children. They are sick. In the new village just south of us. More coming by the day according to the man who brought us the news."

"Where is he?" Toya stared past her elders and saw no one on the trail behind them.

"With Albertine." Opa's gaze met Rad's. "I told her to go with him and ring the alarm. Everyone will be gathered when we get there."

"They came for Ash to see if he would conjure something to help, but he said Rad would know best what should be done." Fredricka wiped her tears and searched Rad's face, lifting her chins so high, both faded into one. "Good decisions you make, Conrad Wagner? *Ja?*"

"What can he do?" Toya imagined frightened parents watching their young ones grow ill. The German people who settled the Republic had suffered their share of grief these past few years. Would the land demand more? "What can any of us do?"

"He can start by putting back on his shirt." Opa nodded at Rad's bare chest, his gaze lighting with amusement despite the gravity of the situation.

Fredericka's mouth formed an oval, and she swung around as if she'd seen him stark naked.

"First we must learn what is making them ill." Rad gathered his torn shirt and put it back on. "Then we will decide how to remedy that."

Toya gently touched her aunt's arm. "He is fully clothed now."

"Please, save the children." Fredericka spun around to grab Rad's hands and press them against her cheek. She kissed the back of his hand as if she were paying homage to a king. "Without them, what will there be left but endurance?"

"I give you my word that I will do all I can, Frau Reinhart." Rad's promise reverberated through the orchard. "I am no physician, but I will find a way . . . this I vow."

Rad was a man of his word. A man of principle. The fact eased Toya's fears for the children. She raced down the row of trees beside him. If anyone could solve this dilemma, he could. He would not give up until he did.

The reality of what had almost happened between them hit Toya full force, nearly staggering her. Tempting him into ignoring his principles had been wrong. When his lust was sated, when he had time to consider what they'd done, would Rad feel that making love to her had been worth the breach of honor? She couldn't take that from him. Rad's integrity was the core of his entire being. Giving in to their desires would make him betray himself . . . and that she could be no part of!

Grateful for the distance and slower gait that kept Opa and Fredericka from following too closely, Toya attempted to talk to Rad before they reached the others. "What almost transpired back there should never have—"

He held up a restraining palm. "I was an equal partner, if I recall. I'm not sorry it happened. We must talk about this. Decide what we will do. But now is not the time."

She had to make him listen. He was stubborn, her Conrad, and there was only one way to get through to him when his mind was set. Toya deliberately laughed. "The time will be of my choosing. When the mood strikes me."

Rad halted and grabbed her by the arm. "Be careful, *Liebling*. This is a dangerous game you play. I can be impulsive too. Next time, think twice before you come so readily into my embrace." His gaze ravished Toya as surely as if it were a wildfire sweeping over the land and leaving devastation in its wake. He turned her loose and moved away, calling back over his shoulder, "You will finish what you start next time. No matter what the cost we both pay. I guarantee it."

12

The peal of the bell stationed atop the maypole in New Genesis's town square rang out the alarm. Doors flung open. People rushed into the street, shielding their eyes from the afternoon sun to see what transpired. Sidewalk vendors stopped hawking their wares, and heads turned. Wagons changed directions and flowed toward the distress call.

Toya accepted Rad's help from the buckboard. She glanced from Aunt Albertine and the man standing next to her on the speaker's platform to the three covered wagons still harnessed to their teams next to the maypole.

"Opa, stay with Fredericka and Toya while I see what this is all about." Rad handed Toya the reins. "Could you hitch these for me and see that Opa doesn't wander off in this crowd?"

He didn't need to say more. Toya knew Rad was worried the excitement might distract his grandfather. "We'll stay together. And do not concern yourself with the horses. I will see to their care."

It took Toya's best effort to ignore the stirrings of her

curiosity and to complete the task Rad required of her. But complete it she did, rushing to satisfy her concern over why women, several bodies deep, sat on the driver's boxes of those three wagons, peering through the tarpaulins. Worried expressions on their faces and ill-looking children cradled in their arms could mean only that these were some of the families from the neighboring village.

The bell quit ringing. A river of people suddenly swept Toya, Opa, and her aunt along with the others. Spotting Betina in the crowd not far away from her, Toya called, "Over here. Betina! Join us."

"What's happened?" Betina yelled above the heads dividing them.

"Children are sick. Maybe dying," Toya shouted back, trying to carve a path toward her friend.

Everyone nearby stopped, stepping aside to allow Toya and her companions through. Curiosity laced the air around her as she made her way forward. She could feel their questions circling her like a pack of hungry wolves. "I only know that a messenger had been sent to Opa and Rad Wagner, to see if they can help. I know little else."

Many grumbled, turning their attention to the speaker's stand to watch. The lone man who stood beside Albertine raised his hands to herald silence.

"I am Johann Wilhelm of Little Munich, a day and a half's journey south of New Genesis." He motioned to the three wagons. "These are some of the children of my people." His face looked suddenly older, strained. "As many of you know, the journey to America was difficult. Most of us had to walk across land because of lack of funds. Still, we survived these hardships and have made a good home for us all. But our crops have failed these last two years. The Society offers no variety to the staples they allot us. Nothing the children eat stays down. Our people are growing sicker by the day. But especially our little ones!"

One woman began to rock back and forth on the driver's

box, cradling her toddler close to her breast. "My little Ernst, he will not suckle. He will not eat. Please . . . someone . . . anyone . . . help me save my Ernst. He's such a dear little boy. He has not learned to speak a full sentence yet." She looked up, her gaze sweeping over the crowd. "Anyone?"

"Save my Greta," another woman cried.

"And my Catherine," still another appealed. A chorus of haunting pleas echoed over the gathering.

Fear gripped Toya's heart for the children. She wanted to assure the mothers that New Genesis would do all that was possible to save the children, but she soon discovered she could not be heard above the noise.

People moved forward, wanting to assist but not knowing what to do. Some hurried to the wagons to help the women down, while others converged upon Herr Wilhelm. Many remained where they stood, discussing what could be done.

One clear voice shouted above the crowd. "And what if they have brought this sickness among us! Did any of you think of that!"

Everyone froze at the sound of Lineva Pyrtle's censure.

"Are we rushing off to heal what might, in the end, kill us all?" Like the bandleader heading the parade, the redheaded woman marched to the other side of the maypole, careful to keep considerable distance from the wagons and the man who had brought them. "We do not know what ails our visitors or if they are contagious. I think they ask quite a lot of us, riding in here without warning and demanding sanctuary. Perhaps they should be quarantined. After all, they did leave Little Munich. Were they run out of town?"

Speculation murmured through the crowd, faces turning fearful.

"They can stay at my home," Opa announced to everyone around them. "It will make it easier for me to nurse them." Before the old man could make his offer known to all, Rad stepped onto the platform and extended his hand to Johann Wilhelm.

"There is plenty of room at mine and my grandfather's home . . . for all of you. Opa, will you step forward?" As Opa moved toward the speaker's stand, Rad introduced him. "Ladies, this is my grandfather, Ash Wagner. The finest *Heilkundiger*"—seeing confusion on some of their faces, he translated for those who were not German—"*healer*, in all of the new country."

Toya's heart swelled with pride at the Wagners' generosity, appreciative of their compassion yet equally fearful concerning the logic of Lineva's warning.

Relief made Herr Wilhelm bob his head with gratitude. "I cannot say how much your kindness means to us."

"Think nothing of it. You would do the same for New Genesis, would you not?" Rad deliberately increased his volume so the last statement would by heard by many in the crowd.

"*Ja,* we would. A friend lends a hand when another is in trouble. So must a village to its sister."

"How can I help, Opa?" Toya followed the old man as he made his way to the wagons. Betina kept pace alongside her.

"Meet the women. See how many there are. Betina, you know the lay of the house. Determine how we should divide them according to rooms. If need be, put them everywhere except the third floor. That's too much walking for someone who's ill or taking care of the sick. We'll keep Rad's room for our own use."

He placed a hand upon Fredericka's shoulder and squeezed gently. "Fred, I ask you to fetch every extra blanket and pillow you own. We'll need them for makeshift beds."

"I have several," Betina reminded Opa. "I keep them well stocked for those passing through to the gold fields."

"And me?" Disappointment filled Toya as she realized

A TASTE OF HONEY

he had assigned Betina and Aunt Fred important responsibilities. Did he, like Rad, think she was incapable of following through on anything he assigned her?

"You and I will have the hardest task." Opa stared at Toya. "We'll need strong coffee for the adults, herb tea for the children, plenty of broth. We must try to get something down them. And I need you to help me think."

To help him remember, Toya discerned. He trusted her to understand. Feeling the weight of *his* responsibility as the sole healer in this part of the Texas hill country, Toya scolded herself for being so self-centered at the moment. Children's lives were at stake, not her pride. She hurried to the wagon holding baby Ernst and his mother. "May I help you, *Frau*? The Wagner home is only a few streets away. I can carry little Ernst for you if you like?"

"*Nein.*" The woman shook her head vehemently. "I will hold my son . . . *danke.*"

Toya asked another of the women. She received the same answer time and again. Each seemed afraid to let go of her child, afraid that it might be the last chance to hold her baby in her arms.

"Please follow me, then. I'm not sure we can move your wagon through the crowd fast enough. It will be quicker on foot." Toya waited until they'd formed a line and pointed in the direction of Rad's house. "See that three-level chalet. *Ja*, the big one. That is the Wagner home. You will find comfort there."

As she passed the speaker's stand, Johann Wilhelm called out to Toya. "Frau Hinger? I did not see you among the women? Did you come alone?"

Toya stopped for a moment and shook her head. "You must have me mistaken for someone, Herr Wilhem. My name is Reinhart. Toya Reinhart."

"But I'm certain . . ." The man teetered on his feet. "Are you not Sonya Hinger, married to Kirk Hinger, the tailor? I thought you quarantined your home when little

Dante was so ill. The others"—he pointed to the women—"said that's why you refused to leave the house until he was better." Hope lit his eyes. "Did he get better? Have you found a cure, then?"

If only she didn't have to disappoint him. The man was clearly ill and not seeing well. "I am not Frau Hinger, sir. I must look like her."

"I could have sworn." The man swayed, grabbing hold of Rad. "I'd better sit down. I do not feel well."

"Karl, Hans, help get this man to my home." Rad barked out orders, quickly obeyed by two of the strongest men in the crowd. "Do not worry about the others, Johann. We will see that they are cared for. You did right coming to New Genesis."

Rad joined Toya and urged her to continue leading the way to his home. "When we get to the house, will you stay there until I can return? Johann says others may follow. A new group of immigrants arrived in Little Munich two days ago, suffering from exhaustion and sickness. Their leader, one of those who is not well, said they would move on as soon as all had rested and gathered badly needed supplies. But his own fever raged. He collapsed and is being cared for by his people. Once the fever leaves him, they will complete their journey."

Rad glanced back to make certain none of the women had trouble following. "Johann believes they will not linger there if this epidemic among the children continues. And we are the closest settlement with a doctor of any kind. I am not sure if Opa is prepared for this, and I must count on you to be by his side."

"I will help all I can," Toya promised. Rad's words sank in. "A new group of immigrants in Little Munich? Their leader ill? You don't suppose it could be Peter, do you? He said he wanted to be here before the bluebonnets bloom, and they're already beginning to bud."

"It may be him."

A TASTE OF HONEY　　　　131

Silence filled the afternoon with the likelihood that Peter had returned from Germany and lay ill miles south of New Genesis. Toya had dreaded his return but never wished him harm.

They reached the stone gate to the Wagner home. Toya faced Rad. "What if he dies?" Her whispered words seemed to echo into the evening shadows.

She had yearned for some way out of the pledge given to Peter, but Toya had never wanted it to happen this way.

"He won't." Rad placed a reassuring hand upon her arm, though he looked off into the distance. "And you will be ready to care for Peter when he returns. Quit worrying. You did not wish this upon him, no more than I have. Now, make certain Opa doesn't leave without you being at his side."

He stared at the end of the line where Opa walked with one of the women, talking earnestly. "I'll go have a word with him to let him know I need him ready to concoct some potions. I have an idea how we might help these people . . . or at least begin to."

"Help us?" Hope filled the woman's face who carried baby Ernst. She stepped closer. "You have something to cure him?"

Rad reached out to stroke the child. "I am not certain of it, *Frau*, but I believe that if things are as you say—the children are not keeping anything down and their food supply has been the same for several years—then we must find something they can eat. What have you tried to feed them?"

"Potatoes. Corn. All that was not destroyed by the drought. We even sent for sweet cane from the Austin colony, but it was too green."

Rad nodded. "*Ja*, something sweet to add flavor to the medicine. Fruit perhaps, a natural sweetness? Mixed with . . . honey. A healer of many ailments." Excitement rocked him as one mighty fist slammed into the open palm of the other. "Honey and peaches! It is worth the try."

The loud smack of flesh against flesh startled baby Ernst. "Shhh, little one, do not cry. Mama will make it better. Mama will—" The woman stared at Rad and Toya with anguished eyes. "Where can we get the fruit? I have not seen peaches in two years."

"My orchard set early this year. I have hundreds of peaches, maybe even thousands to trade with our sister settlements. And"—he smiled—"I am a beekeeper by trade. The honey is abundant."

"*Lieber Gott!*" the woman praised, turning to pass on the news to the others. For the first time since their arrival, the mothers of Little Munich braved smiles.

"Herr Stoltz was right," Ernst's mother announced. "He said that if anyone could help us, they would be in New Genesis. *Danke Schön! Danke!*"

"Herr Stoltz?" This could not be mere coincidence. Toya stared squarely at Ernst's mother. "Is he the leader of the group that just arrived in your town?"

"*Ja.*" The woman's head bobbed. "Peter Stoltz he said his name was. And he said the finest people in all of Texas lived in New Genesis. It is a shame he is so sick. He told us he is to marry when he returns home. I should like to meet his intended when we are all better . . . *ja*. To tell her how fondly he speaks of her and how he is eager to become her husband."

"I'm sure you will." Toya could not share her identity with the woman any more than she could ignore the intensity of Rad's gaze burning into her skin.

"And I am sure," Rad quietly assured the woman, "his bride-to-be is equally enthused about his return."

Several wagons rolled up outside the Wagners' gate as the evening progressed, each one filled with people, scared, hungry, and ill. After Rad helped them down, Toya softly welcomed each one and offered an assurance that they could rest here while help was being found. Each hugged her in return, making her aware that they were so adrift with fear, they needed someone to anchor themselves upon.

As she greeted each new patient, she carefully watched for a sign of Peter. People came until the house was filled and others in New Genesis took the influx of patients. Those more critically in need were put downstairs closest to the kitchen. Others filled every room on the next level. Hour by hour, Toya continued, rocking a baby for its mother, boiling more coffee, sponging away a fever. Still, she searched the night horizon for sight of a wagon bringing Peter.

But no more came. An hour earlier, Rad had taken the last group to the Reinhart home to be cared for by Albertine and Betina. Opa asked Fredericka to stay behind and be his aide. Toya was pleased by his decision. Not having to worry about him or his whereabouts allowed her to concentrate on the children and their mothers.

Albertine was efficiency incarnate and needed someone spry, like Betina, to help her. Fredericka's diminishing eyesight, Toya feared, would only cause Fred to get in her sister's way. Whereas here, Opa had become Fred's eyes, and Fred, Opa's memory. Together they had ministered to the ill for hours. When they finally retired for the night, they both looked exhausted but pleased by all they'd accomplished. Rad would be proud of them when he returned. To have watched them work, no one would know that either suffered from an affliction.

Though he hadn't said anything to Toya since discovering that Peter was only miles away in Little Munich, Rad had nodded his gratitude to Toya before taking off the last time.

Unable to sleep, Toya needed to escape all the sadness within the Wagner home. The tiny whimpers and deep sobbing heard from every corner of the house was almost too much to bear. Should she go out to the barn and sleep in the hay? The idea of sharing the sweet-smelling hay and curling up next to Monarch's warm little body seemed appealing. Then she remembered. Herr Wilhelm bunked there, wanting to leave the the house to the women.

A map of the home filled Toya's mind. Every place she recalled housed a woman and her offspring. With nowhere else available, she sought the one place left to her, a place she preferred never to enter again—Rad's room.

The distance of his sleeping quarters from the rest of the house reminded her that she couldn't hear what transpired below. Tonight that would be a blessing. She needed a short time away from the painful sounds of suffering.

Toya opened the door and stepped inside. She quickly closed the door behind her, settling her back against the wood and willing the tension from her weary shoulders. When her eyes at last opened again, she saw that the curtains had been pulled aside. Moonlight bathed the room in a soft glow. The beauty of the furnishings calmed her turbulent emotions, allowing a sense of peace to settle into her weary bones.

When her gaze drifted to the portrait Rad had painted with such love, the flood of tears she tried diligently to hold back undammed itself.

Rad wandered through the shadows of his chalet, looking for Toya's familiar form. A thorough search left him wondering if she had gone home after all.

Remembering that he had told Opa to stay on the third floor so that they could offer all other rooms to their guests, Rad took the stairs three at a time. He slowly opened the door to his bedroom, careful not to wake Opa. To his surprise, he heard crying. As his eyes adjusted to the moonlit shadows, he saw Toya sitting on the edge of his bed, her face cupped in her hands.

"Do not cry, *Liebling*," he said as he moved forward.

Her face shot upward as though she'd been caught doing

something wrong. Even in the darkness, tears glistened down her cheeks.

"Whatever is wrong, Toya, I am here." He wanted to hold her, but he would not take advantage of her fragile state of emotions.

"I don't know what has unnerved me." She brushed back the tears. "I suppose it is all the children, and feeling so helpless."

Rad sat down next to her, unmindful of where they were and how intimate the setting. "It's been a long day, and you need sleep."

"Where?" Her eyes met his. "I seem to have no place here." The tears came in earnest now as her words hinted of what had been lost between her and Rad. Of what could never be now that Peter was so close to home.

Rad pulled her against him. "Toya," he whispered over and over as he stroked her hair. "Everything will be all right."

Her crying stopped, but her hold around his neck didn't. "You can sleep here. I'll bunk down with Opa."

"I'm fine now. I cannot take your bed. I'm sure Aunt Fred will allow me to join her."

He felt Toya's back straighten. Rad forced himself to pull away. "You'll find a fresh shirt in the armoire to sleep in if you like."

"*Danke*," she whispered without moving away.

Slowly, a fraction of an inch at a time, he pulled her against his chest. She hesitated, but his voice was so low, it could have passed as a thought between them. "I want only to hold you, Toya. To offer you what you have given to others all evening. I promise not to do anything more."

She allowed him to continue. The heat of her body radiated through her clothes, warming the chill the night breeze had instilled within him during the last few trips to settle the remaining visitors. Her breath blew gently across his earlobe as her hands slid around his neck and she cradled her cheek against his shoulder.

Damned if this wasn't the hardest promise he'd ever made.

"If your peaches can provide a cure, won't it take a lot of hands to harvest them?"

"*Ja.*" Like a bee lusting for pollen, Rad's nose nuzzled the strawberry-blond curls that had loosened from her braid, drowning in the scent of her hair.

"Why not ask the others to help us pick them?"

"Lineva Pyrtle might have something to say about that." He positioned himself so he could unbraid her hair. The thick texture felt like silk beneath his fingertips.

Toya sighed, a throaty sound that sent streamers of desire racing through him.

"True, but with more of us helping, more can concoct recipes of whatever you and Opa think we should try."

"I've always taken care of my own problems." Not one to ask for assistance, he felt most of the townspeople might react as they did tonight. Better to count on himself than to waste time asking for the unlikely.

"This is not just your problem. It's ours, the whole town's. And if you are too proud to ask for help, then I will. It's time you learned, Conrad Wagner, that you are not the only one capable of resolving things. You do not have to walk alone in this."

He started to argue, but the look of caring in her eyes made his heart stop its beat. As long as Toya was willing to join him in the undertaking, he did not have to feel the incredible loneliness that had become and would remain long after she and Peter married.

"Tell her you will, Grandson, so we can get some sleep."

"Opa?" Rad and Toya asked in unison, breaking apart as if they'd been caught naked. Rad stared into the shadows that formed an ell into the part of the room that wrapped around the entire third floor. When he'd not found his grandfather sleeping in his bed, he presumed Opa had chosen to bunk down elsewhere. "Are you there?" The possiblility that Fredericka might be with him instigated a further "Alone?"

"*Nein,* this is my spirit night-talking. I am truly over at Fredericka's, stirring up—"

"Enough, old man." Rad could have sworn someone other than Toya giggled.

"Such a wicked mind you have, Grandson. I was going to say stirring up some magic for tomorrow's cure. Listen to Toya. It is wisdom she speaks. If you are too stubborn to seek help, then the peaches will be too wilted to cure. Pride is an anvil upon the shoulders, no matter how big they are."

Rad walked to the curtains and pulled them back farther, staring out into the moonlit night as if he could see past the rolling hills of South Texas and count each and every one of his peaches. He finally faced Toya. "You've taught me one thing, Toya, if nothing else."

"Which is?"

"Sometimes a man just has to take a risk and see what happens."

13

Dawn arrived, bringing with it a reprieve from the troubles under the Wagner roof. Toya insisted upon staying up all night. She claimed someone needed to watch over the patients in the event of an emergency, and that everyone else needed to rest while they could. Truth was, she would not have been able to close her eyes. Not in Rad's bedroom.

Neither Rad, Opa, nor Fredericka could change her mind, so Rad conceded to her wishes. But at the crack of dawn he took Toya and Fredericka home. The baker and his wife offered to help patients while Toya and Fred rejuvenated themselves, Opa tested remedies, and Rad picked peaches.

Out of sheer exhaustion Toya slept soundly for a few hours. But as the room heated with growing sunlight, she felt the need to rise and pull a chair close to the window. This new fondness for watching the land awaken to the day had become a habit—one provoked by mornings spent in Opa's and Rad's company.

Toya stared into rolling hills now greening with spring. Wildflowers blanketed cedar-lined knolls. Milkweed and butterflies floated on air currents. With them drifted the smell of peaches ripening and an image as sure as the man himself. Rad would be up already, harvesting the orchard.

The great expanse of Texas sky swept troubles into the far horizon, making them seem insignificant and leaving quiet reassurance that no concern was too big to overcome. The breadth of Rad's shoulders had always seemed wonderfully large. But were they big enough to take on the task of saving the children?

With a sigh Toya glanced at the box of ribbons held in her lap. Her fingers searched through the collection used to hold back her hair. Her favorite, the emerald calico one that matched her eyes, was nowhere to be found. Memory seeped through her exhaustion. Toya realized she had dropped it in Rad's bedroom and never asked for its return. But her ribbon should be the least of her concerns at the moment.

The door opened and closed behind Toya, drawing her attention.

"Up already? I hoped you would sleep longer." Betina set a tray of food on the small table next to Toya's bed. "But I brought you something to eat, if you happened to be awake."

"*Danke.* You're always so thoughtful." Toya shrugged. "But I am not hungry or sleepy."

"Are you watching for him?"

"Who?" Toya stared out into the horizon, knowing full well who Betina meant.

"Who do you think? Peter, of course." Betina moved alongside, gently squeezing Toya's shoulder. "Put Peter out of your mind for now. Rad says what will be will be."

"I cannot continue with this farce." Toya spoke without realizing. Even if she and Peter couldn't marry, Toya would not stand in Betina's way if her friend loved Rad.

So noble you sound, Toya scorned herself. *Yet you take every opportunity to test Rad's love for you. Some friend you call yourself!*

"Neither your nor Rad's honor will allow your word to be broken." Respect for the beekeeper softened Betina's voice, yet her grip tightened. "I hope Peter's fever rages so high that he forgets this vow. That he cannot remember it is your hand in marriage he has asked for. Cannot remember that it is you he desires to mother his—"

Toya bolted to her feet, shaking her head. "Do not wish such upon him. Do not even think it. Peter does not deserve this ill will—from you, nor me, nor anyone." Her stomach knotted at the possibility that the town councilman might never return. How easily his demise would solve her dilemma.

Toya knew Betina was not insensitive to the attraction between her and Rad. She faced her friend, curious as to why Betina sought Peter's undoing and the possible ease it would offer her and Rad's growing fondness for each other.

What she saw there surprised her. Instead of anger, a certain sadness filled her friend's eyes. "Why do you dislike Peter so? What has he done to harm you?"

"Harm me? Never!" Startled, Betina looked away. "It is not that I dislike him." She hurried to Toya's bed, busying her hands with its making. "I—I just do not think you can be happy with him. That is what I detest. What I mourn."

So, the sadness was only empathy for Toya's predicament. No truer friend was there than Betina Bram. All the stolen moments with Rad sent shame coursing through Toya. Not only had she wronged Peter but her best friend as well. She didn't deserve their friendship.

Toya reached out to touch Betina, but the dressmaker shifted away, jerking the sheet up with so much force, it ripped.

"I will repair that or make you another," Betina mumbled, not meeting Toya's gaze directly.

Something was wrong. Something more than to what Betina alluded. In the past, Betina had never avoided Toya except when she'd been afraid to say something that might distress Toya. Had she witnessed one of the kisses?

"What is it you keep from me?" Toya pressed a restraining palm over Betina's hand. Her friend stopped making the bed. Did Betina resent her for not stepping aside where Rad was concerned? She wanted to... had tried to... for Betina's sake. But Toya's heart kept daring her to do things her mind spurned. "Are you angry with me?"

"Nein."

"Then what are you protecting me from? Bad news about Peter?" *Oh, God, he has not passed from this world, has he?*

"Rumors." Betina shrugged and grabbed the quilt to straighten. "Peter was seen kissing another."

Toya exhaled a pent-up breath. Those rumors were as old as their wedding plans. She was too guilty of the same to challenge Peter on the subject. "Is that all? I feared something worse."

"Do not take it so lightly. Anyone who would betray you like that does not deserve your allegiance."

Is your admonishment meant for Peter or me? Embarrassment swept through Toya as Betina's words chastised her.

"No one, no matter how close they are to you, has the right to treat you that way." Betina's voice emitted something other than anger. "You're too good a friend to suffer that."

Relief washed away the embarrassment. Betina's accusation was aimed at Peter. Could this be true? Peter in love with someone else? A seed of hope planted itself. Toya's mind raced to determine which of the young ladies in their village had captured his interest. Or had Herr Wilhelm mentioned a beauty among the immigrants returning with Peter? "This kissing. When did it happen and with whom? I thought he was ill when he arrived in Little Munich."

"It happened several years ago," Betina answered in a

tight voice. "Three to be exact. And he was perfectly healthy."

Hope plummeted as the identity of the kisser became clear. Had her friend brooded all this time, indignant for Toya's sake? The dressmaker's dislike of Toya's twin would only increase when she learned that Peter was guilty of kissing only Tilly.

Toya sought a way to help her understand. "Dear heart, such a loyal friend you are. There's no need to fret yourself over this matter any longer. Peter was fond of kissing my sister. And I also know Lineva Pyrtle long ago started those terrible rumors about his and Tilly's courtship developing into something more intimate. In fact, given that Tilly died not long after that, I have always hoped the rumors were true. That she didn't die without knowing the touch of the man she loved."

Betina rubbed her hands over her arms as if she were staving off a chill. "But he is to be *your* husband. Only you have the right to such . . . to share Peter's secret longings. Do you not feel envious of Tilly? Do you not care that she was the first to—"

Realization hit Toya full force. She didn't care, but she should have. "For three years I have tried to take her place. I've reacted to situations the way I thought she might, planned my life to achieve the dreams she had, even promised my hand in marriage so that I would bear the children that would have been hers."

Toya laughed bitterly as the truth settled in. "I know you think I am impulsive and adventurous, but those are Tilly's traits. I've tried to be all that she could never become. Live her life as she would have. I've only now discovered that about myself."

Her fingernails sank into the flesh of her palms. "No wonder I never finish anything. I start impossible causes, knowing I am too cowardly to face the result because I will be found lacking. I have resigned myself to be a substitute.

A hand-me-down heart, if you will," she mocked. "Something went astray inside me when Tilly died, and I have been searching for it ever since. I didn't realize until just this moment that it was me, *Toya* Reinhart, I had lost."

Toya squared her shoulders and lifted her chin, not wanting pity. She pulled the quilt back enough to allow room for the pillows. "But it is a bed I have made and now I must lie within it—comfort or not."

"You must listen, Toya." Betina shook her head. "There is more of which you are not aware."

Green eyes met brown and demanded unwavering attention. "I refuse to listen to anything more. If Peter has dallied with another, what good would it do but ease someone's conscience after all these years? My sister went to her grave believing he loved her. She asked that the two of us would marry and see that Father's plans for us be fulfilled. That's all that I want to remember. To know more would desecrate what my sister and Peter shared and what my father dreamed. Now, help me finish with these pillows and let us put this behind us."

Betina fluffed one pillow and draped it across half the bed, then Toya did the same. Perhaps she needed to reassure Betina that she would not go into this marriage blind. "All this I know about Peter and yet do not blame him. I knew I would be second in his heart when he proposed. Do not concern yourself. You worry that I have lost something I never had."

"I have dared every adventure with you along the way." Betina's words started out low as she pivoted and strode to the door. "I have faced every backlash when our curiosity got the best of us."

With a yank of the handle, she glared back at Toya. "But I cannot in good conscience watch you sacrifice yourself to Tilly's last cruel whim. Do not ask it of me. Do not ask it of yourself. If you mean what you said before, then find yourself, Toya. Find who you are, what you want. Do not choose to live this lie."

Toya's knees suddenly felt like butter that had not yet hardened. She sank upon the corner of her bed and gaped in astonishment at the slamming door.

The rift growing between her and her best friend suddenly widened. How ironic that loving Rad seemed the remaining bridge they might share.

The day spent at the Reinhart home offered little time for relaxing. Toya woke early again on the second morn, repeating the countless tasks of caring for the ill. Just before noon, Toya longed to refresh herself before returning to the Wagner home to relieve the baker and his wife. Several of the children had gotten sick while Toya held them, soiling her clothes. Toya stretched tired, sore muscles and longed for a breath of fresh air.

Slipping into her bedroom, she filled a washbowl and splashed her face with cool water. A quick rummage through her chifforobe located a dress of emerald linen that would ease the heat of the day. It would seem frivolous to some, but the dress's prettiness might lift the worried mothers' somber spirits. Toya stripped off her soiled clothing and underthings, sponged her arms and legs, then put on the clean dress.

Pulling open the doors that led to the balcony running the full length of the Reinhart home, she ventured into the brisk, refreshing wind.

"Peter's coming home."

Toya turned and noticed Betina standing at the top of the stairs that led to the balcony. "I thought you weren't speaking to me."

Her friend hesitated a moment before joining Toya. Tightness pinched her mouth, her forehead furrowed. Leaning against the balustrade, she folded her arms across her breasts. "You would not *let* me speak to you."

"Not if it is about the past."

"What I tell you now will bring you face-to-face with your future." Betina pointed to the town square. "See those wagons? Those have brought some of the new immigrants from Little Munich. Rad is out gathering peaches, but he sent a party of men to fetch Peter and his voyagers. Lineva Pyrtle, who is in the kitchen with your aunts, said the immigrants were halfway here when the men met them. It was kind of Rad to offer them escort." Admiration eased the rigidness of Betina's face. She brushed back a wisp of dark hair. "Care to walk?"

Betina surprised Toya by catching Toya's arm and hooking it through the crook of her elbow. The dressmaker smiled, then motioned toward the stairs.

The town was alive with activity. The streets swarmed with wagonload upon wagonload of newcomers. Toya's gaze searched the conveyances for one face alone, though her words spoke of all. "Where will we put everyone? Those who were willing to open their homes to the new families Peter brought with him are not so ready to greet them now."

"Perhaps many of us will have to reevaluate our promises to Peter."

The two friends continued walking silently. Betina seemed to have shed the anger of the day before, and Toya relaxed in her friend's company. Their friendship was a godsend. Betina offered the support of a comforting arm and the silence of understanding. Toya knew, if she wanted to cry, she could. Betina had never experienced the loss of a man she deeply loved, but she would understand Toya's tears.

Lineva Pyrtle stood at the kitchen window, her eyes focused on the two friends walking arm and arm in the distance. "Fraulein Bram will be trouble," she stated to Fredericka, who sewed at the table.

The chubby woman put her needlework aside. "Has it ever occurred to you, Lineva, that you should mind your own business?"

"The refinement of New Genesis *is* my business." Her red curls bobbed. "Betina spends too much time with Conrad Wagner, and he has his mind set on Toya Reinhart. There are transgressions abounding, and I plan to see that they stop."

"Leave them alone. Betina is only being a friend to Rad, which is more than can be said of you. You should not have denied those Munichers help, nor caused dissension among our people. What if *you* needed assistance? Conrad did right by taking them into the Wagner home."

Ignoring the reprimand, Lineva sat in a chair opposite Fredericka's. "Are you aware that Betina and Peter Stoltz once spent the day picnicking at the Comal?"

Fredericka leveled critical eyes on the townswoman and asked in controlled patience, "What harm is there in a picnic?"

Lineva lifted a teacup to her lips and stared out over its rim. "None, I suppose . . . if that is all that transpired."

"You asked Betina about this picnic?"

Frustration lifted on auburn brow. "She denied anything happened."

"Then we must assume that is true."

Lineva studied Fredericka, watching as her fingers deftly wove the thread in and out in a straight line despite failing eyesight. She hurried back to the window and watched as Betina and Toya strolled away from the Reinhart home. "Still, something here swims beneath the surface," Lineva whispered, unwilling to ignore an impropriety left unchallenged. "I wonder . . ."

For a while Toya actually forgot the worry that consumed her. Betina played quite the storyteller that morning, entertaining her with tales of Rad's exploits as a child. "It is hard to believe he was such a mischief maker." Toya laughed, grateful that the tale was humorous enough to quell the envy she'd been experiencing while they walked. Betina had gotten to know Rad in ways Toya did not. And her friend seemed bent on telling her everything she knew about the man.

"He is normally such a stone face." Toya's lips formed a straight line, mimicking Rad.

"*Ja*, he is. But only when he believes someone watches." Betina grinned. "But not always. In the old country, Opa once gathered all the great healers from the surrounding villages. Remember how our families used to do? Everyone endowed with sacred abilities came. The big event took place on summer solstice—the longest day of the year. A time for harvesting seed and hope."

Images of solstices spent in the Lahn Valley brought back fond memories for Toya.

"For moons, Opa invoked the spirits of the oaks to lend strength and wisdom so that this solstice would be the most powerful and prove the most beneficial to all." Betina waved a hand as if encompassing the whole of the Texas hill country that stretched before them. "Herbs of every kind were boiled and brewed. The finest flax was poured in a circle around his conjuring place to ward off those that walked the night and might vanquish the good he summoned."

Her voice hushed as if someone other than Toya listened. "On the very eve of solstice, when Opa and his fellow enchanters meditated near the river, Rad lay in his bed, certain that he might actually see a specter or two. As we both know, our Rad is too determined to assure his own fate. He crept from his bed and buried swine *düngen* amid the kindling. Rad said that no flax was needed to ward off the spirits that night! The smell alone drove everyone away."

Toya's nose twitched in sympathy as she laughed. What

other antics of Rad's past did he share with Betina?

"Rad's father ordered him punished and said that it was Opa's right to do so since Opa's friends suffered. Ash Wagner grabbed Rad by the ear and dragged him behind the chalet. Rad was certain his backside would need some of the soothing those brewed herbs offered. But instead of taking a stick to him, Opa pointed to the sky and raised his lips like a howling wolf. Then he grabbed a willow and started beating the chalet's outside wall."

Amusement lit Betina's eyes, softening them to warm chocolate. "With every whack he pointed to the moon and signaled for Rad to wail. When it was all over, both Rad and Opa returned to the group with tears in their eyes... from laughing together."

"With a grandparent like Opa, Rad comes by his mischief naturally." Toya grinned, wishing she could have known Ash Wagner when he was younger. "I wonder if he was always so mischievous, or if Opa is merely trying to relive his youth before he cannot."

"I think we all have a bit of rascal within us."

"You?" Toya grinned at her best friend. *Me, undoubtedly, but you?*

"Once," Betina responded in a lower voice. Her face grew more solemn.

The dressmaker caught Toya's hands in hers, an act that had become a signal to each of them that what was being shared was important. Something to remember. Something that affected the harmony between them. After the rift healed that morning, Toya paid close attention to Betina's gesture.

"I shall never repeat that devilment again." Betina sighed. "I am ashamed to say that it put something very precious to me in jeopardy. All because I was feeling a bit selfish at the time and had no one else's desires in mind but my own."

Looking up, Toya got the impression Betina believed she

had harmed their relationship. "I am sure whatever you did is easily forgiven."

Betina squeezed Toya's hand. "I would prefer to die rather than hurt—"

"Perish the thought," announced a male voice.

Toya and Betina twirled to their left and found Peter leaning among the drooping branches of a live oak tree. His tall, muscular form pushed away from the trunk and moved toward them.

Betina dropped Toya's hands and took two steps closer to the councilman. She halted, allowing Toya to move ahead of her.

"Hello, Peter. Welcome home." *You look fit and handsome as ever*, Toya thought with considerable admiration. She could see why Tilly had been so attracted to him. His disposition only strengthened his appeal. A red rim around his eyes hinted at a faint truth to the tale of his illness. Gray. His eyes were definitely gray. *Remember that*, Toya told herself, ashamed that she had forgotten their color.

"Peter," Betina cried, "what a relief to see you!"

Peter's face lit with pleasure at her enthusiasm. "Betina! A heartier welcome I have not received this day! *Danke!*"

The welcome from others would have been less than enthusiastic considering he brought sickness into New Genesis. Stung by his compliment to Betina, Toya attempted to garner the enthusiasm of a bride. "It is a relief to see you. We've been worried."

She forced herself to study him carefully. His dark hair hung almost as long as Rad's. Peter had braved many hazards to bring homelanders to New Genesis. He was a handsome man . . . a good man . . . and she should be proud to marry him. Anyone should. Why, then, did she keep thinking, *He is not Rad Wagner*? "Have you just arrived?"

"An hour ago."

"Let me look at you." Betina circled him, surveying him

like a merchant gauging her inventory. "You have lost weight but look better than we expected."

Where? Toya found no change in him.

"The way Herr Wilhelm described you, we feared you would need a lengthy recuperation." Genuine relief softened Betina's tone.

Toya's attention averted to Betina. Curiosity rooted itself in her mind. As if she'd been caught pilfering a cookie, Toya turned away, afraid Betina might read her thoughts. Surely that softness in her friend's voice was nothing but kindness and concern toward a returning Samaritan and not aimed directly at the man himself.

Betina smiled expectantly. "Shall I have Albertine and Fredericka make you tea or coffee?"

"Either will be fine." Peter nodded. *"Danke."*

"Then I shall leave you two alone." Betina's gaze locked with Toya's. "I am certain the two of you have a great deal to discuss." She swung around, making her eyes impossible for Toya to read. "Most important... your wedding day."

14

"Now is not the time to plan a wedding." Toya stepped forward and embraced Peter, turning her cheek at the last moment so that his kiss would not meet her lips. "You look like you need to sit, *ja*?"

She returned his hug as she would any long-absent friend who had been ill. No matter what else Peter might become to her, he had been a good friend. His happiness and well-being mattered. Instantly pulling away, Toya held him at arm's length and, like Betina, pretended to survey him. His dark beard and mustache made him look older than his twenty-seven years. But those would soon come off. The councilman preferred a clean-shaven face. "They say you were bedridden with fever."

"A result of an arduous journey, not the scurvy that is affecting the others. I am better now. And you?" His gaze swept over her, as if sensing she held something back.

"Busy." Toya motioned toward the Reinhart home. "As you know, many from Little Munich came here for help. Aunt Albertine and Betina have set up a makeshift hospital at our home, while Aunt Fredericka and I have been helping at the Wagners so Rad can work the orchard."

She explained as briefly as possible her role of companion to Opa and the turn of events that led to the Wagners offering their place as the main infirmary. Then it dawned on her that Peter had put a name to the patients' plight. "Is it truly scurvy?"

"Everyone down south says this is so. They think it is some form of scurvy unique to the Republic. I believe they have labeled it that because it has similar symptoms. But no one really knows. The only thing everyone agrees upon is that the sickness arises from the lack of fruit and vegetables to eat. And that was caused by the drought."

Excitement filled Toya. She could hardly wait to tell Rad and Opa. Somewhere in the old man's memory, Opa might know a particular remedy for scurvy. Maybe variations of the recipe would determine the cure for this form of the malady.

"Rad . . ." She decided now was the right time to enlist the others' aid. Surely the new immigrants who were healthy would help. "*Conrad* Wagner thinks a blending of peaches and honey might help the children's appetite. If what you say is true, then he may be on the right trail to finding a remedy. He is in the orchard now, gathering peaches and taking them to Opa to cook. We must enlist enough people to help him harvest the fruit."

"You say his name with such admiration, I wonder if I should be jealous."

A sudden gust of wind billowed Toya's skirts and flung wisps of hair across her eyes. She saw a wagon in the distance heading their way. Where would they put anyone else? A lone man? Perhaps one more would not be too much trouble.

Grateful for the distraction, she garnered her courage to meet Peter's challenging stare. "Of course, I admire him. I would admire anyone compassionate and unselfish enough to put others' needs before his own. He and his grandfather did not hesitate to lend a hand to the needy."

"I have reason to feel about Rad Wagner the way I do. We both know it, Toya."

"I told you—"

"He has kissed you in the past," Peter reminded her. "Everyone in town knows he proposed. A man like Wagner does not take defeat lightly. You put yourself in temptation's way by working so closely with his grandfather."

"It was your proposal I accepted, not Rad's. Remember?" No matter how much his suspicions warranted it, she had to make Peter understand. "Working for Ash Wagner is not the wrong here, Peter. I don't want to be anyone's *duty*. Not yours. Not *anyone's*. I am perfectly capable of taking care of my own needs." Her chin lifted defiantly. "I am healthy and strong. Being Opa's companion gives me income I need."

The wagon drew closer. She suddenly recognized the driver. *Please, no. Don't let it be. Not now.* "You spoke to Lineva Pyrtle?" *The witch!*

A frown shaped Peter's mustache. "*Nein.* Who could get a word in when that woman talks? I *listened* to her. And what I heard I did not like." His gaze swept over Toya as if tallying her every asset.

Without warning, Toya threw herself into Peter's arms, kissing him exuberantly. Closing her eyes and pressing herself farther into his chest, she attempted to block out the image of the man driving the wagon—the man who had warned her to make very certain Peter's kiss was better than his. That was exactly what she intended to do—with Rad to witness the affection.

Toya's tongue gently probed the councilman's teeth to nudge them open. He chuckled and allowed her entrance. Though any other woman might have been lost in Peter's kiss, Toya's heart refused to let her enjoy the moment. As

Rad had warned, this deeper sampling of Peter's passion fell far short of the savory sensations experienced in Rad's embrace. Where was the intoxicating taste of danger, excitement . . . eternity promised in Rad's kiss?

Toya pulled away, ashamed that she had used Peter to prove a point. The knowledge that she did not and could never love the councilman weighed heavy on her heart. Peter reached out and grasped her arm. Had he sensed she meant to escape these turbulent emotions and the inevitably of Rad's scorn?

"Where did you learn to kiss like that?" Peter exhaled a heavy breath.

The wagon came to a halt next to them. "Please, Peter, let me go," she whispered, doubting she could keep the truth from him while in Rad's presence.

"Let her go, Stoltz," a low baritone echoed her command.

"This is between me and my intended, Wagner. It is no concern of yours." Peter stared up at Conrad on the driver's box, meeting the glint hardening the bee charmer's eyes. "Or is it?"

"Perhaps I should make her my concern. If you insinuate that Toya has done anything to warrant your disrespect, then you know your bride-to-be too little."

Anger flared in Peter's face, then instantly faded as he caught the implication of Rad's words. The councilman offered Toya a smile. His hands slid slowly to his sides, while his gaze turned back to Conrad. A silent challenge layered the space that separated the two rivals.

"We all are out of sorts." With her entire being Toya wanted to run for the house. It seemed every time she turned around lately, she came face-to-face with another truth that no longer could be ignored. "We have had little rest."

Toya suddenly felt as weary as she claimed. Once, she thought she could honor her sister's wish. Once, she believed she could work as Opa's companion and ignore the longing that raged within her every time she looked at Rad. Once, she even supposed she could grow to love Peter as easily as Rad nourished his peaches. Now she knew all of these things were impossible.

Everything else would suffer her lack of commitment to it . . . because she loved Rad. Everything else would never see completion . . . because as Rad accused, she could not finish what she started out to do. Everything else was a lie . . . and only her love for Rad an indisputable truth.

Drums of tension pounded at her temples, forcing Toya to grasp any subject other than the men in her company. "Let us all go back to the house and tell everyone of Peter's return. Aunt Albertine has been particularly eager to see you, Peter. And I'm sure Aunt Fred will be just as happy to know you have recovered."

Toya shaded her eyes to buffer the glare of the sun as she looked up at Rad. His stare sent heat skimming across the surface of her skin and ignited beads of moisture in its wake. She fidgeted and fanned herself with her hand. "It is too hot to stay out here much longer. Let us all go in and have some tea . . . perhaps something to eat. Then Aunt Fred and I will be ready to return with you to help Opa." Needing to break Rad's possessive gaze, she smiled at Peter. "I'm sure you have many things to tell us."

"*Ja*, but there is one thing more important than any other."

Hearing the reservation in Peter's tone, she blinked. "What?"

"Climb aboard, and I'll take you to the Reinharts so you don't have to walk," Rad interrupted. "Then you can tell us this most important news."

Unable to satisfy her curiosity, Toya moved to the wagon. Before she could lift her foot to boost herself, Rad lent a powerful arm. Not to be outdone, Peter grabbed Toya by the waist and propelled her upward. With the added impetus, she almost landed in Rad's lap. Her breasts pressed against his chest, her body locked in place by a band of iron flesh. Toya could feel the beat of his heart against her own, noticed when its rhythm altered and began to race.

"Excuse me," she whispered.

"My pleasure," Rad murmured in return. "Entirely."

"Forgot my own strength there for a moment," Peter apologized.

"You might want to get in back." Conrad motioned behind them to the wagon bed. "There are plenty of blankets and bedding to make it more comfortable. I assume there will be additional patients to transport on our return home, and I hoped some of the healthy would want to lend a hand in the orchard. I hear you've been quite sick, Councilman. Stretch out and rest while you can."

Peter drew himself up, straightening his shoulders as if wanting to intimidate a bully. "Save it for the ailing, Wagner. I shall sit next to Toya. The three of us will fit on the driver's box. Unless you have objections, of course."

Rad muttered something unintelligible. Having heard part of what he said and only guessing at the rest, Toya blushed. He certainly was spontaneous with his cursing! She elbowed him.

"Oof!"

"Do you need more room?" Glancing at the bee charmer, Peter scooted over. He wrapped a possessive arm around Toya and nestled her closer to him. "There, that ought to do it."

Toya glanced at the set of Rad's jaw as he flicked the reins into motion and stared directly ahead. With a huge intake of breath, she heard the telltale sounds of teeth gritting. Exhaling slowly, she muttered, "*Ja* . . . that ought to just about do it."

• • •

Toya's teeth ground together. She attempted to listen to Peter's experiences during his journey to the fatherland. But it was the tale of one immigrant particularly that she found difficult to ignore. "And where is this eight-year-old you have adopted... Liesl, is it?"

"The child needed to freshen up, so I left her at my house. Gunnar Williams's wife volunteered to watch her until I had time to have a private reunion with you. The child becomes frightened of too confining a place, I suspect from hiding wherever she could among the street people. But I've told her your home is much larger than mine."

Rad strolled to the kitchen window and stared into the distance. Ever since they'd returned to the Reinhart home, he'd said little more than a greeting to her aunts. He merely offered a polite nod to Lineva Pyrtle. Toya fidgeted in her chair, aware the women who sat around the kitchen table—Albert, Fred, Betina, and Lineva—were all looking at her and giving her a knowing grin at Peter's reference to *private reunion. It is not what you think*, she wanted to scream. If only it could be.

Lineva's mouth stretched into a grin that seemed as if someone had pinned its corners to her ears. Aunt Albert, though she would never interfere with Toya's decisions, tended to favor the marriage to Peter as well. Her aunt's smile caused Toya's stomach to knot with tension. Lineva, she could ignore. Toya's fingers traced the handle of her teacup, searching for the pair of eyes that would hold understanding. Instead, Toya was surprised to see a shimmer of tears in Betina's lashes.

Betina glanced away, murmuring, "Rad, would you pull the curtain a bit? The sunlight is hurting my eyes."

Toya might have believed her had Betina not instantly sipped her tea to hide the tremor in her voice.

"Frau Williams should be arriving shortly with Liesl." Peter took a sip of the chamomile tea, then nodded at Albertine. "I wanted the child to meet Albertine... and Fredericka as well. After all, we'll soon be family. And since she lost all of hers, it is my hope that you will welcome the waif into your fold. She's really quite an amiable child. When I found Liesl stowed away on the ship and realized what her fate would become on the streets of Nassau, there was nothing else to do but bring her with me."

He stilled Toya's fingers. "I know how you adore children, Toya, and thought that we might start our marriage out with one a bit older than we first anticipated. I promised her that she could live with us."

"I see." So that's why he wanted to rush the wedding—to offer the orphan a replacement father *and* mother. Disappointment, even a little resentment, swept through her. The decision had been made without consulting her. Without considering her feelings on the matter. At least Rad asked her to do things. He never forced her.

Yet what blame was there to cast when kindness was Peter's transgression? What wrong was there in yielding so readily to a motherless child? If no blame could be given and her heart was willing, why, then, did she balk against the yoke of a responsibility that would further harness her to Peter?

"How compassionate you are, Herr Stoltz." Admiration radiated from Lineva's face and dripped so sweetly from her lips, it could have jelled.

"If she is to be yours and Toya's child, then we need to make this her home now, not after the marriage," Albertine insisted. "The two of you will take your wedding trip as planned, while Fredericka and I care for the poor thing. Better that she has a bit of time with us before that happens."

"I quite agree." Lineva nodded her approval.

"No one asked you." Fredericka flashed a blaze of white teeth at the townswoman. "But then, it is always nice to know when you agree with something, Lineva."

All heads quickly bowed over their teacups to take a hurried sip of the refreshment.

The hint of Rad's masculine chuckle sounded from the direction of the window. The others waited for him to speak, but he merely stared out into the countryside.

"I will help." Betina set her cup down and stared at Toya. "You and your aunt will be busy with Opa and his patients. I planned to help Albertine finish your wedding dress and nurse the patients we have here. I'm sure if Liesl"—she glanced at Peter to make certain she spoke the correct name—"is anything at all like us when we were her age, she'll want to help with the wedding decorations."

Betina toyed with her linen napkin. "The word must have spread that there is illness among us. If you noticed, no more strangers have arrived in the past two days ... at least those who are headed to the gold fields. I am filling no clothing orders, so I have plenty of time to help."

Peter's gray gaze swept over the dressmaker, affection and appreciation softening his angular features. "That's kind of you, *Fraulein*. You are a true friend."

Betina's lashes dipped against her cheeks. "*Nein*. I do nothing out of the ordinary. All of us would offer the same."

Toya noticed a blush sharply contrasted against Betina's porcelain skin. With dark hair and rosy cheeks, Toya thought Betina never looked so becoming. A glance at Rad to see if he witnessed this radiant look revealed that his attention was focused on her and not on Betina. Toya turned back to Peter and was surprised to see his regard of Betina lingered. Was it possible an attraction had grown between Betina and Peter? Had Betina been trying to tell her earlier and Toya was too caught up in her own troubles to listen?

"All of us need to forget the wedding for now." Toya wanted to change the subject and the direction of her thoughts. She needed time to think of this new turn of events—the possibility it posed. "We should concern ourselves with finding a remedy for the children. We *must* convince everyone to help Rad harvest his peaches." She explained Rad's plan to the others, frustrated that he didn't turn from his silent watchtower to add his conviction to her request.

With a shrug, she plodded on. Rad was accustomed to doing everything himself and not asking for help. Did something else besides pure stubbornness and pride drive his obsession for self-reliance? She vowed to find out before her employment with Opa ended.

Peter rose and placed his teacup in the washbowl. Sudsy water awaited the flow of dirty dishes that increased with each new patient's arrival. He returned to the table and grabbed Toya's hand, bowing gallantly to press a kiss upon her knuckles. "A remedy is important, *ja*. Getting everyone to help gather the fruit is wise too. But you are too overwrought about the children, Toya, and not thinking correctly. We'll wait until after I've helped Conrad gather his peaches, then we'll talk more about the wedding."

Toya exhaled a pent-up sigh, grateful for the reprieve.

"Why not have a singing festival?" Lineva demanded everyone's attention.

"And have you sing?" Fredericka stopped her sewing and leveled a glare at the redhead. "That will *increase* the sickness. We want them well."

Everyone sipped tea again, bubbles rising to the cups' surface as laughter hid in the brew.

"What better way to gather everyone and ask for help?" Lineva wouldn't let go of the idea. "It should take less than two or three days to send word to the other communities and arrange things. We can welcome the new immigrants and make the needs of the ill known. Our sister settlements could decide whether they would like to lend a hand as well as join in some hearty vocal competition."

She clapped her hands. Her all-occasion starched white

gloves muffled the sound. "Why not announce the day of your wedding, then? Perhaps even combine the *Sängerfest* and the actual wedding? Such an event will be fun for everyone, including—"

"That remains to be seen."

All heads turned to watch Rad walk away from the window. His eyes were narrow slits of blue. To the others, it might seem as if he'd squinted too long into the Texas sun. Toya knew he had just set his mind to battle Lineva's plans. The reason defined itself when he continued.

"I wonder how many children will be sacrificed while you plan your little festival." Rad nodded briefly at the women, then jerked open the door, stopping to look back at Peter. "The time to act is *now*. I plan to pick every single peach in my orchard. Even if I have to do it myself."

15

A subtle fragrance lingered in the orchard, like the delicate perfume of a passing woman that tantalized the imagination long after she departed. People worked in the trees, shaking and plucking the peaches, while others collected the fallen fruit into baskets. A swift-footed relay team carried the filled baskets to a wagon that would take the precious cargo to Opa's kitchen.

"Can I help?" The amber-eyed eight-year-old Peter had brought back with him stared up at Rad, her hands on her hips.

Rad glanced down from his perch atop one of the branches of the peach tree. Normally, he started at the top, where the fruit ripened first, and worked his way down. But his weight and brawn made it too dangerous to work any higher. Had the children not been ill, he would have hired several to climb to the lofty branches and salvage many of the unreachable peaches.

The brown-haired girl was so small, she seemed at least two years younger, but the agility and boundless energy she'd shown since dawn proved Liesl had mastered the dexterity of someone much older. Perhaps he should give her a try.

Rad assessed where he should be in the event he needed to catch her. He adjusted his position and pointed above him. "Those branches could use a good shaking, but it takes someone smaller than me. Someone not afraid to climb."

A look of importance washed across the freckled face. "I climbed lots of trees back home . . . like a monkey. And I am not afraid of anything . . . almost."

The lithe child grabbed a low-hanging branch and swung herself up. Before he could tell her to slow down and be careful, Liesl scurried past Rad until she was at least three feet above him.

"Stop!" He feared the girl's exuberance would put her in danger. "That is far enough."

"See . . . that was not so hard. Now what do I do?" She grabbed a branch just higher than the one she perched on. "Shake?"

"*Ja*. Be careful. Shake hard but slowly so you do not lose your balance. Herr Stoltz and Fraulein Reinhart will hang me from this tree if you get hurt."

Brown braids swayed back and forth as Liesl fought to get a clear view of Rad. "Does Fraulein Reinhart like Peter?"

"Why do you ask, little one?" It was obvious to Rad that Toya liked Peter well enough to offer him a hearty welcome-home kiss yesterday.

"No reason. She just looks at him strange. Not all soft and dream-eyed like Fraulein Bram does."

Betina? Dream-eyed over Peter? "Fraulein Bram has a gentle heart. She is glad Peter is home and has recovered from his illness. That is all." If Peter and Toya were to become Liesl's parents, then he needed to assure the child that her new home would be a happy one. "As for Fraulein Reinhart, her mind is focused on helping Opa and the others. Do not concern yourself, little one. She will be a good mother to you. Now, change branches. That one is done."

"But I like Fraulein Bram...Betina." Liesl scooted over and began to shake another branch. "She looks like my mother." Liesl lifted a dark braid to remind Rad of Betina's similar coloring. "She's pretty, and nice too."

Rad motioned to the branch. "Always keep both hands on the limb while you shake. Do not get distracted."

"*Ja,* I will."

"And you are right, Fraulein Hartz, Betina is very pretty and will make a wonderful mother someday."

After a few minutes of watching Liesl to make sure she didn't endanger herself, Rad concentrated on his own task. He squeezed some of the fruit nearest him. The amber flesh gave slightly, a sign that they were almost ready. He would leave some to pick next week...if the orchard yielded enough ripened fruit to ensure the needed remedy.

The falling peaches knocked against ladder steps and pattered on the ground, building from a light tapping to a thunderous crescendo as the workers picked up speed.

Rad and Liesl moved from tree to tree, allowing the others to gather the lower rounds, while he and the child dispersed the fruit on top. All morning she worked above him, alongside him, sticking to him like thistle blown against a fence. The girl was diligent to a fault.

Hearing a loud sigh, Rad glanced up. Liesl rubbed her golden-brown eyes. The midday sun beat down through the foliage, staining the cherubic face a ripening pink.

"Come down now," he instructed gently, offering her a hand for balance.

"I'm tired." She turned backward and stepped her way across branches until she reached him.

"Now, turn around, little one, and wrap your arms around my shoulders." When she did, Rad encircled her with one protective arm and used the other to descend one-handed.

Her cheek lay against his shoulder as she whispered, "I just need to rest a little while, Herr Wagner. Shaking peaches is hard work."

"*Ja*, it is, and you have done a fine lot of shaking." The warmth and smallness of the willowy body hugging itself against his own tugged at Rad's heartstrings. She was so small. So fragile. So willing to pull her share.

An overwhelming sense of protectiveness consumed him, and he vowed to do whatever it took to settle this child in New Genesis. Hers was a heart that needed mending, yet she was determined to be part of a remedy to restore the others' good health. From what Peter had said, Liesl suffered tragically from the loss of her parents and living on the street, hungry and cold. The fact that she had managed to escape the sickness seemed a miracle.

But Liesl needed more than a miracle. She should be given a proper, loving home. Rad decided to speak with Peter and Toya about making such a home for the child or finding her one. "Such a diligent peach picker deserves more," he promised her, pressing a kiss against the child's head.

"What's this?" Betina hurried down the row of trees, carrying a basket. Concern furrowed her brow, widening her eyes to chocolate-colored ovals. "Is she ill?"

Rad patted the small back. A snore blew a puff of breath against his neck. He smiled. "Only tired, I believe. Such a worker our Liesl is." Rad explained how the child had toiled with him all morning.

"Here, you take this." Betina set the basket down beside him. "Opa sent food. You eat while I hold Liesl. After Toya parcels out baskets to the others, she said she would join us for lunch. Then I am to help her and Opa in the kitchen again. When I do, I will carry Liesl back with me and let her rest."

Rad gently unthreaded Liesl's arms from around his neck and allowed Betina to take her. The child moaned for just a moment before snuggling against Betina. Pleasure radiated from his friend's face as she cradled the little girl against her. "You should be a mother, Betina."

"She needs one." Betina's gaze swept over Liesl, then focused on Rad. "Toya will make a fine parent."

"It is not Toya now that I speak of, but you." Rad grabbed the basket and Betina's elbow, urging her to return down the path. "The child adores you."

"She does?" Betina smiled affectionately at the sleeping ragamuffin. "She has a way of tugging at my heart, the imp." The dressmaker qualified her attachment. "But the same will happen with Toya. She's just too busy with Opa now to give Liesl the attention a child needs."

"Let us talk while we walk back to camp."

Betina nodded, her gaze darting toward the area where Peter had last been picking. Rad wondered if there was any truth to what Liesl inferred about the dressmaker's interest in Stoltz. "Are you looking for someone in particular?"

She shook her head. "*Nein,* just wondering how much you've harvested already."

"Many . . . thanks to the little one there."

Betina's words said one thing, but Rad read something else in her eyes. Curiosity hurried his steps. What if the councilman shared a mutual fascination with Betina? This needed further investigation. He had noticed Betina and Toya were not as friendly of late. Could it be because of Peter's return? Could jealousy have risen between the two women? Rad preferred the direct approach.

"Are you and Toya arguing today? You do not seem as"—he struggled to find the right English word—"*cordial* to each other. Has she done something to anger you?"

"Toya and I are the best of friends. Nothing she could do would annoy me."

Her pace quickened, and he suspected her words were deliberately vague. They had come too swiftly. The many hours he'd spent in the dressmaker's company gathering information about Toya assured him Betina was protecting their friendship. *She* could complain about her friend, but she would not give anyone else the right to do so.

"Does she feel the same way? What if you did something she disapproved of, would she be so forgiving?"

"You talk nonsense," Betina blurted out. Liesl stirred in her arms, causing the dressmaker to pat the child back to sleep. In a lower tone Betina continued, "Nothing will ever be so fierce that we could not forgive each other. I am sure of it."

Are you? Rad wondered, sensing that something had happened, something that Betina refused to tell, something she feared might be fervent enough to test the friendship.

As they made their way to the others, Rad formed plans that would force Peter to resolve his suspicions. and free Betina from this secret she obviously would not share. Such plans that might prove the pledge between Peter and Toya *could* be altered . . . and with honor. Hope surged through Rad. If what he suspected was true, there still might be a chance for him and Toya to share a life.

It all hinged on making Peter—and Toya—jealous.

Rad guided Betina to a tree heavy with fruit and considerable shade. "Did you bring a cloth to spread the picnic on?"

She nodded.

"Good, we will have our lunch here. We are close enough if anyone wants to find us." Hopefully, it would be Toya. He could put his plan in action.

Toya had to gauge carefully where she stepped. Hundreds of peaches littered the ground. The workers had accomplished much that morning. A handful of the children back at the Wagner house already seemed better, though they weren't completely well. She wasn't certain if their partial recovery was a result of the concoction she and Opa stirred up. The peach-and-honey mixture alone could be strengthening merely because the children were finally keeping something down. Enough remained sick that Opa said the recipe was not all it should be. He kept mumbling that there was a missing ingredient he hadn't found. Toya didn't have the heart to ask Opa whether he really meant he hadn't *remembered* it yet.

The rows of peach trees seemed endless. Only the thud-thud-thud of peaches against ladders warned her that someone worked overhead and that she should duck. Toya gingerly stepped her way over the blanketed ground, straining to see into the shaded distance for a glimpse of Rad. He could be anywhere. The orchard stretched far into the horizon, reminding Toya of the monumental effort of harvesting the fruit.

She was about to try another section, when a deep masculine voice caught her attention.

"Toya! Wait!"

Her gaze settled on the rugged features of Peter Stoltz. She handed him one of the baskets she carried. "I've brought you some lunch."

Peter wiped the perspiration from his brow. "*Danke.* It has been a long morning. I saw the others eating and thought you had forgotten my return to New Genesis."

"Hardly." Her gaze swept over him. She noted the pallor around his eyes and mouth. "Perhaps you should stop for the day. You push yourself too hard, Peter."

"*Nein.* We need every able hand."

"No one will find fault with your effort. You've been ill."

He waved away her concern and smiled gently. "You worry too much about me. I will stop for lunch, but no longer."

Glancing up into the nearest trees, Toya asked, "Have you seen Conrad . . . or Betina?"

His smile seemed slightly forced now, or perhaps it was just her hopeful imagination.

"They are together?"

"She took him lunch and has not yet returned." Toya fought down the same feelings she sensed stirring in Peter. But she had played matchmaker to Rad and Betina, making certain they shared more time. Now that they did, she had no right to question when or how long.

"I think it would be wise—I think we should join them." Peter moved past her. He sidestepped peaches and people as his long legs propelled him down the various pathways.

Toya followed, pleased that he was determined to find the pair. A good sign, indeed. Perhaps there was some thread of truth to her suspicions about Betina and the town councilman. Peter certainly acted like a jealous beau.

A burst of laughter reverberated through the foliage in front of them. He stopped too abruptly for Toya to slow her momentum. Together, they crashed through the bushes that clumped around the trees.

Betina pulled instantly away from Rad's embrace, shrinking slightly beneath Peter's frown. Toya took in Betina's blush and the sight of the blanket spread out upon the ground. She wondered if she was only fooling herself into believing an attraction between her best friend and the town councilman had arisen. The fact that Liesl lay asleep on that blanket irritated Toya more. Had Betina and Rad paid court only a few feet away?

Calm yourself. Toya battled the anger building within, telling herself it was righteous indignation for the sake of the child. But her heart had spoken its piece to her too frequently in the past week. Her anger rose for more self-serving reasons.

They were only kissing, Toya reminded herself. She took careful stock of their appearance. Betina's hair wasn't even mussed. They were fully clothed. All buttons were buttoned. Betina and Rad *kissing*!

Toya should have been pleased by the sight of her best friend blushing in a man's arms. She had always wanted Betina to find love and happiness. Toya's stomach roiled with disappointment. Being faced with the reality of losing Rad made this almost too much to bear—no matter how noble she tried to be.

Rad approached Toya. "Is something wrong?"

Toya stepped back, praying he did not touch her. "*Nein.* I wanted to waste no more time. Opa needs Betina and me to help him this afternoon. I knew she was delivering baskets of food to everyone. We assumed she might be with you. And so she is."

Rad glanced at the child and put a finger to his lips to remind them all to be quiet. "You're upset."

"Of course she is." Peter wrapped a protective arm around Toya. "She had expected to see you two working, not kissing."

"And so we were." Betina lifted her chin. "Not an uncommon sight between two people courting each other."

Betina's defiant tone surprised Toya. She wanted nothing more than to be left alone to think about this new turn of events. Toya had always thought that if she found a way out of her pledge, Rad would be there to gather her in his arms.

Now she wasn't so certain.

One of Opa's sayings raced through her mind. *Wish not upon the star unless you can tolerate its shine.* Isn't this what she wanted? For Betina and Rad to become serious about each other? Why, then, was she so angry?

Grateful for Peter's defense, Toya summoned her courage to meet Betina's gaze. "Are you finished here?"

The dressmaker glanced at Rad to silently confer with him. His brief nod irritated Toya for reasons she couldn't discern.

"*Ja.*" Betina nodded.

"Is that an answer to her question or mine?" Rad moved closer to the dressmaker and gently lifted her hand to his lips to press a kiss upon her palm.

The fine hair on the back of Toya's neck prickled. Something more portentous than a kiss had just transpired between Betina and Rad. Certain Peter would see the distress carved upon her face, Toya knew there could be no hiding her love for Rad. Yet, she shouldn't let Peter find out this way. She had to tell him alone, face-to-face, to make him understand.

Fate offered a kindness. Seemingly unaware of her inner turmoil, Peter stared up at the afternoon sun, his own face revealing nothing. "We best end this delay."

"What question?" Toya's curiosity took voice, knowing the answer would only deepen her despair. Blood rushed to her ears as she awaited the dreaded words she had feared since learning of Rad and Betina's courtship. This would alter everything—her relationship with Betina, her commitment to Peter, her love for Rad.

"He asked me to be his bride." Betina's brown gaze locked with Toya's. "And I told him I would give him my decision once the crisis with the children is over."

16

The heat of a half-dozen boiling kettles gusted against Toya's face as she entered Opa's kitchen. Everywhere she looked, peaches—sliced, diced, peeled, and whole—filled counters, shelves, and the tabletop. Jars of honey, stacked in crates, rose waist-high under the tables, along the walls, anywhere there was room. Only a small pathway from the counter to the stove left Opa walking space.

"It is good you've returned." Opa greeted Toya and her companions with only a brief nod before focusing his attention on the pot he stirred. "I need someone to take this batch to Albertine. Everyone here is resting at the moment, and I want to let them sleep as long as possible."

"Toya can stay and help you while Betina and I take Liesl home. Betina said she had to meet Fraulein Pyrtle at two o'clock at her dress shop." Peter halted just inside the doorway and stiffened his arm to keep the sleeping child from shifting against his shoulders. He faced the dressmaker, who followed him. "If Fraulein Bram approves, I will deliver your medicine and put the child down for a nap. Betina will return as soon as possible."

"You have done too much already." Betina shook her head. "You should rest, or your fever might return. I have walked this path often. I shall return on my own. Unless, of course, Toya would prefer to take my place and ask Fraulein Pyrtle to meet me here."

"I am needed here," Toya objected abruptly, letting them think she meant to fulfill her obligation to Opa. The last thing she wanted was to be alone with Peter. And she wanted to get as far away from Betina as possible. This feeling that burned inside her—anger, jealousy, betrayal—needed some cooling off. "Take all the time you need."

"Not so long, Betina." Opa shook his head. "Six hands are better than four. Lineva's dress can wait. Tell her that I said such."

"I will hurry, Herr Wagner. You can count on me."

Toya turned and grabbed an empty crock, silently mimicking her best friend's words, *You can count on me*. She held the crock still while Opa poured it full of the peach and honey mixture. *You can always be relied on, dear friend. Relied on to spend Sundays with lonely bee farmers. To visit the Wagners and play cushion to any of us too weak to maintain our honor. Such conscientious charms you have, Fraulein Bram. A man like Rad could not possibly resist you. And you? Will you resist a marriage proposal from such a man?*

A glance at Betina only intensified Toya's misery. The dark-haired, dark-eyed beauty looked as if she had just emerged from a Parisian salon while Toya's hair winged out in wisps from her braid and peach juice stained her dress. She had almost changed her attire before she delivered lunch but decided against it. Toya knew she and Betina would be coming back to help Opa and would just get dirty again. But not Betina—she elected to clean up before she went to the orchard. Toya brooded. And what had the effort afforded her? A marriage proposal!

"Careful, you will crack it."

"Sorry." Toya realized she had been squeezing the crock so hard, her fingers had turned white. Another aroma wafted from the pinkish-brown mixture. "Mesquite?"

"In this batch. Those two"—Opa nodded at the kettles warming on the back of the stove—"contain ocotillo. I have tried many things."

He didn't need to say more. The true remedy lay just beyond his reach. Suddenly ashamed of her selfish emotions, Toya pressed his shoulder gently, wishing she could ease the concern that deepened his wrinkled face. "You have done well, Opa. The children are getting better. Several of the other townspeople are taking them into their homes. They no longer fear the sickness is incurable."

"But some have not improved. Only those who have been ill a few days eat well."

Toya spun around to hand the crock to Betina, but Peter barred the way. "Excuse me." Toya sidestepped her intended and thrust the container at Betina. "Think you can handle one easily?" Green eyes leveled on brown. "Or would *two* be more to your liking?"

Betina's brown eyes rounded as the implication of Toya's words sank in. They were speaking of Rad and Peter, and both women knew it.

Opa filled one crock with the blend of ocotillo.

"Hand me two." Challenge glared back as Betina stepped around Peter. "If that is too much, I shall choose which appeals to me and will do the most good."

Toya's mouth gaped. She'd expected a reaction from her friend, even relished it, but direct insolence? Betina had certainly changed lately and, apparently, under Toya's nose. The dressmaker obviously assumed Rad's affections for her were greater than those he had held for Toya these past three years. Suddenly the wind went out of Toya's anger, leaving her heart adrift.

"Take one for now." Opa deliberately held back the

second. "But do not stay away long, Betina, or the second might sour. Toya, why the moon face?"

"Because I realize you are right, Opa." She turned to stare long and hard at her best friend, wondering why it had been necessary for their friendship to suffer when their sisterhood had weathered many storms throughout the years. They always promised nothing would be too strong to crush it. But now she had allowed her love for a man to come between them. Wasn't there a way to remain friends and also devote themselves to love?

Perhaps she had tarried too long. "Waiting can only damage what you once believed would work." She echoed Opa's words, but his concerned the medicine. Toya prayed Betina understood what she truly implied.

When Betina returned from the dress shop, Toya would apologize for her insinuations and rude remarks. It wasn't Betina's fault alone that their friendship suffered. It took two to argue and ignore each other. And it certainly wasn't Betina's fault Toya lacked the courage to tell Peter she did not want to marry him.

Most important, Toya could blame no one but herself for losing the devotion of the only man she would ever love. She had been the one who denied loving him all these years.

"Why the sour face?" Peter quietly stepped out of the room where he had put Liesl down for a nap. "You should be happy. You've promised your hand in marriage today."

Betina glanced down the hall, looking to see if anyone could hear their conversation. Albertine was busy somewhere else in the house, while Fredericka, they were told, had grown ill. Betina shook her head, afraid to stare into Peter's eyes and see the pain there. "I have not given Conrad my answer."

Peter gently grabbed her arm to keep her from turning away. The heat of his body emanated through his clothes, reminding Betina of another day, when she had pressed her cheek against his chest and allowed him to hold her close. But that was long ago, and she needed to put the memory away forever. He belonged to Toya. He had always belonged to Toya. Betina knew she had no right to long for his touch now, just as she had no right to indulge his embrace on the day he left for Nassau.

The councilman pulled her closer. His gray gaze smoldered as his husky demand whispered against Betina's cheek, "Will you marry him, or is this some game the two of you play?"

A game, ja. *One Rad thought might rouse your true feelings.* Betina kept the words silent within. She would have to answer him eventually. Peter was not a man who waited easily, and she could deny him little. *A game we play to persuade you to take action against this imprudent pledge you and Toya made. One too difficult to perform because of its possible ramifications.*

What if Toya continued to believe Betina would accept Conrad's proposal? If Toya's attitude in the kitchen was any indication, their friendship had caught in a mire of deception and was sinking fast. Only Toya's cavalier innuendo had kept Betina from crying out the truth. She'd wanted to say *I went along with this plan of Conrad's only to make you and Peter jealous.*

But Toya's ire kindled a quiet fury that had burned within Betina ever since Peter left for Nassau, a fury that Betina held back, refusing to acknowledge its source. For her friend's sake, she denied her feelings for Peter. For her friend's sake, she accepted that neither Toya or Peter would dishonor their word. Now, for her friend's sake, she played this game with Rad, hoping that his plans to make Peter or Toya—or both—jealous might convince them to find a way out of this marriage pact. So Toya would know true love.

So that I might too, she reminded herself, disgusted that her own personal aspirations stoked her fury enough to let it burn openly. Betina seldom argued with Toya, seldom allowed herself an opinion or voiced a preference. Being a peacemaker maintained the harmony between them and suited Betina.

She did not mind being second to Toya in most things. She rather liked basking in the attention that often followed Toya. It was a position common in their years as friends, but one she *willingly* condoned. Toya was the star, Betina, the star's caretaker. But not this time. Not when it came to Peter. For once Betina wanted to shine more brightly than her friend.

Today Betina found out how fiercely she wanted to fight for her right to love Peter. The only thing that kept her from doing so now was that she truly believed the councilman would never forgo his promise to Tilly. And that meant marrying Toya. As long as Peter honored his word, Betina would let Toya believe Conrad was the man they battled over.

Denial tasted foul on Betina's tongue, but she did not know any other way to test Peter's sense of rivalry. "I play no game. You have been gone a very long time, and now you are to marry my best friend. Would you deny me happiness?"

Peter's lips hovered only inches away from her own, driving Betina to distraction as their breaths mingled.

"I want nothing but happiness for you, Tina. But you will not find this in his arms."

Peter's mouth enveloped hers in a demanding kiss, but she didn't care. The same longing claimed her now that kept her watching the trails leading into New Genesis for sight of his beloved face these past months. Betina answered Peter's kiss with all her heart, wrapping her arms around his shoulders. She opened her mouth to his, savoring its warmth and trembling at the feral possession of his tongue.

With a need that consumed her every thought, her breath,

her entire being, she clung to him. He lifted her just enough to slide her down the length of his torso until their hips pressed together. Betina felt as if their bodies were two sides of a matching pattern being sewn together by threads of destiny. Somehow she knew no one would ever fit her this way again. No one would ever make her feel so wanted, so needed, so . . .

The last feeling remained undefined. Being held like this, kissed like this, was not enough. It would never be enough. She moaned into his lips, not knowing what to ask for but sensing he knew the answer that would make her feel complete. That was the indefinable . . . she felt incomplete without him.

"I thought I might find you here."

Peter abruptly stepped away from Betina, pushing her behind him to shield her from view. "Just making certain Liesl is tucked in. Betina and I were about to see if you needed anything."

"It is good that you both have taken such a liking"—Fredericka strode closer, then paused—"to the child. And, *nein,* I will tend myself . . . *danke.* I wonder if I might have a talk with you, Betina, before you leave."

Betina's eyes blinked, willing away the sensations Peter had aroused. The effort was no easy task. Her body vented a rhythm his kiss had kindled, as if it were harp strings that hummed long after the last stroke.

She prayed her cheeks were not as red as they felt. Pressing a hand gently upon Peter's back, she whispered a low "*Danke schön,*" then moved around the councilman to see what Toya's aunt needed. Her embarrassment at being caught quickly faded. Fredericka looked hollow-faced and unsteady on her feet.

"You should be lying down, Fredericka. Whatever it is you wish to talk about can wait until later. I will go back to the Wagners and tell Toya of your condition." Betina linked her arm through Fredericka's and looked at Peter expectantly. "Ask Fraulein Pyrtle to come to the Wagners if she cannot delay our appointment until tomorrow. That way, I can help Opa while Toya checks on her aunt."

"Certainly."

"Nonsense." Fredericka broke the link of arms. "Albertine will be near and will enjoy the opportunity to boss me. There is little Toya can do here but much she can do to help Opa. Opa needs Toya. Tell that old *Bier* brine that I will try some of his latest remedy. Better me than the children, *ja*? If he becomes forgetful and puts in too much of one thing or the other, then only I endure the result."

Though she said it in a teasing lilt, Betina worried that there might be more truth to Fredericka's concern than any of them wanted to admit. "I will try to make her stay, but you know our Toya."

"*Ja*, child, I do know our Toya." Fredericka hugged her, whispering so only Betina could hear. "And if you do not tell her what you have confided in me, the sickness she and your young man there are feeling will soon be incurable. Be the first to remedy this wrong, Betina. Be friend enough to give Toya the cure."

"Did anyone visit while I spoke to Lineva? Peter? Conrad? Lineva wanted to pay a call on Frau Liedermann and baby Ernst upstairs before she leaves."

Annoyed at Betina's question and Lineva's sudden sense of charity, Toya watched the dressmaker stare out the kitchen window into the evening shadows instead of paying attention to the task Opa had given them. They were supposed to be making custard rolls for those who would work in the orchard the next day while Opa prepared the next batch of medicine. But not much was getting done.

The tension between her and Betina had become an invisible bunting board to separate them. They'd barely spoken since Betina's return. The few times they did, each had been as polite as a stranger.

"Do it like this," Toya instructed, demanding Betina concentrate on her assignment. The dressmaker may be a genius with fabric, but she couldn't melt butter. Rad liked a good meal; she'd watched him eat. Betina had a lot to learn before she could appease that particular hunger for the bee man.

Then again, Toya realized, she was no prodigy with a needle. At least Betina could outfit the house with beautiful curtains, bed linens, and upholstery for the furniture. She could even help with the saddle making in the barn. Rad already had the best cook in the Republic, what did he need Toya for?

Brooding, she attacked the piece of dough with a vengeance, rolling it as far as the batter would stretch. After sprinkling the confection with cinnamon, she cut the dough in quarters, then added a spoonful of the honey, butter, and custard mixture Opa wanted added to each. Betina attempted to do the same. With great precision Toya folded the pastries so that all the ingredients fit snugly inside.

Betina's concoction leaked at both ends.

"You will soon learn." Opa's laughter filled the kitchen. He patted the dressmaker's shoulder. His cheeks shone like two cherry ovals, heated from working over the stove all day. "Some of us have a knack for cooking, some for sewing. And"—mischief lit his eyes—"some for building fires . . . of various kinds."

Betina laughed with him, dusting her hands free of flour. Sprinkles splattered Toya's face. Toya blinked and stared at the dressmaker to see if Betina had deliberately coated her.

"My regrets." Betina held her hands up in mock surrender.

"Accidents happen." Toya didn't like Betina's smug expression. Letting her hand slip, Toya pressed hard upon one of the custard-filled rolls. Cinnamon-colored goo squirted on Betina's apron. "Strange how accidents seem to follow one another."

Betina gathered the glob from her apron and held it in her open palm. "How right you are, Toya Reinhart. But I heard they always happen"—she started to walk past Toya, then stopped, plopping the glob down on top of Toya's head—"in threes."

"You . . . you . . . hemstitcher!" Toya yelled, unable to think of anything worse to call her best friend at the moment. She grabbed a handful of cinnamon and threw it at Betina.

"Doughroller!" Betina cursed back, and threw a piece of dough at Toya's head.

Toya ducked, her nose barely missed by one of the less-than-perfectly rolled confections.

"A sage I am not on women things. . . ." Opa dodged first one way, then another. He grabbed the remainder of the filling on the table and rushed it to the stove. "But I warrant the two of you have a difference of opinion to settle, *ja*?" He spread his arms wide to protect the pots warming behind him.

Looking around for something else, Toya decided against using any of the precious peaches, but the peelings were another matter. She launched a handful of skins at Betina.

Opa swatted them away. "Keep your opinions on that side of the room, doughroller. I spent too much time measuring for you and hemstitcher to fling such into my pots."

"Watch where you aim and what you waste," a deep voice warned from the back door.

Toya spun around as cool air, twilight, and the reprimand filled the room. There, blocking the doorway, stood Rad. She felt suddenly younger than her twenty years, her actions more damaging than any threat posed by the mountain of muscle stepping toward them. Neither she nor Betina seemed capable of speech.

"They discuss reproduction"—Opa explained with a grin—"of misfortune."

"They are supposed to help you, not make more for you to clean."

Toya stared at the giant of a man standing in the doorway. So proper, this Rad she loved. Her do-the-right-thing-at-all-times Rad. Never-have-any-fun-and-always-plan-ahead Rad. Before she could change her mind, Toya grabbed another handful of peelings and threw them. The skins hit Rad with more force than she intended. A smear of yellow juice ran down his forehead to drip into one eye.

Opa chuckled. Betina gasped. One golden brow winged over the look of surprise registering in Rad's other eye.

Something slippery oozed down Toya's hair. Betina's glob! Toya reached up and grabbed what was left of it, cupped it in her hand, then winked at her best friend. Betina shook her head vehemently.

"Did I miss something?" Rad wiped his face with the back of his hand.

"*Ja*, this!" Toya rose on tiptoe, smacking the gob of filling against the top of his head. An ironlike fist locked around her hand before it could return to her side.

Though his tone was stern, bluebonnet-colored eyes lit with challenge. "Is this to be a contest of wills, Toya? Do not forget . . . I finish all I start. Are you prepared to do the same?"

She tugged her wrist from his grasp, realizing it loosened only because he allowed the freedom. Toya followed her impulse, raising her other hand to accept his challenge. Though he made no move to stop her, Rad's look warned that she was dangerously close to being swept into his arms and kissed. Ever so gently, she wiped the juice from his brow and cheek. To her chagrin, her fingers trembled, voiding any show of courage she displayed.

When Rad's flesh hardened beneath her touch, triumph

blazed through Toya. He was just as affected as she by their nearness.

"A small victory, *Liebling*." He searched her face. "I wonder how you would fare a *thorough* retaliation."

Her eyes widened as he took a few steps away, poured fresh water into a pan, then wet a towel and began dabbing at her hair. As he stood beside her, she became more aware of his height and brawn. He was taller than Peter, outweighed him by twenty pounds, but not an ounce of it was fat.

"*Danke*," she said almost shyly, aware that Rad made no attempt to hide the innuendo of his words or his actions. And this in front of Betina? What game did he play?

As his cleansing focused on her nose, cheeks ... lips, pleasure blazed through Toya. A sigh escaped her before she realized the others must have heard it too.

Betina finally found her voice. She dropped the dough and wiped her hands on her apron. "I must go soon ... after we clean the kitchen. The hour grows late, and I would like to walk back before it gets much darker."

"Do not concern yourself. Toya and I can clean what is soiled." Rad's attention never left Toya's face. "I will escort you, Betina."

Mesmerized by the blue eyes that traced a path wherever his hand cleaned, it took Toya a moment to realize he was asking *her* permission to usher Betina home. "Of course, you should." Toya's heart skipped a beat as he smiled, deepening the cleft of his chin. "It is a gentleman's way."

Both of them were so lost in touching and being touched that neither realized the dressmaker had slipped from the room.

"I will ask Lineva to walk back with her." Opa cleared his throat to get their attention. "I am certain baby Ernst and his mother are growing tired of their visitor."

A slow, knowing smile spread over the old man's face. "While I am gone, keep watch on those fires for me, Grandson. Especially the new one that builds."

17

"The heat is quite noticeable," announced a familiar baritone.

Opa seemed to dance a jig, stepping first one way, then another, as he blocked the newcomer's entrance into the room. "Decide which way you intend to invade my kitchen, Councilman. You make an old man dizzy."

Toya realized the crafty cook was giving her and Rad time to step away from each other. She moved first, grateful for Opa's quick thinking. "Peter! Why have you come? I thought you had gone home to rest."

His gray gaze swept over her, making Toya aware that her hair was disheveled and damp from Rad's administrations.

"I thought you and Betina might need an escort home. You look . . . tired."

She fanned herself elaborately. "Tired . . . and hot." *And guilty.* Of what? Thoughts? She'd done nothing to be ashamed of except glow with passion—and in front of her best friend no less. Her chin lost its loftiness.

"But not too exhausted to enjoy your company." Rad

poked Toya in the back, making her jump forward.

Toya hurriedly dipped her hands in the water bowl and wiped them on a towel. "Just let me see if Betina and Lineva have already gone."

"The ladies should take advantage of such thoughtfulness." Rad motioned to encompass the kitchen. "Do not concern yourself with the disorder, Fraulein Reinhart. I will put everything back in order."

Toya swung around. "Oh, I for—"

"*Danke,* I'm sure Lineva and Betina are equally ready to retire for the evening."

Peter's announcement prevented Toya from changing her mind. She glanced apologetically at Rad, hoping he understood that she sincerely did not mean to leave him with the mess. But despite his congenial words, his eyes lacked their former warmth and were now frosted an icy blue. Another task she'd left unfinished, and to a man who could be no less tired than all of those who had labored today.

"Tomorrow," Toya promised, "I shall arrive early and finish whatever you—"

"It will be done tonight." Rad raked peelings into a trash bin. "We will begin anew tomorrow."

Peter remained silent on the ride back. He would say nothing in front of Lineva. But now that they were pulling away from the Pyrtle home, Toya wondered if he would suppress his irritation with only Betina to buffer his mood. Anger exited in his sharp commands to the horse and exuded from him like heat waves from the sun.

"What transpired between you and Conrad Wagner in my absence?"

His question was low, meant only for her to hear. Toya glanced at Betina, who sat in the rear of the wagon, her shoulders ramrod straight. From the way she'd acted in the kitchen with Rad, Toya was certain Betina was just as irritated with her as Peter was.

Perhaps she could evade Peter by pretending to misunderstand which absence he meant. "All I did was help Opa with his cooking. Then, when Betina returned, we made treats for the workers." She laughed deliberately. "We let ourselves get out of hand with the cinnamon and custard."

"I didn't mean today. What happened between you and Wagner while I was gone to Nassau? Did he kiss you, Toya? Has more passed between you?"

"Peter! How can you ask her such questions?" The voice behind Toya drew closer as Betina shifted in the wagon. "The dress we sew for her wedding is white. Toya has kept her pledge, this I promise."

But you can make no such promise about the kisses, can you, Tina? Toya appreciated Betina's defense of her but equally resented it. What transpired between her and Rad should be no one else's concern but their own. Yet Betina had made it her business. And now Betina was to become Rad's bride. Another stone added to the wall being built between Toya and her best friend.

Peter's questions were warranted. He was a perceptive man, and the time to talk to him about her true feelings must come soon. But would he understand that she intended to break the pledge, not to dishonor her word, but to free him from a loveless marriage? And when everyone learned of the broken vow, would Rad then dismiss it as another commitment she'd left unfinished?

She needed to talk to her aunts—to someone wiser than she. Her aunts had enjoyed wonderful marriages and held great respect among many of the men in the village. "I want to check on Aunt Fredericka before we turn in, but tomorrow, when we are not so weary, we will have a long talk, you and I. *Ja?*"

"*Ja*, we must make time for this talk."

"How is she?" Toya tiptoed inside Aunt Fredericka's room and halted beside the chair Albertine had pulled up next to her sister's bed. Fredericka seemed to be sleeping soundly, but her skin looked pale and her cheeks devoid of their normal rosy hue.

Albertine held a finger to her lips and pointed to another chair for Toya to move alongside her. "Just went to sleep a few minutes ago. Opa's last batch made her more ill, I fear. She lost everything that was in her stomach several times this past hour. Poor thing is exhausted."

Toya bent over and kissed Fred's forehead, tucking the blanket more firmly around her shoulders. Perching in the chair adjacent to Albertine's, Toya waited quietly and observed Albert watching Fred. After a few moments of silence, Toya whispered, "You two fight like hens over a prime nesting place, but you truly love each other, don't you?"

Albertine smiled. "She's all I have left in this world . . . but you, of course." Albertine reached up and smoothed a lock of Toya's hair, securing it behind her ear. "You will soon be a married lady and have a life of your own."

"My life will always include you and Fred, you know that." Toya raced to reassure Albertine. A second glance at their patient made her realize that her aunts were getting older. Their health would become more fragile. How precious Albert and Fred seemed to her now. She couldn't imagine her and Betina ever growing old. *Betina.* Would her friendship with Betina last until the end of their lives? Would they care for each other as Fred and Albert obviously cherished one another? The recent turn of events cast doubt in Toya's mind, and she sighed heavily.

"What is it, child?" Albertine patted her hand. "What weighs so heavy upon your shoulders?"

The words came slow at first, hesitant. Then, like a great flood washing through her, Toya spilled the turbulent emotions she'd kept dammed inside. "And so you see, though I have not dishonored Peter, I dreamed of doing so a thousand times. I know I must break this pledge, but how can

I? If I do, I lose Rad's respect and slight Tilly's memory. If I do not, then I hurt Peter."

Her eyes searched for understanding in her aunt's face. "And what of Liesl—she needs a mother. But most important, what of Betina's and Rad's affection for each other? How can I stand back and watch the man I love marry another . . . even if it is my best friend?"

"Do you not think Fredericka and I suffer from this same dilemma? Both of us care very deeply for Opa, yet he will choose only one someday."

In the back of her mind Toya knew this, but her aunts handled their rivalry skillfully. "Will it be easy for you to step aside if Opa chooses Aunt Fred?"

"Easy?" Albertine reached over and smoothed the blankets that covered her sister. Fredericka stirred, her lashes fluttering. Her eyes opened to stare at them, then instantly closed. "*Nein,* but I love them both enough to want their happiness as well as my own. And if Opa will be content with Fredericka, then I shall step aside."

Toya bowed her head, wondering if the virtue so inherent within her beloved aunts had diluted itself when it reached her. "I have tried to play matchmaker between Rad and Betina, but when I see them together, I care not for her happiness. I only mourn my loss of Rad's love. And it is Rad I love, Aunt Albert. Not Peter, as you might wish, but Conrad Wagner."

Waving a hand of dismissal, Albertine frowned. "No matter what I may have led you to believe, I do not truly favor your marriage to Peter. I have spent forty years taking the opposite view of whatever Fredericka chooses, and it seemed you were adamant to honor the pledge made to young Stoltz."

Albertine smiled, her gaze slanting toward her sister. Fredericka's lips curved downward, hinting that she only pretended sleep and was eavesdropping. The slender woman rose. "There seemed no reason to give in on this issue ... as long as I felt you were marrying the man you wanted to wed. Our Fred may not see well, but I was the one blind to your feelings for Conrad."

"Then I'm confused, Aunt. You do not want me to marry Peter. Yet you tell me I should care enough about Rad and Betina to step aside since he has asked her to marry him?"

"*Nein*, dear heart." Fredericka's eyes opened and she scooted up. Her hand flew to her mouth as if trying to fight off a wave of nausea. When Albertine took a step forward, Fredericka held a palm up to stop her from moving closer. "I am fine, Sister. Would you be kind enough to brew me some tea? Toya can sit with me till you return."

"See, even in sickness she must have the last word." Albertine looked sternly but lovingly at Fredericka.

Fredericka's multiple chins lifted. "You expect no less."

Though wagging a finger at her sister, Albertine directed her warning at Toya. "Listen to about half of what she says. The correct half is what I mean. The other, she makes up to seem more wise."

Fredericka laughed and winked at Toya. "She knows me too well. Now I see what Opa sees in her."

"And everyone knows you do not perceive well, Sister." Albertine exited the room with a laugh.

Warmed by her aunts' playful banter, Toya wondered if their cheerful rivalry held something more. If they suffered the kind of jealousy she felt toward Betina, they hid it well.

"Why the frown?" Fredericka studied Toya.

"Just thinking." Toya wrapped her arms around herself as if to ward off a cold breeze.

"You think with your heart in your eyes, Niece. All is not as tragic as it seems."

"You heard what I told Aunt Albertine." *Please do not make me repeat the hated words.*

"*Ja,* I heard." Fredericka reached out to stop Toya's hands from rubbing her arms. "And I know you are troubled about not only Rad, but your friendship with Betina as well."

"I may not have to worry about that much longer. Our accord fades by the hour."

"Then do something about it."

"What? What can I do but tell Peter I cannot marry him?" Toya rose and began to pace the room. "Even then there's still Betina to consider."

"First things first, *ja*? Come." Fredericka patted the cover next to her. "Sit beside me and listen to this old woman. I cannot see, but I can still help you find a way."

Toya sat and stared at her pale face. "Do not tire yourself, Aunt. This can wait until another day. It has gone on this long, it can—"

"Enough! It has gone on far too long, and we both know it. There are two reasons this pledge must not be fulfilled. One, you felt you owed Tilly something, and that is no reason to marry. It was no fault of yours she could not deal with the reality of her life. You had no say in being born two minutes before her. You did not make her second to Betina in your affections. Tilly chose to believe she was slighted."

Fredericka's hand cupped over Toya's. "I wonder if you even know that it was *you* your father wanted to marry Peter in the first place, but Tilly persuaded Herr Reinhart to change his mind. She convinced him she *loved* Peter and wanted to marry him. Your father granted her permission out of belief that the marriage would not only be one that would benefit both his daughters but would provide a love match for at least one of you."

Toya had been unaware of all the details that prompted the betrothal. She knew her father had wanted to ensure they were well taken care of after his death, but she never suspected her sister of such blatant scheming. "But why would she go to such lengths? If Father had demanded I marry Peter, and I knew that Tilly loved him, I would have stepped aside. All she would have needed to do was talk to me."

"Just as you are willing to talk to Betina now about Rad?"

Embarrassment stained Toya's cheeks. "This is different. I love Rad. He's asked her to marry him. I cannot find it in me to overcome this envy that she will have all I dream of. I do not know what to say to her anymore. And I like myself even less for how I feel about Betina because of all this. I promised to be her friend forever... even when it came time for both of us to marry and spend less time with each other. I do not see that happening now." Toya glanced away. "It's different than with Tilly."

"No different, really. Tilly wanted for one time in her life to be first in your father's eyes. All she had to do was tell him the truth and it would not have mattered to him which of you married Peter. Instead, she chose to lie, and now the lie has followed you all these years. Be stronger than your twin, Toya. Speak the truth. Go to Betina and repair your rift before it is too late to mend the damage. I believe you will be surprised at her true feelings."

Something nagged at Toya as she mulled her aunt's advice. Then she remembered. "You said there were two reasons I must break the pledge to Peter?"

Fredericka stared at her long and hard, then nodded. "*Ja*, I think you are finally ready to listen to what Albertine truly meant. She says, do not blind yourself to the truth, Toya. See all of it, not just what seems apparent. Face it with open eyes. Listen with an understanding heart."

"What have I not been told, Aunt?"

"The second reason, and only Betina can tell you that."

18

*L*ight finally streamed through the dress shop's windows. Toya waited for the silhouette outlined in the lamp's glow to move to the door. When she heard the bolt slide back from its latch, Toya grabbed the handle and turned. With a slight push, she stepped into the shop.

As the bell overhead announced Toya's entrance, Betina grabbed her night wrapper and pulled it more closely around her. "Toya! You frightened me. I could not imagine who—what are you doing here? I did not expect anyone so early."

"*Nein?*" Toya moved farther inside, forcing Betina to take a few steps backward. "Then why did you unlatch the door?"

The dressmaker walked past a hat rack that held colorful bonnets and moved around the edge of the counter, where she worked when shoppers browsed. "I did not expect *customers* so early. I always unlatch the door for Opa. He is kind enough to set the milk bottle inside when he makes his morning rounds."

"Peter has offered to deliver the milk for the Wagners

so Opa can remain at his stove—did you know?"

"I knew." Brown eyes met green, challenge glaring back at Toya. "It is kind of him." Betina took a ledger from one of the shelves beneath the counter and opened it, pretending to scan the written entries.

"Peter has many fine qualities." Toya lifted one of the bonnets from the rack, admiring its stitching. Her friend's disposition was anything but warm and welcoming; still, that would not deter Toya from asking what Fredericka had meant by the second reason. "I'm sure he will be willing to deliver the bottle inside."

"And just what does that tone imply?" Betina slammed the ledger shut.

Toya folded her arms beneath her breasts, surprised that Betina lost her temper. "What we both know. Peter is particularly thoughtful where you are concerned."

"What is it, Toya, that you've come to say this morning?" Betina tossed her one braid over her shoulder as she smoothed back wisps of dark hair from her face. "Did I not leave at just the right moment for you to enjoy Rad's hands all over you in the kitchen? Did I not defend you to Peter and swear that you can still wear white on your wedding day? What more do you need to appease your vanity?"

The anger behind Betina's words stunned Toya. She returned the bonnet to the rack and moved to the counter, splaying her hands on either side of the ledger. "Is that what you think? That this is a matter of vanity? Surely you know me better than that."

Betina leaned over the ledger, her eyes darkening to coffee brown. "You're wrong. I do not know you anymore, Toya Reinhart. The Toya I know would see that I am not the one of us guilty of deceiving the other. The Toya I know would not have to ask why I walked out so easily last night." Her fingers rounded into balled fists. "You swore all those years ago to be my best friend. To never let anything come between us. To let no man divide us. The Toya I know would not be so consumed with herself that she is blinded to the needs of everyone else around her."

"Blinded?" Toya stared out the window at the dawn of a new day. Fredericka's and Albertine's words came back to haunt her. "I see the way you look at Peter." Toya's tone sharpened as the hurt swelled inside. "I saw you blush in Rad's arms." Still, her affection for the men was not the hurt Toya felt deepest.

She swung around and glared at Betina, ever aware that her aunts' goodwill and status in the community granted the dressmaker the privilege of living unchaperoned above her shop. For no one in New Genesis questioned their stewardship over Betina. Toya had gladly and willingly shared everything with Betina—until now.

"You have confided in Aunt Fred these past months, yet you will not talk to me. You complain that I'm not being a friend to you, yet you allow Rad to court you without telling me. You notice things about Peter that only a fiancée should, yet you consider a proposal from Rad. Open my eyes, Betina, if I am so blind. Tell me what it is I do not see. I think, perhaps, I see too clearly."

"How many times I've tried to tell you... and you looked the other way. You did not want to see, Toya. You did not want to hear." The blaze of anger in Betina's tone subsided to a simmer. "And as you said, what good will it do now but ease someone's conscience? Go on believing whatever it is you believe, feeling whatever you feel. But do not expect me to sit back and tolerate your actions anymore. I cannot. I will not."

Betina folded her arms in front of her as if to put a barrier between herself and Toya. "I have a right to expect you to choose whom you will marry. Whom will it be, Toya? Peter? Rad? Or do you trifle with both just to humor yourself? Is that what they are to you... a game? I will no longer sit back and settle for your leftovers. It is time you faced the truth and I no longer pamper you."

"What truth do I not see?"

"Peter Stoltz and I went on a picnic to the Comal one day. Your twin saw us kiss. Tilly's demand that you marry him was only to drive a wedge between you and me. It had nothing to do with honoring the arrangement made between Peter and your father. She thought that if you found out I had kissed Peter, you would think I dishonored our friendship."

"She would do no such—"

"You defend her because it is unkind to speak ill of the dead. But you knew her as well as I. Tilly was envious of our friendship from the time we were little." Betina's eyes narrowed into slitted chestnuts. "You saw it many times. Even in death, Tilly saw the ultimate revenge—making sure you and I could not remain friends. She thought if you married Peter, it would destroy our friendship completely. What she did not realize was that at the time, our friendship meant more than Peter's kiss. I wanted you to honor that pledge . . . because it was what *you* wanted. I would not give her the satisfaction of knowing she had won. That's why she ran off into the hills to die. She could not stand to watch the two of us remain friends despite your pledge to Peter."

"That's a lie!" Toya's hand shot out to slap Betina, but she yanked it back, horrified that she had almost allowed her anger to become physical. "Betina . . . I'm sorr—I never would . . . what has become of us?" Betina leveled a gaze so direct that Toya found it hard to meet squarely.

"The truth stands between us. And you refuse to hear it."

Toya yearned to deny the claim, not wanting to believe her twin capable of such deception, such cruel manipulation. But as she wrestled with the accusation, she recalled the many times Tilly had resented her and Betina's closeness. Had their friendship declined so much that there was no salvaging it? "It seems she succeeded after all."

"It does not have to be this way."

Like a bee sensing nectar, possibility rang in Betina's tone. Toya finally met her friend's gaze.

"Make your decision, Toya. I have made my choice. And as much as I cherish our friendship, I will not let it keep me from telling—"

The bell over the door rang.

"—Peter," Betina said hurriedly. *"Guten Morgen."*

"Not so good, I fear." Peter set the bottle of milk down just to the right of the door, then raised worried gray eyes to focus on Betina. Instead, they found Toya. "Oh, it is good you are here, Toya. Liesl took ill during the night and I . . . do not know how to help her. I asked Frau Williams to watch her while I deliver milk."

He ran a hand through the dark hair at his temple, his eyes red-rimmed from lack of sleep. "I wonder if I might convince one of you to relieve Frau Williams. Or perhaps I can carry Liesl to your house, Toya, where she can be watched more carefully."

"Of course. She can have my bed."

When a finger touched Toya's shoulder lightly, she spun around, uncertain what to expect.

"Let me change clothes. I will stay with Liesl while Peter delivers the milk," Betina suggested. "When he's finished, I will go with him to your house and remain at Liesl's side until you return. That will let you help Opa as long as possible."

"Danke." Toya thanked Betina, not only for her kindness, but for the reprieve she'd granted. Betina had clearly made up her mind to give Rad an answer to his proposal—an answer that threatened to test the frayed bounds of her and Betina's friendship. "I will think about what you said," Toya promised. *I will search my own heart for this*

truth you say I do not see. "And I hope, Betina, that you know I never meant to hurt you or anyone else."

"How are Liesl and Fred?" Toya climbed wearily upstairs behind her aunt.

Albertine escorted Toya to her room but paused just outside the door. "Not much better. You look exhausted, child. Tell me of your day at the Wagners?"

Toya laughed, more to relieve tension than out of humor. She swept back hair that dangled in her eyes. "Difficult? Exasperating is a better definition. I watched Opa at every turn today and, still, he managed to get away from me when we delivered lunch baskets to the workers. I spent the afternoon looking for him." She didn't mention how difficult concentration was with her own mind preoccupied on the conversation with Betina that morning.

"Did you find him?" Dismay deepened the creases in Albertine's face.

"*Ja*, Aunt. Do not worry. He found some rosemary and jimson near his fishing cove. Fortunately, when he decided to mount and ride farther downstream, his horse took a different notion and came home. We found him cursing the poor beast at the barn. But at least Opa was physically unharmed. Though I cannot say as much for his mental faculties."

Toya rolled her shoulders, trying to relieve the day's tension. "He made the same remedy three times today because he could not remember if he had or had not put in the jimson. As you know, jimson can be quite deadly, so we had to throw out three batches. Three batches, Aunt, of precious peaches."

"Is he all right now?" Concern softened the dismay.

Toya nodded. "Rad made him lie down and sent me home. He said we both had been pushing too hard. But no more than he has." She yawned. "He drove me home, yet

I know he will return to the orchard and work far into the night."

"Conrad will not stop until the remedy is found."

"That is why I love him . . ." Toya thought, then realized in her exhaustion she had allowed the thought to take voice.

"I know, dear heart. I know. But only you can decide when it is the right time to tell him."

Tears welled in Toya's eyes. She tried to blink them away so Albertine wouldn't see. But when her aunt opened her arms, offering silent comfort, Toya threw herself into Albertine's embrace and wept.

"I'm so tired, Aunt," she whispered. "Tired of keeping a pledge I do not feel in my heart. Tired of hurting my best friend. Tired of pretending I do not love Rad. Why can't I just tell everyone how I feel and face what comes?"

"You can, dear heart. But only after you've done the most important of these three things."

"Telling Rad that I love him?"

Albertine nodded. "*Ja.* Once you can do that, then together you can face anything else."

"But what if I am wrong? What if he does not love me in return?"

"Then you must be strong enough on your own to do what is right. To step aside."

Toya knew her aunt's wisdom was sound. But she was mistaken about one thing. She needed to correct the first wrong she'd committed. This was of her own doing, not Rad's. She would end this marriage pact now. "Have you seen Peter this afternoon? I thought I would look in on Aunt Fred and the child, then have a talk with—"

"He and Betina are with Liesl in your room." Albertine let go of Toya. "He's been near panic about the child and remained at her bedside since delivering the milk this morning. Betina has stayed with them both."

"I thought she was acting a little too spry even for her

age and hiding something from us. But she wanted to help in the orchard so desperately that I didn't have the heart to deny her. I should have listened to my instincts. But then, what do I know of children?"

Albertine reassured her. "I do know of children, dear heart, and yet I did not see. We all did not see. When someone is dedicated to a task, it is difficult to stop them. Even in one so small."

Just as I must now commit myself to this task. Toya took a deep breath, gathering her courage to step inside that room and speak with Peter. Tired as she was, she refused to let another night go by without telling him she could not become his bride. "I would like a word alone with Peter, Aunt, if you will excuse us."

"Of course. I shall check on Fredericka. When you're finished, come down and eat some supper. I kept a plate warm for you."

Toya thanked her aunt and waited until Albertine walked down the hall to Fredericka's room. Plastering a smile on her face, Toya opened the door and stepped inside. The smile froze at the sight before her.

Candlelight danced along the walls, illuminating the room in a soft, welcome glow. But the bed drew all her focus now. Liesl, Betina, and Peter lay spooned one behind the other, with Betina's arm protectively locked around Liesl and Peter's around Betina. Though fully clothed, there was an intimacy to the way Betina and the councilman fit each other—an intimacy that reminded Toya of how perfectly she had fit Rad at the well.

Staring at them, emotions warred within Toya. Was she relieved more than angered at her friend's duplicity?

Is it possible you were trying to tell me you love Peter? Toya silently challenged Betina. *Or do my eyes see only what they wish to believe?* She recalled Betina's greeting when Peter delivered the milk this morning. *Make your decision, Toya. I have made my choice.* And, as much as I *cherish our friendship, I will not let it keep me from telling—*"

Betina finished her sentence with *Peter. Guten Morgen.* Had his name been spoken, not in greeting, but to define her choice?

A light tap sounded at the door. "Betina, are you hungry?"

Toya tiptoed into the hall, holding a finger to her lips to silence Albertine.

"Is all well?"

Toya nodded and wrapped her arm around Albertine's slender waist. "There's a chance it could be, Aunt. There's a chance it could be."

19

"There is no time for such folly." Rad reined the buggy to a halt and called to his grandfather, who rode ahead of them. "Hold up, Opa! She wants to have the picnic here."

The old man turned his mount and pointed to a section of Toya's land fed by the creek. "You and the *Fraulein* get settled. I shall water my horse and join you in a while."

"Stay close."

"How can I wander off? This four-legged barn-lover is too afraid to miss his oats. He is loyal only to his belly."

Rad laughed despite his distraction since leaving church services. "Just be careful, and tell me if you decide to go anywhere else—without the horse."

"*Ja, ja.*" Opa turned back and nudged his mount into a canter. He waved impatiently. "Eat. Drink. Do not watch every move I make. I am fine this day. I need time to gather more herbs. My patients need time between batches, and you, Grandson, need a dose of relaxation."

Rad secured the reins and jumped down, frowning at

Toya as he offered her a hand out of the buggy. "Did you put him up to this?"

Perhaps this picnic hadn't been such a good idea after all, Toya decided. Rad grabbed her waist like she was a sack of flour and lifted her with little effort... or effect. "Opa needs some time away from the cookstove," Toya said, unable to meet the deep blue gaze staring at her for explanation.

Discouragement enveloped her. If touching her meant so little to Rad, then the path she walked today would only lead to heartbreak. "The workers are tired. The least we can do is give them a few hours with their families after church services. If he rests, maybe he will not make so many errors with the medicine. Fewer mistakes mean fewer wasted peaches."

"You heard the reverend this morning." Rad grabbed the picnic basket and handed it to Toya. He motioned to the meadow that spread before them like a tapestry of blue. Everywhere her eyes could see bluebonnets blossomed in all their glory, their hue so vivid, it rivaled the cloudless Texas sky. Though the field no longer droned with thousands of bees as it had before, the warm scent of honey permeated the countryside, hinting that not all obeyed their keeper and had taken up residence nearby.

"Three Oaks Crossing is now suffering from the illness. Other settlements are too. I should be in the orchard, picking." He strode several yards ahead. "Is this a good place, or do you want to move a little closer to your sister's grave? Perhaps near one of the trees for shade."

The wind whispered through the upper branches of the trees, gently swaying them and staving off the afternoon sun. Toya shook off her dark mood and joined him, thinking this would give the horse room to graze. She spread the blanket and let it settle amid the bluebonnets. "Here will be fine."

"While you prepare lunch I will check the bees and

A TASTE OF HONEY

make sure they are not rogue. I know you fear them.''

Not as much as I fear your reaction to what I plan to tell you, Toya wanted to say.

"Did you bring something I can use for a container?"

She searched the basket, then handed him one of the wineglasses.

"*Danke,* that will do."

Toya watched him walk toward the trees. Rad's sleek and powerful strides resembled a predator stalking his prey, certain of victory. The drone grew louder as he approached a trunk that looked darker in color than the others. It was then she noticed the darkness shifted; hundreds, maybe thousands of bees coated the tree trunk.

Rad stood perfectly still. A haze of bees danced about his head, diving, dipping, landing on him, only to spiral into the air again. Toya's heart leapt into her throat. Gooseflesh rippled along her skin as she imagined the number of stings he would suffer if the bees became angry. But they seemed to be testing him, cautiously examining him to see if he posed a threat.

"No, stop," she whispered as his hand slowly disappeared into the dark mass. Had he lost his mind?

The arm sank deeper.

Instead of retreating quickly, Rad delved deeply into the trunk. The bees must have built a hive in the tree's inner sanctum. Toya held her breath, certain any moment Rad would begin swatting away the insects and running for his life. Instead, his arm eased out ever so slowly. Along with it came a piece of honeycomb dripping with the bees' precious treasure. He placed it gently in the wine goblet and stood motionless again.

Allowing them time to enrage themselves over his theft? Was he so confident of his ability that he had lost all sense of danger? What was he saying? She couldn't hear it, but his mouth definitely moved. Toya sat transfixed, realizing that what others had said about him was true. She'd seen it with her own eyes. The man had charmed the bees out of their honey without suffering a single sting!

As he moved toward her, fascination for this man she loved spread through Toya like butter melting over hot biscuits. Wind rustled the blond mass of hair hanging to his collar. His shoulders blocked the sight of the tree now, their expanse big enough to obscure any concern she might have. His thighs flexed with each powerful stride, sending a salvo of desire coursing through Toya. She fanned herself with one hand.

"Care for some honey?"

The huskiness in his voice rippled through her bloodstream, skimming along the surface of her skin in pebbled gooseflesh. Her eyes blinked away the vision of him offering something more. She swallowed and licked her lips. "I—I think I will have some of Opa's wine first. Would you care for some... wine?"

Rad held up the glass, allowing sunlight to shine through the amber-coated honeycomb. "I used one of the glasses. We shall have to share."

Their gazes collided. His lips, then hers, would touch the glass rim. "I suppose we could," Toya whispered. She uncorked the wine bottle, poured the glass full, and offered it to him.

"You first." Rad sat down beside her, then stretched out his legs, setting the glass of honey on the edge of the blanket so it wouldn't be knocked over. He waited as she took a long sip. "Though I grumble, I needed this, Toya. Thank you for making me rest. It is difficult to hear the clock ticking away and watching the children suffer—"

"Shhh." Toya handed him the glass and started to refill it. He shook his head, denying the need for more. She recorked the bottle. "Everyone is concerned. But we're all so tired, we cannot continue. I ask nothing but this afternoon. We'll begin picking again this evening."

"That's one of the things I like best about you." Rad's

lips dipped against the glass's rim, leaving his compliment unexplained.

A shiver of longing raced through Toya as if he had pressed his lips against her neck instead of the rim.

When he finished, his tongue darted out to lick his lips. Toya fidgeted, her body suddenly tensing. The meadow vibrated with life, anticipation ... promise. Even the bluebonnets deepened in hue, or was it only her imagination making it seem so? All she knew for certain was that her blood had begun to hum some nameless tune with words she did not yet know but yearned to discover.

Rad smiled at the expression softening the contours of Toya's face. For one small fragment of time, he would enjoy the sun upon his back, the wine to soothe his woes, and, most of all, the opportunity to be with the woman he loved.

He stared at her cherished face, aware of the exact moment her curiosity lost its patience.

"Well? Am I to guess what it is you like about me?" Challenge sparked the emerald of her eyes.

Her skirt spread around her like a shawl, blanketing the lovely legs he'd seen at the well. He'd sworn that he would find a way someday to have the right to admire them openly. Today he sensed it might actually happen ... if he allowed himself to hope. To dare. But this was only a reprieve from their duties—his to harvest the peaches, hers to marry the councilman. "Your impulsiveness."

Rad thought she'd never looked more beautiful ... or engaged.

He didn't know why he loved this infuriating woman.

When Toya heard him sigh, she knew he had shut her out again, sitting behind the iron will of honor that separated them.

They spoke little while they ate, each pretending that all they shared was a meal. Opa returned, talking incessantly about the plants growing along this portion of the creek.

Toya pretended to listen as the Wagners discussed the medicinal qualities of one herb over the other, but she finally blocked it all out, longing for something she had only dreamed and could not put into words.

"What do you think, Toya?"

She looked up, startled and embarrassed that she hadn't been listening for quite some time now. Then she realized whatever her answer should be, it pertained to Opa. The old man paced back and forth in front of the blanket, reeds and bluebonnets clutched in one hand.

"I am old enough to see myself home, Grandson." He stressed the last word to remind them of his greater maturity. "And even if I become lost, that swayback will make sure I return home. See the way he chomps his bit? He is ready to head for the barn now. I might as well go with him. Betina said she would come by later this afternoon. Between the two of you *Frauleins*, I am well corraled."

Rad began to rise. Opa motioned him to remain sitting. "You two stay. Enjoy the day. Leave an old man alone to his conjuring."

"You are as subtle as a sandstorm, Opa."

The corner of Opa's frown tilted just enough for Toya to see why Rad mocked him.

"Then ease an old man's heart. At least try to show her you have inherited some of my oomph."

Toya giggled. That was the most unusual definition she'd ever heard of Opa's charm.

"And you"—the old man glared at her—"you quit swimming with four-legged frogs when you prefer three."

"Go, old man, before I change my mind," Rad groused.

Opa mounted and grinned. "That I will do. Now, take advantage of that soft grass and change hers."

He spurred the willing beast into a full gallop, yipping and yehawing like one of those vaqueros herding longhorns up from Mexico.

"When Opa told you to change my mind...?" Toya

searched Rad's face, noting the stubborn set of his jaw. She was playing with fire, challenging him to define his grandfather's words, but the time had come to lay all pretense behind them. "Does he speak of my pledge?"

Rad shoved away from the blanket and stood. He walked to the buggy and braced his hands on it. "Unless there is something else that keeps us apart."

Toya crossed the distance that separated them until she stood directly behind him. He stiffened as she slipped her arms around his waist and pressed her cheek against his broad back. His chambray shirt was soft and warm from the sun, the skin beneath it issuing an even greater warmth. She could feel his every breath, heard the exact moment the steady beat of his heart sped up to match the racing of her own.

"It is you I love, Rad."

"Do not say this to me. You gave your word to—"

"I owe him nothing but the truth."

Rad turned away from the buggy and braced his feet as if warding off some unknown attack. "And what is the truth, *Liebling*?"

His endearment was all Toya needed to hear to know how hard he fought his own conscience not to touch her. She gently brushed his arms, urging them to slip around her and pull her closer.

She leaned back into the curve of his embrace, letting her gaze take in the golden thatch of hair, the blue of his eyes, the heaven waiting at his lips. "The truth that keeping one's word when the heart is not in it is meaningless. That only when your word is heartfelt does the promise become a gift. Otherwise, you only satisfy an obligation, nothing more."

Her eyes flooded with tears as she searched his face for a sign of understanding, of acceptance. Toya knew she might never win this battle of honor, but her love for Rad was too great. Telling him the truth about her feelings was the one thing she would not—could not—leave unfinished. "No marriage should be a matter of duty. I shall never marry Peter."

Rad's gaze seemed to study her, gauging her in some way. Did he doubt her sincerity? "Th-the only thing that p-prevents me from throwing myself at you this very minute"—Toya's voice broke on every word—"is that you asked Betina to marry you. I want to know. No, I *must* know—do you really love her, Rad? Should I turn away and keep these words silent within me?"

Though she suspected Betina had already made another choice, Toya's heart needed to hear the words from Rad's lips, needed the reassurance that he loved *her* and no other.

Rad groaned. "I have loved only you, Toya Reinhart, and no one else before or after you. My proposal to Betina was an agreement between us to make you and—if my suspicions are correct—*Peter* jealous."

"You succeeded."

Their lips met instantly. Toya's arms flew up to wrap themselves around his neck as he crushed her against him. His tongue traced the seam of her lips until she opened her mouth and met its delicious heat with her own. A heady feeling engulfed her, overwhelming Toya with a need so torrid, she thought she would melt in his arms.

She moaned against Rad's lips, shoving her hands into the mass of sun-burnished hair that hung about his collar. As she tasted him deeper, he swept her into his arms, carrying her toward the blanket they had spread earlier. His boot raked aside the empty tins and wine bottle to clear away the remnants of their picnic. But as he did, the jar containing the honeycomb turned over, spilling some of the amber treasure onto the blanket.

"I have made a mess of things," Rad muttered against her lips.

"The bluebonnets," she whispered. "Make love to me in the bluebonnets."

Gently he lay her amid the blue and gray flowers, worshipping her with his eyes. When his hands reached toward her breasts, Toya sucked in her breath in anticipation of his touch. Instead, his fingers found the calico ribbon holding her braid in place and pulled it loose.

A grin flashed white against his bronze face. One hand delved into his pants pocket to bring out the emerald ribbon she had lost in Rad's bedroom.

"I collect these," he teased.

"I offer them gladly." Toya marveled at how his smile alone could hold her a willing captive.

"Mine to keep forever, *ja*?"

She knew they talked of something more than ribbons. She gazed deeply into the hooded blue gaze darker now with banked passion. "Forever."

The ribbons disappeared into his pocket, then Rad began to slowly unthread her braid. She watched him measure the weight and length of her hair with his hands, run his fingers through it, then spread it out around her shoulders like a golden shawl.

His slow, methodical caresses drove her to distraction. Frantic to touch him, to have nothing between them, her hands pushed aside the open front of his shirt. Two buttons popped off, causing Rad to chuckle.

"Always in a hurry, my Toya."

Toya laughed with the pure joy of the moment, then kissed him fiercely, wanting to breathe in his chuckle before it faded from his lips.

Suddenly, a fierce impulse to satisfy her curiosity, to press him closer, overwhelmed her. She grasped the edge of his shirt where it disappeared into his waistband and began to tug it up and out of his pants.

Without breaking the kiss, Rad let go of her hair and started working the dress off her shoulders and down her arms. When she realized what he was about, her fingers raced to help him.

He gently halted her hands. "No, let me. There is no hurry now. I want us never to hurry."

Ever so slowly, Rad peeled away the garments that hindered their closeness—the dress, her chemise, the pantaloons. With aching slowness, he shed his own clothes, allowing her to view all his magnificent manhood, giving her opportunity to change her mind one last time.

But there would be no going back for Toya. The only path she sought led to a future with Rad. "I want you, Rad," she encouraged. "I want to know what loving you means."

He heard the words from somewhere far away and tried to shake them off. It was only his mind playing tricks with him after all his silent longing.

She meant it. Toya Reinhart, the woman he had dreamed of sleeping in his arms, working by his side, nursing his children at her breast. The woman he believed would marry Peter Stoltz now welcomed him into her heart forever. He blinked away the sting of tears that threatened to blind him to the beauty offering her heart, gladdening his soul. He pressed his length against her and kissed her ever so gently, the miracle of her love tasting like honey upon his lips.

Toya's hands traced a sensuous trail across the expanse of his shoulders, down the flat plain of his abdomen to explore the hard shaft of desire pressing like velvet stone against her thigh.

In a move rougher than he intended, Rad covered her mouth with his, his tongue diving between her lips to find its mate. Toya moaned, her arms wrapping themselves around his neck. He wanted to inhale her, to consume her, to absorb her until there was nothing left of either of them but one all-enveloping flame.

Rad held her fast, pressing her against him with a possessive hold, unable to let her go now that he had her in his arms. She had been another's in the beginning, but now she belonged to him. She had bound him to her from the first day he met her, at first with her beauty, then with her curiosity and radiant smile, finally with her kindness to Opa. He had endured the thought of letting her marry Peter for the sake of honor, but Toya was right. Marriage for duty's sake was the worst breach of honor they could commit against Peter.

Toya clung to him as his lips moved over hers possessively. She ran her hands through his hair and decided she liked this sudden wildness within him very much. She knew as she lay there locked in his embrace that she would never love another man the way she loved Rad Wagner.

She tore her lips from his long enough to demand the one thing she wanted more than anything else in this world. "Make love to me, Rad. Show me how to belong to you and only you."

"You are so beautiful." He nuzzled her neck, scattering kisses along her jaw, tracing his tongue around the lobe of her ear.

Toya moaned and lost herself in the pleasure that invaded her senses.

Rad captured her lips again and kissed her long and hard, his hands roving over her back, along her sides, then to cup her breasts. He caressed one nipple until it grew taut and strained against his thumb. She clung to him, wordlessly begging for more. Rad bent to suckle one hardened peak, then the other, causing her to cry out with need.

His hands played over her body, explored the silky length of her. When his fingers brushed the curls between her legs, she surged upward, pressing herself against his palm. Rad slid down the length of her, kissing his way to the hollow of her abdomen. Finally he buried his face against the golden apex of her thighs, nipping and kissing until she whispered his name over and over again.

His hot tongue moved over her, setting her flesh afire. Toya gripped his shoulders with her fingers, clinging to him in an effort to ground herself to the bed of bluebonnets, but her senses swirled unrestrained. Slowly, he drew one nipple into his mouth, gently tugged on it with his teeth, then sucked until he extracted a tortured moan from her lips. She wrapped her legs around his hips to draw him even closer, writhing against him in a dance of wanton desire.

Rad moaned against her lips, knowing he could wait no longer. But he had promised not to hurry. Determination broke into beads upon his brow as his hands cupped her hips and lifted her to him. Gently, Rad probed the welcome waiting at the entrance of her womanhood.

Toya thrust her hips toward him, gasping when he slid inside her. Suddenly he held still. Toya sensed his intense concentration, wondering why he paused. Did he await some move from her? Barely breathing, Toya memorized the wonder of their joining. But then she could endure the wait no longer. Softly, she implored, "Please, Rad, please, don't leave this unfinished between us."

Before the exquisite torture drove her over the edge, he silenced her with another kiss. Slowly, he started to withdraw. Misunderstanding, Toya moaned softly and clasped him tighter.

With a savage growl, he gave way to his passion. She gasped with the pain but did not cry out. He filled her completely then, slowly, gradually, giving her time to open to him and swell around his length. He was breathing heavily now, but his every breath matched her own, as did the wild beat of his heart.

She buried her face against his neck, tasted his sweat-sheened skin, and began to move with him.

Bluebonnets swayed in rhythm to their lovemaking. The scent of warm honey permeated the meadow. But it was the sound of his endearments whispered in her ear that forever imprinted itself in Toya's heart.

The tension mounted as she met his driving thrusts. Higher and higher they climbed toward some unfathomable release. "Please," she entreated against his lips. "Please."

Yet she had no idea what she asked. Just as she thought she might scream from the pure ecstasy of being in his arms, Rad buried himself completely one last time. She began to shudder. The world spun out of control. Toya clung to him, crying out his name, her soul shattering into countless contented fragments.

Several minutes passed before their ragged breathing subsided. Rad kissed her slowly, reverently, drawing himself up on his elbows to look deeply into her eyes.

Their sweat-glistened bodies glimmered, alive with light and shadow from the afternoon sun. The buzz of a bee captured her attention as it landed where honey had spilled on the blanket. Her gaze darted to the insect, then back to Rad. He reached out and dipped his finger in the amber treat and rubbed it gently upon her lower lip. Unable to resist, Toya's tongue darted out, hungering not for the honey but for the sweetened roughness of Rad's flesh.

His lips curled into a smile that set Toya's heart to pounding so loudly, she was certain it would draw the attention of the entire swarm of bees. But all fear fled her instantly. Staring back at her from the blue depths of Rad's eyes was a love so bold, she would never again fear anything. From this moment on she knew she would never belong solely to herself.

Her fingers delved into Rad's thick, burnished curls, combing them and watching the light shine against them. How Toya wished she and Rad could stay this way forever, warm and wrapped in each other's arms with their bodies entwined so exquisitely.

"I love you, Rad." Tears stung her eyes as powerful as the emotion giving voice to the rapture she shared with him. "I will love you forever."

"Then there is someone we must tell, *Liebling*." Rad leaned down to nip the lobe of her ear, trace the hot edge of his tongue against the curve of her jaw, and halt only a breath away from her lips. "For I will never again allow a pledge to keep us apart. You belong to me, Toya. To no one else. It is the vow our *hearts* have made."

Fierce was his kiss, branding her with a possession that left no corner of her soul unscorched, unclaimed, uncharmed.

20

Betina watched Peter march up the steps and go into the apothecary, glad for the reprieve from his stony silence. All morning he had said little more than ask her to attend church with him and pray for Liesl's health, which she had done gladly.

But while Betina prayed, other anxieties kept creeping in to shadow her thoughts. The sound of anguish rumbling from Peter's throat when he woke and found himself spooned against her echoed like a discordant howl, making it difficult for Betina to concentrate on her prayers. Though she diligently prayed for the child's sickness to end, her mind kept wondering why Peter nearly flung himself off the bed as if he'd touched a smoldering ember.

Betina doubted she would ever know. He hadn't even looked in her direction during and since leaving church services. She sat very still on the driver's box and watched townspeople pass along the planked walks in front of the stores. Everyone seemed to be taking advantage of the sunlit afternoon away from the work in Conrad's orchard.

As a familiar thatch of red curls bobbed into view, Betina

shifted on her seat, pretending to focus her attention elsewhere. Lineva Pyrtle was definitely the last person she wanted to encounter at the moment.

"Fraulein Bram, how good it was to see you at church." Lineva hurried forward like a buzzard swooping to the kill. "I could not help but notice that you were sitting alongside Councilman Stoltz. Where is Fraulein Reinhart? I hear Toya's aunt is ill with whatever is affecting the children. Did she stay home with dear Fredericka, or is she still playing nursemaid to Ash Wagner?"

Before Betina could answer, the woman's questions surged.

"I noticed how diligently you prayed today." One brow shot upward, and she darted a glance at the apothecary. "Is something lying heavy on your heart, *Fraulein*?" Lineva leaned closer, as if to secret her tone from the other women. "If you need an ear in which to confide your transgres—er ... your worries, child, please allow me to—"

"You bear too much, Fraulein Pyrtle." Betina leveled a gaze so direct at Lineva, the older woman blinked several times as if warding off blazing sunlight. Betina thought of climbing down and going into the apothecary, but evasion would only fuel the redhead's meddling. "How kind it is of someone with such ... maturity ... to extend your inclinations and precious time to those of us whose value it is often lost upon. I worry you will collapse beneath the weight of everyone's concerns you count so zealously as your own."

Lineva's smile angled into a frown.

Several of the other women snickered, understanding completely that Betina had just called the woman a babblemouth. Not only a babblemouth, but an old one at that!

Lineva was the head of the local kaffeeklatsch, a group of eight ladies whose venture was conversation. The discussions usually centered around harmless subjects such as household chores, children, relatives, and recipes. But Li-

A TASTE OF HONEY

neva's kaffeeklatsch sowed the bad seeds of gossip. Betina didn't care. Let the criticism sink into those supposedly natural red roots.

"Have I kept you waiting?" Peter startled Betina as he placed a box in the back of the wagon. "I had a few more things to get than I planned on." His attention averted to the redhead and her friends. "Is there a problem, ladies?"

Betina didn't mistake his direct look at Lineva, though his words addressed all. Nor did she miss how quickly Lineva mumbled some excuse, then turned away. They might snub *her* for sitting with Peter when he was promised to another, but they would not dare confront Councilman Stoltz!

The dark-haired man who ran the apothecary filled the store's doorway. He motioned to the box Peter had placed in the back of the wagon. "You come back if that does not help the young ones. We will try more." His massive hands looked as if someone had tarnished them with berry juice.

"Are you bleeding?" Betina hadn't realized she'd spoken until he grabbed a kerchief from his pocket and began wiping the stain from his hands.

"*Nein.*" Gunnar Williams wiped furiously as he hurried forward to show her. "It is a mixture I have tried with the berries along the riverbank. The honey and peaches, they do not cure all. My Lucia, she is ill now. I fear she has taken the fever just as Frau Fredericka. We must try other remedies if the peaches do not work."

"Here, let me take that for you." Betina reached for the kerchief, and he offered it to her, curiosity lifting his brows. "I shall clean it for you since Lucia does not feel well," she insisted.

When the middle-aged man half smiled, his eyes disappeared above rounded cheeks. "It is kind of you, *Fraulein*. When she feels well enough to complain, she will be angry that I stained it."

Looking over Gunnar's head to Peter, Betina noticed he

was busy tying the supplies down and didn't look up. "I promise to make it look as pretty as the first time I saw it."

"Oh, then you have seen this before? It is my wife's favorite."

"*Danke* for your help, Gunnar, but we'd best be on our way if I'm going to deliver this to the Wagners." Peter tipped his hat to the older man, saving Betina from answering. He handed her a box and climbed into the wagon. "I promised Albertine that Betina and I would take this to Opa as he requested and would return as soon as possible. Liesl's still quite sick." Peter flicked the reins, urging the horses to action.

Betina couldn't help but smile as they passed Lineva and her gaggle of grumblebums. The women pretended not to notice Peter's wagon moving down the street. She couldn't resist the impulse and waved at Lineva, laughing when the redhead tilted a parasol to one side in order to block Betina's view.

"I hope you're as pleased when you open the box." Peter's low baritone breathed softly against her ear.

Betina lifted the container to look at it more closely. She had assumed it was something from the apothecary—more medicine to give to Opa. "What is it?"

"If you were Toya, you would have already had it opened by now."

Nein, Betina silently pleaded. *Do not compare us. I am not Toya. I will never be.* She tucked the kerchief into her pocket for later. "Patience is a great virtue, I am told." She tried to keep the anger from her tone but failed miserably. "But I tell you nothing new. A man who lives by honor surely knows the value of patience far better than I."

"Honor is a lonely word, Betina, just as patience can be. Where this conversation leads, I cannot go. You know it. I know it. Do not deprive me of this one moment I can share with you."

Slowly, Betina opened the box. In a swatch of white linen lay a kerchief of sapphire blue. Lifting it gently, she noticed an elaborate *B* embroidered in one corner.

Words of gratitude raced to her lips but remained unspoken as she softly brushed her fingers across the silk and marveled that he had gone to such lengths to please her.

"It can never replace the one you lost, but I thought it matched the color of your—it would serve the purpose."

A silk kerchief? Betina sold none finer in her own dress shop. The embroidered stitches of the monogram were so evenly spaced, they looked as if they were woven by magic. She was afraid to glance at Peter for fear he might see the tears welling in her eyes.

He had been gone all this time, yet he cared enough to consider her. She had hoped, dreamed, all the days he'd been in Nassau, that some miracle might end the pledge between Toya and Peter. But her friendship to Toya kept those dreams and hopes locked away in her heart, daring not to give them credence beyond the shadows of night. Now, here, in broad daylight, Peter offered a gift of... what? Thoughtfulness? Caring? Friendship? Was she reading more into the gift than what he offered?

Betina trembled, half in reaction to the man sitting so closely beside her, half in dread of the disappointment she surely would face if she let her emotions get the best of her.

"Are you cold?" Peter moved the reins to one hand and reached behind him. "There are plenty of blankets back there. I didn't know how long we would be at the Wagners nor how many might want a ride home, so I brought several. Wrap up in it and get warm." He handed her a blanket, concern darkening his eyes. "Are you becoming ill?"

"*Nein,*" she whispered, deciding it was easier to pretend she was cold than to find a reasonable explanation he would believe. She allowed him to drape the blanket across her shoulders. *"Danke."* She lifted the kerchief. "It's lovely."

"I wanted to get you something... as Toya's maid of honor."

Betina glided her hands across the silk and silently pleaded for Peter to say no more. Part of her wanted to give him back the gift if he had bought it only because she would stand attendant to his bride. Yet another part of her wanted to hold it against her cheek and imagine his hands caressing the material, testing its texture, choosing its shade because he admired the color of her eyes.

Instead, her hands found the other kerchief—the stained one she'd demanded from Gunnar. She knotted it between her fingers, remembering too well that it once held a value as great as the kerchief Peter gave her.

The material felt as if it were liquid fire, and her touching it, a betrayal of herself. I cannot, Betina reminded herself, letting go of the soiled kerchief. She blinked away the hot sting of tears brimming in her lashes, aware that one kerchief represented the man she loved, the other the friendship that stood in the way of loving Peter.

The fact that the kerchief she lost suddenly appeared must have some purpose—a reason more profound than Lucia Williams's possession of it.

Peter guided the team onto the road that led to the Wagner chalet, seemingly totally absorbed in driving. As the road made them sway back and forth on the driver's box, he braced his hand behind her back, steadying her.

At first Betina remained stiff in the seat, battling the tossing wagon. But slowly she realized that had it been Lineva Pyrtle sitting beside him, Peter would offer the same courtesy. Betina relaxed against his arm, enjoying the comfort she found there.

In a low voice Peter spoke as if to himself. "We must discuss a few matters before we take the medicine to Opa."

"Ja." She knew he meant before they saw Toya and Conrad again. "A few matters."

Peter reined to a halt in front of Rad's house, studying her. "I am promised to Toya, and nothing will make me break that vow, Betina."

She met his gaze. He had a strong, handsome face despite the firm set of his jaw. She knew she should not ask the impossible, but her heart had longed for him so deeply that Betina could no more stop the words than she could corral the Texas wind. "Nothing? Not even after this morning?"

Peter stared at the Texas hill country rolling into the distance. "I am a man who makes my living by my word. If I break it, then how can I ever expect anyone to believe me? What happened this morning was nothing. Two tired people who found warmth and comfort after a long night without much sleep. We did nothing but lie beside each other."

Turmoil darted across his expression before he masked it behind an iron will. "I promised Herr Reinhart and Tilly I would take care of Toya. I've made a pledge not only to my betrothed, but to all three. Nothing happened between us this morning, Betina. Nothing *can.*"

She sat still, the chill of his words sending gooseflesh to bead down her neck and arms. She shivered beneath the blanket despite the warmth of the afternoon sun.

But love burned hot and deep within her. She could not let him go without telling him how she felt. She would not. "You're wrong, Peter. Something did happen this morning. Just as it did the day you left for Nassau. We fell in love with each other. We did not mean to. We tried not to, but we did. Your misguided sense of responsibility may allow you to hide it during the light of day, but don't you see— this morning is proof that we cannot continue to conceal how we feel about each other."

Peter reached out to touch the tears spilling down her cheeks.

Betina twisted away from him. "You truthfully cannot see it, can you? You do not want to marry Toya as dearly as you want to *save* her, Peter. Delivering the immigrants, rescuing Liesl and offering her a home... even marrying Toya—none of these things will mend whatever has been torn. Forgive yourself, Peter! Forgive yourself for whomever you failed!"

21

Betina wished Peter would say something...anything, but he remained silent as he helped her down from the wagon. His hands lingered for just a moment at her waist while Betina gained a firm footing, then he nearly shoved himself away from her.

He grabbed one of the boxes in the back of the wagon and headed up the stone walk that led to the porch. She quickly took another, sensing that if she let him walk away now, he would leave her forever, if not physically, then emotionally. She could not let that happen. Not until he heard what she had to say.

"Peter, I—I did not say that to hurt you or anger you, but it was something you needed to hear." Betina followed. "You try so hard to be everything for everyone, you do not consider what *you* want—"

Peter spun around, nearly making Betina drop her box of supplies. "Enough. I will not hear this from you. Especially you. You have always walked behind as if you were not equal. You held your silence and refused to claim what you wanted. Do not talk to me of saving when you are so willing to sacrifice love for the sake of angering a friend."

"Is that what you think?" Betina felt as if he'd slapped her. "You think that I *wanted* to stand aside and watch you and Toya marry? You think that it is easy to hide my tears that might stain her wedding dress each time I help her aunts sew its beads? You think that my love for Toya is any greater than the love I bear for you? Peter, I stood aside *because* I love you. Because I believed your honor would never let you break your vow to her and her family."

Betina's voice lowered to a whisper. "I can see now that whatever it is that drives your will, whatever possesses you, may be too strong to alter. It festers so deeply within you, it demands accountability. Do not ask the question of me, but of yourself, Peter. Why are *you* only too willing to sacrifice love?"

"Don't love me, Tina. It is Toya I will marry, because where there is no love, there is no harm. It is better this way."

She laughed, trying to mortar her heart from the sorrow threatening to break it into tiny pieces. "So, Herr Councilman, that is your reason! You are so afraid of taking a risk, of feeling you can't control or predict the outcome, you hide behind your word of honor because it is safer."

Betina glared at him, wishing she could find a way to stop loving him, yet knowing any possibility of that had been taken from her long ago. She flung words, cruel and hurtful, praying that they would veil her crumbling emotions.

"And all along I thought you were a selfless man. A man who put his community before himself. A man whose honor demanded the highest esteem. Now I see that it is pure selfishness that influences you. All your kindnesses, your hand-lending, merely masks a man unwilling to face the truth. You're afraid, Peter, afraid of letting go and allowing yourself to live. Afraid that somehow by giving your heart to me completely, you will lose control of your life. Of yourself."

She rushed past him, then spun around. "Go. Help the immigrants. Rescue Liesl. Marry Toya. When all the immigrants have made their happy homes and you go back to Nassau for more, ask yourself why you must always feel the need to save someone else's life, why your own must remain so dispassionate. Then question why Toya's goodbye kiss will always hold something in reserve."

Betina turned her back to him and began to walk away, unwilling to see the effect of her words shadowing his eyes. Calling back over her shoulder, she thrust the dagger she knew would cut deeply. "Toya's touch will never blaze quite as ardently as your passion for duty."

"Where are you going?" he demanded.

"Inside. To give this to Opa. After that, anywhere but where you are."

"Something's wrong." Toya tugged on Rad's shirt-sleeve as he reined the buggy to a halt in front of the Wagner home. "There's no smoke in the stack. Opa's not cooking. What if he never made it home? I should have . . . we shouldn't have—"

"Taken so much time?" Rad brushed her cheek with a quick caress, then secured the reins and jumped down. He lent a hand to help Toya out of the buggy. "Go inside. I will see if Opa's horse is stabled. Opa may be there but not cooking. Meet me out back if he's gone."

They held each other for just a moment, for there was no time now to talk of what had transpired between them that afternoon. Finding Opa was the priority now.

Toya rushed up the stone walkway and into the Wagner home. A search through several rooms proved fruitless. She hurried to the kitchen, hoping the lack of smoke from the stack stemmed from Opa allowing the stove to cool awhile.

But when she reached her destination, she found it full of disarray and empty of its cook.

Quickly, she searched several rooms, beginning with Rad's, since that was the one the Wagners shared because of their houseguests. Working her way down, she asked the patients if they had seen Opa recently. Most assured her that he'd returned to the house and that, *ja*, they had also spotted him with the dressmaker. But no one had seen him in at least two hours.

"Berta says you are looking for Herr Wagner. May I speak to you alone for a moment, Fraulein Reinhart?" Baby Ernst's mother exited the room where Rad had drawn pictures on the walls.

"No one is in the kitchen at the moment. We can talk there." Toya blinked away the memory of the night she'd spent alone with Rad in that once-empty room. She had changed since then, and their relationship blossomed and developed into a love that would last beyond eternity. That simple sharing of supper seemed like another lifetime. "Do you know where I might find Opa?"

The woman reached their destination first. Her mouth gaped at the sight before them. "I thought I heard an argument." A hand rushed to cover her dismay. "Now I know I did! He was with the dark-haired woman and Herr Stoltz."

"Betina? Peter? Arguing with Opa?" Toya scanned the room with a critical eye. Peaches were scattered on the floor. Stems lay on the table where they had been separated from whatever flower once adorned their crowns. Now cooled, the peach concoction was left congealing in two pots on the stove. Something was definitely amiss. Opa would never have wasted the mixture or squandered the peaches. Had there been a struggle? "What were they arguing about?"

"I could not hear all." The woman's cheeks darkened with crimson. "I was upstairs and did not hear anything at first. Then I became hungry and thought I might ask Herr Wagner for something to eat. When I heard the angry voices, I did not enter . . . for fear of intruding. So I decided I would wait in the room with the pretty paintings until the argument stopped. It finally did, and I was able to satisfy my hunger. I took only one peach.'' The crimson deepened.

"No harm done.'' Toya reached out to hand the woman another piece of fruit. "Opa would want you to make yourself at home and, with a cook, that means to feel comfortable enough to eat whatever is available in the kitchen.''

"*Danke.*'' The woman smiled gratefully. "I will mash this and give it to Ernst. Perhaps it will be the peach that makes him better.''

Toya hurried to agree, understanding the woman's worry but needing to ease her own about Opa and the argument. "You said that you did not hear all of what was said. Can you tell me what you did hear?''

With her gaze suddenly focusing on the fruit she'd been given, the woman shifted her weight back and forth from one foot to the other.

Why was she fidgeting? Toya realized whatever Ernst's mother overheard had something to do with *her*. "The argument was about me, wasn't it?''

"*Ja.*''

"Do you know why?''

"*Nein.* But after I heard your name, the two men shouted at each other and soon Herr Stoltz left. The dressmaker and Herr Wagner remained. About a half hour after that, the councilman returned. This time he did not sound angry but quite concerned. He said someone named Fredericka had taken a turn for the worse. Herr Wagner and the dressmaker left here so fast, I did not have time to ask about the snack. They carried one of his pots between them.''

"Did they say anything else?'' Toya's mind raced to her beloved aunt. *Don't die,* she begged silently. *Please don't die, Aunt Fred.*

"All Herr Wagner kept saying was 'This is it. This is

it.' I am sorry I do not know the 'it' he spoke of."

Toya thanked her for helping, then told the woman that she would be leaving. "Should Herr Wagner—Opa—return, please tell him to stay here and do not go anywhere else. I will tell his grandson what has happened, then I will be at my aunt's home."

"I'll watch for his return, *Fraulein*. Fredericka is someone you know?"

"Someone I love very dearly." Toya quickly thanked her, then hurried outside to the stable.

"His horse is here." Rad took quick strides toward her. "So he's been here. Was he inside?"

"*Nein.* I need to go home. Aunt Fred is worse."

"I'll take you there."

She nodded her thanks. "As you drive, I'll tell you what I know."

Toya waited until they were seated in the buggy and Rad had flicked the horses into motion, then repeated what she'd been told.

"Perhaps the argument was whether you would be angry about his leaving without us knowing his whereabouts. But his words could mean that he had found it—the true cure. Let's hope that is so. And remember, Toya, Betina is with him. I think our concern should be with Fredericka at this moment, not with Opa."

Toya linked her arm through his, needing to feel the powerful flex of Rad's arm as he commandeered the team. His strength buoyed her and his reassurance lessened her apprehension. "I pray you are right, Rad. If only you are right."

Toya paced the floor outside Fredericka's room, waiting, praying for the door to open.

"I need to see Aunt Fred!" She felt unable to endure another moment of not knowing whether her aunt would survive.

A TASTE OF HONEY 233

Rad rose from the chair he had pulled alongside Betina's and went to Toya. He reached out and touched her gently, bringing her to a halt. "You cannot go in now, Toya. Opa said it would take some time. Now, come sit beside me and Betina. Relax, or you will wear a hole in your aunt's fine rug."

"I have to see her." Toya despised the lack of control, the waiting. Patience had never been one of her strongest virtues. She'd always managed to take care of Fredericka, being there to comfort her when her stamina failed, careful to remove obstacles to her failing eyesight. Why, then, when her aunt needed her most, did she feel so helpless?

"Look, Toya." Betina rose from her chair and walked to the end of the hallway. She drew back one panel of the flower-patterned curtain that graced the window. Dawn streamed through. "It's morning already. Opa will let you see her after she's been through the worst of it."

Rad tried to be kind but firm. "She would not be able to keep her eyes open enough to see you."

Toya wanted to scream at both of them. "That is why I must see her. Fredericka Reinhart not talking is like the wind not blowing. It's too quiet in there."

Gently, Rad wrapped an arm around her shoulder and led Toya to the chairs. He pulled a few together, sat down, then urged Toya to settle against him. "Come, rest here. Close your eyes awhile, and I'll watch for you."

"You should be rested when she comes around. She'll not want to see how you have worried." Betina sat in the chair next to Toya's.

"Still, it is not easy to wait." Toya collapsed against the warm security of Rad's strength, pressing her cheek against his chest as his arm tightened around her. Her eyes closed abruptly, but her mind and body were too tense to sleep. "But"—her eyes opened to stare at Betina—"I am glad I do not have to wait alone. *Danke.*"

Slowly, Betina's hand reached out. Toya stared at her

friend and hesitated, a thousand emotions coursing through her. But in the end only one reigned supreme—the one that had followed her and Betina into adulthood. Toya's hand raced to meet the one offered her, and she gently squeezed her silent gratitude.

Hours moved slowly. Finally the door to Fredericka's room opened. Though Opa's face looked haggard, the light of miracles shone from his eyes. He gave a silent nod. Toya brushed by him and hurried to Aunt Fredericka's bedside.

"Hello, Aunt Fred. Trying to sleep through spring, are you?" Toya forced the worry from her tone. She hoped her face didn't show all she'd been through the past few hours.

Fredericka opened her eyes, staring blankly at her niece. "Albertine?" Her voice was raw and a bit hoarse from coughing.

"She went down to make some tea." Toya reached for Fredericka's hand and patted it. "She'll be back as soon as she can."

"Is Betina still here?"

Resentment swelled inside Toya that her aunt would be more concerned about her friend's whereabouts than her own. Realizing she was being petty, Toya decided the only thing that mattered was keeping Fredericka calm and rested. "She's waiting to see you. Rad and Opa too."

"Whatever you do, don't let the men in until I've—"

"Until you have what, Sister?" Albertine marched into the room like a Viking longboat under full sail. "Opa's seen you at your worst, so there is no need to fuss and fume."

"You let him in here on purpose." Fredericka scowled. "You wanted him to see me like this so I would look frumpish."

"I can yell just as loud as you can, Fredericka. I've had more practice. As you take pride in informing everyone, I *am* a year older." Albertine grabbed the brush and began to ease the tangle from Fred's hair. "So stop acting like a spoiled child and look at me."

"What are you doing?" Fredericka's head spun around as she glared at her sister.

Challenge flared in Albertine's eyes. "I am brushing your hair to make you more presentable. And if you'll sit still long enough, I might even help you change into a clean gown."

"Halt!"

Startled, Albertine nearly fell off the edge of the bed. "I was just trying to help you—"

"Albert, I'm not dressed beneath these covers!"

Albertine willingly released the sheet. Her fist knotted on her hips as she rocked back on her heels. "And just when did you plan to make the exodus to your wardrobe? When Opa came to re-examine you?"

Fred's cheeks turned rosier than they'd been in days. "I was hot. A fever raged within. What do you expect?"

"I expected you to play fair. You know how Opa loves to care for the infirm. Being naked and frail is taking unfair advantage."

"Come on, Toya." Rad touched her shoulder and nodded toward the door. A glance at Opa showed he understood. They silently moved into the hallway, aware that the two sisters had forgotten everyone else at the moment—even the man whose affections they fought over.

"They both sound healthy to me." Opa rolled down his sleeves and buttoned them.

The deep sigh that escaped Toya drained the worry that had kept her and the entire village of New Genesis in a state of communal tension. Suddenly she felt weary, but it was a good exhaustion. Things would be fine again. Whatever Opa's latest concoction, it had worked, and virtually overnight.

Toya's gaze focused on Opa. What had his last batch contained? "Opa, let us go have tea downstairs. We're all a bit curious about this last remedy you gave Fredericka. It obviously worked."

"*Ja*, it worked. Worked very good." Opa's shoulder straightened slightly as he beamed with pleasure and pride.

"What ingredients did you use this time?" Toya noticed Betina fidgeting and wondered if the batch of medicine had anything to do with their argument.

"I—I do not recall." Opa ran a hand through the gray hair at his temples and yawned. "It has been a long night."

"But you must remember, Grandfather," Rad insisted. "There are so many lives at stake. The children. More settlements are reporting in every day. This recipe obviously works. You *must* remember."

"Perhaps I can retrace my steps from yesterday, and that will shake my memory." Opa began to describe his day, starting with the morning delivery of milk, church services, the shared picnic with Rad and Toya, the herbs and flowers he selected while there. Just as he mentioned the batch of peaches he'd last cooked, a blank expression filled his face and he shrugged his shoulders. "I cannot seem to remember."

Betina rose from her chair. "I can be of help, Herr Wagner."

Puzzlement creased Opa's brow. "Did I tell you what I used?"

She shook her head. "No, but I was there when you made this batch . . . remember?"

Opa seemed to be studying hard. Focusing on a memory that eluded him until finally recognition danced in his eyes. "*Ja*, you and your young man came." A frown replaced his smile. "The councilman said a falsehood about Toya. Accused her of consorting with my grandson. I got mad and swung at him with the bluebonnets. They landed in the peaches steaming on the stove. I suddenly remembered the bluebonnets have the same properties as one of the lupines along the Alps. I was certain it was the missing ingredient to ward off the scurvy. Fredericka is my proof!"

"Are you certain it was the bluebonnets, Opa?"

Toya realized Rad's question came only because Opa had a tendency to embellish. It was difficult to know if he was spinning tales or telling the truth. She caught Rad's gaze and silently begged him to trust his grandfather in this matter.

Rad grabbed his grandfather and gave him a bear hug. "*Danke schön*, Grandfather, *danke schön!*"

"It was the bluebonnets." Betina motioned for them all to head downstairs to the kitchen.

Toya was pleased Rad accepted his grandfather's word before Betina verified it.

Rad grabbed Toya's hand and pressed a palm warmly over it. "Round up everyone and tell them what we have discovered. We need every available cook in the community to prepare the mixture for the settlements. But we may not have sufficient wagons to get the cure to the others fast enough."

"Ask Councilman Stoltz if we may borrow his. He has many to transport the immigrants." Worry etched Betina's face. "And be sure to give some peaches to Liesl while you're there. She's still quite sick."

"Done," Opa promised. "Toya and I will begin work immediately.

"Not yet." Betina held up a palm to halt everyone. "There is one more thing that must be said before everyone goes about their tasks."

The happiness that had increased Toya's pulse to a lively beat suddenly chilled to dread. She knew exactly what Betina was about to say.

Betina looked Toya squarely in the eye. "About your proposal, Conrad . . ."

22

Please do not speak the words. Toya had never seen such an expression in Betina's eyes—one quite so full of determination, yet somehow empty as well. Why did she stare at Toya when her words were meant for Rad? Had spite crept in to tarnish their friendship?

A dozen memories enveloped Toya. Of she and Betina running along the River Lahn, of them laughing over their games of skat, of Betina's arrival in America. What a day that was!

Toya had bent to lift the next piece of laundry to be hung on the clothesline, when her hand stopped. There, atop the wet garments, lay the kerchief her mother had sewn for her. Toya thought she merely imagined that it was the same one, then began to suspect that Tilly played a cruel joke.

An intense desire to see Betina tormented Toya for several weeks as Betina's birthday loomed. Toya spent afternoons walking the Comal and doing things she and Betina shared as children. But the repetition only deepened her despair, intensifying her yearning.

To make matters worse, Tilly scorned the tears that

flowed shamelessly when Toya stood at the window, fingers spread, looking out into the dawn and recalling the most poignant of those memories.

Toya's hand rose, as if to spread her fingers against the emotional restraint that separated her and Betina now.

Betina blinked and shook her head, holding up a palm as if she had read Toya's thoughts and meant to ward off the bond. Something thick and heavy threatened to choke off Toya's breath. Her fingers rushed to her lips to seal them, certain her heart had broken in two and was now lodged in her throat.

As Betina walked over to Rad with a grace uncommon to most, Toya was reminded of how she had noticed that same elegance silhouetted through the wet sheets, sunlight spotlighting the approach of a woman. When Toya caught sight of the dark crown of hair just above the rope, she knew. The kerchief was, indeed, her own. Her shout of joy announced to all of New Genesis that Betina had finally come to America. How happy they'd been that day! How naive. Toya realized miles were the least separation one might have to endure.

Betina drew so close to Rad, Toya wondered if the dressmaker intended to embrace him. She inhaled deeply, awaiting Betina's intent. If Betina accepted the proposal, how in all that was holy could they tell her the marriage would never be?

If Toya's heart had not already broken in two, it now shattered into tiny pieces. She couldn't bear that Rad be the one to tell her. *She* owed Betina the truth. "Betina." She exhaled her friend's name in a rush of breath. "Please, may I speak with you? There's something—"

The dressmaker shook her head and gently reached up to caress Rad's cheek. "This must be said first."

"But you do not—"

"I understand far better than you think." Betina smiled at Rad. "You have been a good friend to me, especially these past few months. But there is a time when even friendship is not enough."

Toya willed herself to hold back the words of explanation. *I am so sorry, Betina. So very sorry. I never meant to hurt you.*

"I must demand nothing less than love from the man I marry, Conrad. And that, dear friend, was not what you offered me." Betina shook her head. "I shall not accept your proposal."

Toya leaned against the wall to steady herself, a wave of relief buffeting her.

Rad pressed a hand against Betina's, held it there for a moment, then gently guided hers back to her side. "Though my heart shall always belong to another, it holds the deepest respect for you, Tina. It is I who have done you a great disservice. Even as I offered you my respect"—his gaze diverted to Toya—"my own heart yearned for a deeper devotion. Similar gifts, yet not the same."

"There are some too *devoted* to standards to know the wisdom of your words." Tears brimmed in Betina's eyes, but she brushed them away with an angry wipe.

"Peter?" Toya heard the wounded anger echoing in Betina's tone and knew that it had been made raw by what Betina believed was unrequited love. But Toya suspected differently. She had seen Peter spooned against her friend. She had witnessed the melding of their bodies in sleep when a strict code of mores kept them apart in the light of day. Toya shoved herself away from the wall and moved alongside Betina, daring to offer a comforting hand upon her shoulder.

Betina stared at her, brown eyes full of pain so intense, Toya felt her tremble. For one moment she willed all her love for her best friend into that simple touch. *Let me be your strength, Tina,* she silently implored. *Let me be proof that love finds its own way if you believe hard enough. Do not give in to your doubt. Do not let anything sway you from what you feel, for the only honor worth keeping is the truth spoken by your heart.*

A light glimmered in her eyes as if Betina somehow sensed the insight Toya offered. The dressmaker turned away, allowing no one but Toya to see the depth of her heartache.

"He insists that your pledge yet be honored," Betina announced softly, painfully. Then she turned, flicking her wrist as if Peter were of little concern. "But that is argument for another day, isn't it? Now, what can I do to help, Opa? Cook? Gather bluebonnets?" She laughed a little too sarcastically. "Ask Herr Mule Head if we can borrow his wagons?"

Discouragement rocked Toya. Peter? *Insisting?* "Rad," she whispered, her gaze racing to meet his and demanding that this not be true—that this fear was unreasonable. Nothing could prevent her from marrying Rad now. Would it?

Why, then, did Betina's announcement feel as if it had just shackled all her dreams?

"I will speak with Peter when there is time." Rad ran a hand through the hair at his temples. "We have more pressing matters to tend."

Nein, Toya's soul implored, but she nodded, knowing he was right. The first thing to be resolved was the illness.

Silently, everyone made their way to the kitchen. To Toya's chagrin, Lineva Pyrtle stood at the stove, stirring something in a kettle. Her nerves were too raw, her heart too sore to deal with the town tattler. "Fraulein Pyrtle, we have come to relieve you of your duties . . . whatever they are."

Opa chuckled.

Lineva swung around to face the crowd. "Why are all of *you* here? I assumed some of you would be in the orchard." Curiosity animated her usual scowl. "Has something happened?"

"Opa has found the cure." Albertine waved the redhead

to the table. "Please sit and I'll prepare us all a bowl of soup and some tea before we go about our task. Everyone will need strength."

Lineva only too willingly allowed her host to replace her and made herself comfortable at the table.

"What can I do to help?" Though Toya meant with the meal, her mind also raced to think of ways she might convince Peter that he was too much in love with Betina to settle for a loveless bargain.

"It is more how Lineva can help."

Opa's announcement elevated one of Lineva's brows. "Me?"

The old man nodded. "We need you to spread the word. No one does that better or faster than you, *Fraulein*."

Her cheeks reddened to match her hair color. "I should be insulted by that remark."

"*Ja*, on most days, but not this one. You see we *need* your talent for chattering today."

Everyone laughed. Lineva huffed.

Opa asked Albertine to hand Betina the crock that held the remedy he had given Fredericka. "Take that to Liesl and see that she eats a healthy portion of it."

Good, that will force her and Peter together again. Toya plotted ways she might increase the number of encounters between Betina and the councilman.

Conrad nodded his approval. "I'll send a rider to Little Munich and let them know what we've discovered. They seem to be suffering the worst. They can bring a wagon to meet the one we'll send with the cure. Meeting halfway will save transporting time."

Suggestions volleyed around the room so fast, Toya could hardly remember who was supposed to do what, but Rad did not seem confused by the myriad of details and decisions. Her admiration for him grew. Despite what he said, devotion and respect *were* a substantial portion of loving someone. "What about me?" She looked expectant. "How may I help?"

"You will be Opa's eyes and hands when he tires." Her crestfallen expression inspired him to add, "The most important task, *ja*?"

"*Ja*," she agreed, though she imagined dashing off to the other villages, saving the children with Rad's and Opa's cure. She wanted to tell everyone, shout it to the heavens that it had been her beloved and his grandfather who had found this antidote. That it had been their faith, their persistence, their commitment, that led them out of danger.

Rad asked for a piece of parchment and something to write with. Albertine quickly obliged, and handed him the inkwell and paper. He began to draw a crude map, assigning each circle the name of their sister settlements, then marking a meeting spot halfway between New Genesis and each one.

Toya waited patiently until he finished, mulling over what he'd just said to her. Watching Opa was important, even helping him prepare the cure should have been enough, but Toya wanted to be a bigger part of it. Not just for pride's sake, but to prove *herself* in some way. "I want to do more than cook."

"We will need crocks cleaned and pots scrubbed between batches." Rad began to name countless chores she could handle in the process.

"There are a hundred hands that can do as well as I." Excitement stirred inside Toya as an idea took seed. She rushed to Rad's side and traced her finger along the map. "I know this countryside better than most, since I've lived here longer than many of you. You need to stay behind and see to the harvest. The men should stay and help do the lifting and crating. Why not let me take the batch to Little Munich? I can handle a wagon as good as any."

The frown wrinkling Rad's brow was Toya's first warning that he disapproved of the idea. Indecision veiled his eyes, but when her chin lifted stubbornly, he concealed his thoughts behind reason.

"It will be a difficult task, not spilling the jars. The load will be too precious to lose."

"I know every rut from here to the Austin colony, and I also know the peaches ripe enough to pick will soon be spent. Experience with the journey is critical to saving time."

"And I should go with her," Opa announced. "Who best to tell the driver from each village what he must do with the remedy? There are enough here to do the cooking while we are gone. Now that we know the recipe, you do not need these old hands to mind the kettles."

"But if you get tired, Grandfather, you cannot linger along the way. The other wagoneer will fear something happened or you decided not to—"

"You may be right." Toya understood that his words of caution were aimed at her and not Opa. Rad did not believe she could fulfill the task. He did not trust her.

The realization bruised Toya as if he had taken her in his hands and squeezed the life from her. How could their love ever survive if Rad did not trust her? She fooled herself into believing that all was settled between her and Rad. Only her pledge had been resolved.

Now she fully understood Betina's pain. To love a man, to believe that the barriers to marrying him no longer existed, only to discover he did not love unconditionally in return, was a greater misery than any she had ever known. Any she could bear.

"Perhaps you should get someone more skilled at driving a team," she suggested, unable to hide the hurt. Why should he believe she could fulfill this task? What had she ever completed in his company? "The cargo is too precious for you to entrust it to . . . just anyone."

23

Every person in New Genesis capable of lending a hand assembled at the orchard, spreading out into the rows of trees. Rad tried to find Toya's face among them but could not see her anywhere. She had not ridden with him to the orchard, and that alone was enough to tell him how angry she was that he had resisted her request.

But she had caught him unawares. He didn't expect her to want to drive the wagon to Little Munich. That task would be most critical. All their efforts hinged on the success of delivering the cure.

Besides the obvious concern of losing precious cargo, Rad worried that there were too many dangers along the way. She might run into unfriendly warriors. A wheel might break. Toya might tire from handling the wagon. A driver with more experience—more brawn—would have a better chance dealing with any problem that arose.

The responsibility alone would be daunting to anyone. What if she failed? Toya would never forgive herself for the mistake. All the progress she'd made so far would disappear and her self-worth would plummet. She would take on blame for all the illness, not just whatever occurred after her failure. Toya never acted in half measures. It was all or nothing. He could not let that happen. That weight should not rest upon her shoulders.

Yet... Rad stepped forward and raised his hands to signal silence. *The one thing she needed most was for him to entrust her with this opportunity to prove herself.* "You all have been told what our task is here this morning," Rad began in a loud clear voice. "You know what it means to our neighbors."

Everyone faced him to listen intently.

"United, our efforts can make a difference. Let us show the rest of Texas—America—how we appreciate the welcome they extended us, the land they offered us on which to raise our children and free them from the hunger and poverty of the fatherland. Let us show them the power of befriending a German... by saving their children too."

The orchard echoed with affirmation. A chant erupted immediately. "Conrad, Conrad, Conrad!" The sound drifted toward the heavens, and every eye focused on Rad.

He stood arrow-straight, looking solemnly from face to face, searching for the one he needed most to find. Then he saw her leaning against one trunk, her expression rapt.

For a moment, he thought she glowed with quiet pride for him, that she was basking in the warmth of the praise that surrounded him.

She quickly turned away and concealed her expression from him. Rad wished he could make her understand that safety for the driver and the cargo must be his first precaution. But he knew she would only view his decision as a lack of trust.

"I appreciate your compliments..." Rad waved one hand as if to wipe away the cheers. "But only one man is responsible for the cure, and that is Opa, my grandfather."

Thunderous cheers echoed over the hills, calling for Opa to speak.

The old man adjusted his bib and tucker, hooking his thumbs underneath each shoulder strap as he swaggered forward to join his grandson.

"Quiet, babblemouths, or the bees will come and add a little more bounce to this old man's strut!" Opa pinched his hindquarters and made an outrageous face.

After a few moments of reveling in the laughter, he signaled for silence. His grin turned solemn, demanding everyone's undivided attention. Respect for the elder of their community swept over the crowd and all—even Toya—awaited his next words.

"No man or woman alone can fulfill the need of our neighbors. The peaches, honey, and bluebonnets may be the ingredients, but it will be all of us together, working side by side"—he shot Rad a glance—"*trusting* each to carry out his or her assigned duty that shall offer the true remedy. It is the power of our goodwill—hearts willing to trust one another and work together to see hardships overcome and blessings shared that is the cure for *any* difficulty we encounter."

Applause echoed the sentiment, Rad's hands clapping the loudest.

"And now," said Opa, "you are faced with an important decision. Who would you have drive the first batch to Little Munich? The position is one of great responsibility. He or she must not only be devoted to seeing the ride to its end, but must be certain to instruct the proper way for the medicine to be administered. We must choose someone we trust enough with the lives of our children."

Opa's name resounded over the field.

With the lives of *my* children, Rad repeated silently. The depth of hurt he caused Toya began to sink in slowly.

"I appreciate your confidence." Opa waved everyone into silence. "But I believe there is someone more capable we should consider."

Ja, there was. Someone who needed to know how much

he trusted her with his life, the lives of their future children, his love. Someone he would have to believe could handle the obstacles that might befall her along the journey. Rad stepped up alongside his grandfather. "Someone who has worked alongside—"

"Toya Reinhart!" Betina interrupted, drawing everyone's attention away from the Wagners. She began to walk toward Toya. "She helped Opa cook the recipe. It is her bluebonnet field that yields the final ingredient. She knows the countryside as well. We all are aware that she helps Opa when he is troubled. If he goes, so should she. This will allow her to satisfy her commitment to the Wagners, and there are many among us willing to govern his kitchen in his absence." Betina grasped Toya's hand and lifted it above their heads in a sign of unification. "Let Toya and Opa be deliverers for no other reason than they have earned the right."

Though Betina's vote of confidence tainted Rad's chance to make things right with Toya, it gained the result he wanted. The people of New Genesis began to chant Toya's and Opa's name over and over, taking the decision from Rad and giving Toya the opportunity to prove herself.

Perhaps when she returned from the journey, he could convince her that he had meant only to safeguard her. He prayed with all his heart that she would prove each of his misgivings wrong.

"Betina, may we speak?" Toya called after her best friend as Betina turned to leave the gathering.

"I must get back to Peter and relieve him. He will want me to stay with Liesl while he prepares the wagon."

Toya nodded. "I know. But there's something I must tell you before I go."

Betina sighed heavily and halted where she stood. "For a moment, then."

Pointing to a tree that had already lost its fruit to earlier picking, Toya suggested, "Could we talk there, away from the others?"

Betina did not answer but headed for the tree. Toya followed, tension building inside her until it threatened to drum as loud as tom-toms at her temples. There was so much to be said and so little time to say it.

"*Ja?*" The dressmaker faced Toya, folding her arms beneath her breasts and lifting her chin as if to meet a challenge.

Where to begin? Toya wondered. First things first. "You know those old quilts you used for protecting the floor when you repainted the shop?"

"*Ja?*"

"May I use them?"

"What for?"

"I want to wrap the crocks so they will ride easier—provide more padding against the rougher roadway."

"Of course you can use them." Betina's gaze met Toya's and locked. "Now, you called me over here for something more than quilts. What is it?"

Dread dried Toya's tongue and made her swallow, trying to coax moisture into her mouth. The lump of trepidation remained, but at least she was able to find breath enough to begin. "I owe you a debt of gratitude. You cannot imagine how much I needed you to speak up for me about making the delivery."

"You *are* the right person to do this. Opa too. I spoke up for that reason."

"But you could have remained silent and didn't. You were friend enough to ignore the contention that has railed against us for several months, maybe unknowingly even for years, to see that I was given an opportunity to prove myself. I thank you for that, Tina."

"You would do the same for me."

"*Ja*, I would, but I have not been so quick to be your

friend of late. I am ashamed of that. Shamed by what I can view only as selfishness."

Betina's warrior stance eased. She shook her head. "Sometimes loving someone requires a measure of selfishness. Because if you do not show that someone how much you care, if you are too willing to let matters take their own course, then he will focus on those who need him more than on you." She took Toya's hands in hers and stared at her directly, allowing tears to brim in her brown eyes. "Do not repent where love guided you. Had I listened to my heart instead of my wits, I think I would have done very much the same as you."

"Oh, Tina, I never meant to hurt you. I never meant to make you feel that you should have whomever I discarded. I was confused, torn by what I thought was right and what my heart knew I wanted. Then, when I saw you and Peter lying side by side next to Liesl, I finally realized the depth of wrong I had committed against you. I honestly never knew you loved Peter."

"You s-saw us?"

Toya nodded.

A deep sigh escaped Betina as if she had been unshackled from a thousand chains. Tear-filled eyes rose to meet Toya's gaze. "And you know he still insists upon marrying you?"

The futility in Betina's tone reached into Toya's heart to contract it with empathy. "All is not lost, Betina. I love Rad and will never marry Peter. Peter can never demand that I hold to the pledge once I—"

"He will ostracize both you and Rad from the community."

This was not a scorned lover's ramblings but a true warning. Toya could not believe Peter would resort to such measures. "But why? What reason would inspire such vengeance?"

"He has failed someone. I—I believe it is his way of

proving himself. When I learned he still meant to hold you to the bargain, I confronted him. Asked him why he felt such a need to save everyone." Betina repeated the conversation with Peter. "Until he faces whatever made him feel a failure, then he will remain a misguided champion to those he promises to protect. And he did make a promise, Toya. To your father, Tilly, and to you."

Toya grabbed Betina's hands and gently squeezed. "Then while Opa and I are gone, you must find out this thing that stands between his honor and his love for you. Love him enough to help him, Betina. Love him enough to fight for the love you both feel, for what you want. Do not allow yourself or Peter to stand in the shadow of honor ever again."

Betina hugged her abruptly, holding on for just a moment. Then she backed away and wiped at the tears spilling down her cheeks. "I shall pray that you reach the halfway point long before the other driver. You pray that I can find that place in the past where Peter's hesitation dwells. Swift journey, Toya."

"How long have we been traveling?" Opa fidgeted on the driver's box.

Toya stared at the afternoon sun and offered him a patient smile. "Probably an hour or more since the last time you asked me."

Opa yawned. "Just keeping you alert. All this rock and rattle makes me want to sleep."

Toya focused on the pathway ahead. The four-horse team plodded on a winding path through the foothills, following a southbound course toward Little Munich. Toya fought to grip the reins, her hands sore from the many hours of holding the team to task.

The previous day had sped by in a whirlwind of making the first batch. It seemed that she had barely closed her eyes, when Aunt Albertine gently shook her awake that morning to tell her that it was time to make the delivery. When Toya arrived at the orchard, dawn had already brightened the Texas sky, leaving only a haze of gray along the horizon. Opa added two coats to the rest of the supplies secured beneath the wagon's tarpaulin, warning that his bones were creaking and that meant rain would arrive sometime within the next three days.

Studying the horses now from below the brim of her green bonnet, Toya flicked the broad leather straps and encouraged them. "Get along there, horses. Three Oaks Crossing cannot be much farther. We'll rest for the night there, and I would appreciate time to secure our shelter before the rain starts."

The thought of striking camp in a few hours spurred her on, adding energy to Toya's tired, aching shoulders and hips. Beads of perspiration soaked the back of her dress and itched along the rim of her collar, but she didn't dare let loose of the reins long enough to scratch. When they were able to stop for the day, she prayed the spring near Three Oaks Crossing was deep enough to bathe in. A bath and a place to stretch out in the wagon would be wonderful.

A glance at the sky proved Opa's predication true. Clouds hung low, their underbellies sagging with unshed moisture. The wagon's canvas cover would not hold out the rain entirely, but at least it would provide shelter enough to curl up and sleep for a while. The heavy coats Opa brought would reduce the dampness. Thank goodness all the lids to the crocks were secured by rope, or the cureall might become diluted.

Dust from the team's hooves billowed in Toya's face, blasting her with shards of dried buffalo grass and sage. Wisps of hair that had escaped from her braid no longer looked blond but matched the brown-gray of the cottonwood trees they passed along the pathway. Trail dust encrusted Toya's lips, though she kept licking at them at every opportunity until she could no longer abide the taste of grime coating her teeth. The bandanna she had pulled over her nose to keep out the dirt did little to stave off the nuisance. It was layered with so much dust, the air she breathed in beneath its cover grew stale.

Her eyes threatened to swell shut from stinging, and her nose twitched as often as the team's ears, but pride would not allow Toya to ask Opa to take over handling the team. Determined to prove she could see the task through *herself*, Toya bore the discomfort with all the mettle she could muster. Still, it was hard . . . very hard . . . to battle all her sore spots, the blinding dust, and the doubt that traveled with her.

Questions poured through her mind as mesquite trees and live oaks filled the horizon. Had she been too obstinate to prove herself that she endangered the cargo? If Betina had not interrupted and encouraged the crowd to choose her and Opa to deliver the cure, was Rad about to do the same?

Thunder cracked overhead. The lead pair of horses shied, causing the second pair to falter.

"Steady, team. Steady," Opa said soothing the animals. "It is just the Texas sky fussing with the sun. She will shed a few tears to get over her tantrum, then all will be well again. Nothing to worry about. Nothing at all. Steady."

Lightning blinked twice. A loud crack rent the air. A flash of heat struck nearby, its sizzle so resonant the fine hair on the back of Toya's neck stood on end. Blue-white balls of light danced over the horse's backs, plummeting from the tips of their ears.

The team bolted into a full run, wrenching the reins through Toya's hands. She clutched desperately, praying they would not be jerked away completely. With all the force of her fear, she shouted, "Hang on, Opa! Hang on to me and don't let go!"

Fighting the wild rocking of the wagon, she braced both feet on the footboard that fronted the driver's box and leaned back as hard as she could. Inch by inch she fought to regain more of the reins and control of the runaway team. Her palms grew slick with perspiration, loosening the gloves' fit. One foot slipped, then the other.

A rut in the road toppled her backward. Opa's grasp on her arm slipped.

"Grab!" she commanded, thrusting her arm out, praying it would be a long enough lifeline.

"Lean more, Toya!" Opa shouted, battling to regain his balance. "A little more!"

She bent as far as she could without toppling over and still maintain her footing.

Opa clutched for her hand and, in a moment of clenching terror, their fingers threaded, then slipped. With no thought of anything but Opa, Toya gave up the only chance she had of commandeering the reins and groped for him.

"God help us!" she pleaded, and her fingers grasped, finding nothing. "Please, God!"

One hand. Two. Toya clutched at the precious treasure of those aged hands. With every ounce of outrage that filled her heart, she yanked. A primeval yell of conquest echoed from the depth of her lungs as the touch caught . . . held.

The slender, trembling body fell against her own. Toya clung, but instantly grabbed for the reins with her other hand. Their danger was far from being over. The wagon jostled and bumped, throwing them from side to side. Her heart thundered to the rhythm of the pounding hooves. Leather and reins snapped their uselessness, jingling as the Osage orange wheels shuddered beneath the onslaught of hooves and rutted roadway.

Could she grab the straps again? They danced like runaway whips, threatening to trip the team as the leather fell beneath the hooves, then hurled into the air to thrash about and inflict biting stings.

Suddenly the reins tangled in two of the horses' harnesses. In order to reach them, she would have to jump clear of the wagon's tongue and mount one of them as they

A TASTE OF HONEY

ran. If she did not leap far enough, she would land amid the churning hooves. But face death she must if she wanted to save Opa's life and protect the remedy.

The wagon dipped, veered to the left, throwing Toya into Opa. The terrified scream of the horses blended with Toya's as the wagon tilted to one side and overturned.

24

Rain softly pattered against her cheeks, forcing Toya's eyes open. She tried to sit up, but pain rippled to every point in her body. Then she remembered. Opa! The wagon! She jolted to a sitting position, battling the dizziness that overtook her to search the surroundings for sight of him. To her relief, he was bent over the upended wagon, carefully removing crocks that miraculously survived the accident. The scent of spilled peaches and honey wafted with the breeze, emphasizing that some of the remedy had not endured the accident.

We cannot make the delivery. Realization struck Toya hard, and she almost gave in to tears of frustration. Instead, she pounded a fist on the muddy ground, cursing the fate that mocked her determination.

"You curse better than your aunt. I must tell Fredericka you have acquired her fine German temper."

Remembering her command and embarrassed by her tantrum, Toya studied Opa. He moved with no visible injury. Gratitude coursed through her, causing her to thank the same heavens she had just profaned.

"Opa, are you unscathed?" Carefully, Toya rose and let the world quit spinning before she tried to walk.

"I am fine, *Fraulein*. And much of the remedy was saved because of the way you stored it. And you? Do you think you could help me gather what remains?"

"*Ja.*" She nodded, then wished she hadn't. "My head is a bit fuzzled, but I have no broken bones, it seems. We are fortunate to be alive."

"*Ja*, fortunate. I examined you before I inspected the damage to the crocks. You were breathing well and suffered only bruises. I felt I should gather what I could of the remedy while you regained your senses. Now we must get the crocks together and cover them."

"Where are the other horses?" Toya saw only two. One with a bullet in its head and two legs turned in an awkward angle. Opa must have taken his long rifle and put the poor animal out of its misery. The huge Percheron would be a great loss to the Wagners. Donner, Opa's favorite steed, grazed nearby, his front legs hobbled.

"One oat eater took off like his tail was ablaze with hellfire. The other roams nearby. She fancies Donner and will not wander far." Opa motioned toward the wagon. "I managed to hobble him, so we are not entirely afoot."

Wunderbar . . . just what they needed. A mount who would head straight for New Genesis the minute they unhobbled him. If they did manage to get him to obey orders, he would have to carry the remaining crocks and two riders. The swayback was a big horse, accustomed to carving the earth with a heavy plow. But he had a lazy streak and a penchant for his stable.

They brought him along at Opa's insistence that Donner was the speediest of those available. Toya suspected the old man wanted the beast along for other reasons. Riding Donner would guarantee Opa would find his way back if he took the notion to ride alone.

Perhaps Donner's ladyfriend would join him soon. The

prospect of two horses gave Toya hope that all might not be as grave as it seemed.

She joined Opa, quietly examining him with her eyes to verify that he did not hide injuries from her. But he truly had weathered the accident well. Assured he was fine, she surveyed the damage to the wagon. As the rain seeped into the ground, her heart sank at the sight of the cracked wheel. She glanced about, looking through the scattered debris. A chill of dread swept over her, causing gooseflesh to rise in its wake. "Peter did not include a spare?"

"*Nein,* and it would take several days for me to strip the bark of another and mold it into shape. Cottonwood and live oak are not as flexible as the osage orange." Opa's brows furrowed as he ran a hand along the damaged wheel. "Peter is a shrewd man. He would not have left town without a spare, even two. It makes me wonder if he wanted to . . . what is the *englisch* word . . . sabotage our effort."

"Peter?" Surprise filled Toya's tone. The councilman was so respected in the community, she had never heard anyone speak of him with disapproval. "Surely you do not suspect him of wanting harm to come to us?"

"*Nein.* But he has reason for you and my grandson not to proclaim your intentions. A man who is misguided does not think his actions through clearly. Proving yourself to Conrad may be your only obstacle to love, but making certain you do not succeed may be Peter's last defense in facing himself."

Toya started to ask him how it seemed everyone else knew this about Peter but she had no clue. A horse whinnied behind her. Thinking it might be Donner's teammate, she swung around and shaded her eyes to peer into the distance. The outline of a lone rider took form. "Someone comes. This is good. He might help."

Opa's eyes narrowed, squinting to peer into the direction she pointed. "Such good fortune we have, *ja, Fraulein*? I wonder. The rider is Councilman Stoltz."

Peter? Here? Opa's accusation settled heavy in Toya's thoughts. It was odd that the wheel broke, and within minutes—no, she glanced at the sun shadowed through the haze of rain. It was difficult to be accurate, but from its position in the sky, the accident must have occurred at least an hour before. How long had she been unconscious?

No matter how hard she tried to imagine Peter deliberately setting out to bring them harm, the idea would not form. Yet, here he was, an hour or so behind them. Riding in to "save" them. How much would he risk to earn the title "protector"?

"Ho, Wagner!" Peter announced his approach, holding up a hand to greet them. But when he caught sight of the upturned wagon and dead horse, he set his heels to the horse's flanks and urged him into a gallop. Within seconds, he reined the animal to an abrupt halt and dismounted a yard away from Toya.

"What's happened? Toya, Opa, are you both sound?" He gently grabbed Toya by the shoulders, his gray eyes inspecting her from disheveled braid to muddy slippers. A glance at Opa carrying another of the crocks to set alongside the others eased the concern furrowing Peter's brow. "*Lieber Gott!* I was afraid something like this might happen, or worse. Betina told me—"

Toya jerked away from his touch. "You knew this would happen?"

"Knew?" Peter looked startled. "*Nein*, but I worried that we had sent you off with no thought of the danger from neighboring tribes. I was in such a hurry to see that Liesl received the cure that I did not think. I remembered I had not included a spare wheel. Both of those worries ate upon my thoughts until I could not remain behind. When I told Conrad that I felt we had made a mistake in sending you without an escort, he surprised me by agreeing. I set out late a few hours after you left." He glanced at the debris. "I regret I did not find you sooner."

Then Betina didn't talk to you, Toya realized with annoyance. And the hope that Rad had started to speak up before Betina was only wishful thinking. He had not trusted her, after all. "Will you help us get the crocks that survived to Three Oaks Crossing? We are closer to the halfway point than we are to New Genesis."

"It is still a long way."

Peter said nothing she had not already taken under consideration. "But we must get the cure to those poor people. Their children are counting on us. Ra—New Genesis is counting on us."

"One of us needs to ride back home and tell them to send a replacement wagon." Peter eyed the number of crocks that survived the mishap. "That may not be enough."

"It is a start." Toya squared her shoulders, wiping away the rain that continuously fell to dampen her spirits. She might be a sodden strudel, but her determination caught fire. "And a beginning is a good place to hearten hearts. Now, who of us shall ride back?"

"Whoever rides on to Three Oaks should take my horse. Opa's will head back once you set him free." Peter noted the team's absence. "The others fled?"

Nodding, Opa headed toward Donner. "I think we all know who should return to New Genesis. Donner will see me home."

"No!" Toya adamantly refused to separate herself from Opa. "It is too dangerous. You have taken a bad spill. We do not know what ill effects that may—"

"Speak truthfully, *Fraulein*. You fear that I may lose more than my way. You think I will suffer a memory loss."

She stared directly into the alpine-blue eyes demanding the truth from her. "*Ja*, Herr Wagner, and I cannot disappoint Rad twice. It will be difficult enough to learn that I have damaged the load. I cannot let him think that I also neglected my responsibility to you."

"Toya, Toya, Toya." Opa shook his head. "Like Councilman Stoltz said, Donner will return *with* me or without me. Why not save time and trouble? Let this old man go back to New Genesis. You and Stoltz can round up Donner's filly, and the two of you can ride on to Three Oaks Crossing. Besides"—he winked—"an old kettle like me needs to let his pot boil over occasionally . . . if he wants to bring together two who will tend the fire."

His tongue darted out to lick his mouth into a grin, reminding her of Monarch's satisfied expression after the milking session. At first she was unsure what his statement meant. But as his grin widened, realization sank in. Toya's gaze leveled on the old man as she wrestled with her gullibility. "Do you mean to tell me that you have been *pretending* to lose your memory?"

His eyes twinkled with devilment. "Recollection is difficult in my advanced years, but—"

"But what, Ash Wagner!" Toya's fists balled at her hips, her irritation rocking her forward. "Tell me the truth. And *all* of it!"

His lips curved into a pout. "You criticize an old man's fun. I was only trying to play matchmaker. If I lose myself, then you and my grandson must find me. That makes you two forget your disagreements and band together." His gray brows veed so sharply, they touched. "It is only my wish for great-grandchildren while I am still young enough to remember what causes me to act so roguishly."

Peter laughed.

"Do not encourage him." Toya glared at the councilman. "The concern here is that he pretends *sometimes*. When will we know your loss is for real, Opa? Do you realize what you have done? One day you will cry help and everyone will think you tease us. What if we do not race to your aid and you truly need us?"

The old man looked crestfallen. "I meant only to speed my grandson toward happiness."

Toya could not bear to scold him when his misguided intentions stemmed from love. "I am flattered, Opa. My heart is thrilled that you choose me for Rad. But you must promise me you will never pretend again."

"I promise."

"Then it's settled," Peter concluded.

"Ja." Toya saw her opportunity and took it. "It is settled, Peter. Finally and totally. I cannot marry you. I must break my pledge. I will marry Rad as soon as this crisis with the children is at an end. I love him, Peter. I have always loved him. Please forgive me for any harm I have caused you."

"You gave your word." Peter's jaw clenched.

"Words given when my heart was not in it. They are meaningless. Only when the pledge is heartfelt can it become a gift. Otherwise, it's merely an obligation. I am just an obligation to you, Peter. You do not love me. You want to save me, protect me, because you promised Tilly and my fa—"

"Enough! I do not wish to hear this now!"

Something she said touched the core of his wound, she was certain of it. But he was right, now was not the time. Perhaps he would talk more once Opa left and they were on their way to Three Oaks Crossing. "All right, Peter. But talk of it we will. You owe me that much. Betina says you have threatened Rad's standing in the community. You are a better man than that to resort to—"

"What else has she told you?"

"Do you ask whether Betina has told me she loves you?" Toya smiled softly as his expression turned to stone. "She did not have to tell me, Peter. I saw. I see it now. Love is not something that hides behind the gray clouds of concern, but it shines like the sun there, offering a brightness to our lives. You and Betina shine for each other. Shed the gray cloud, whatever it is."

25

$\mathcal{L}$anterns stationed at intervals staved off the shadows of midnight encroaching upon the orchard. Complaints echoed through the workers who had continued long into the night despite the rain.

One man braved to speak louder than the others, "It is too dark to see, Wagner."

Acting upon the first man's bravura, a second man agreed. "We are all exhausted. We should go now and meet back here at dawn."

Rad knew they were right. The fruit was slick and dark from the afternoon rain. Muddied clothing and long hours had robbed the townspeople of their better humor. "We stop then, but any of you who are able . . . please meet me here at dawn and we will resume our task."

"Rider coming!" someone shouted from down the row.

"Problem?" Rad yelled back.

His question was met with such silence, Rad climbed down from his perch and prepared to meet whatever trouble rode in.

"It is Opa!" Lucia Williams waddled forward, struggling for breath enough to share the news. "Alone and riding that swayback!"

Rad picked up the lantern nearest him and took off at a mad run into the shadows of night. A hundred questions raced to mind, but only one mattered. *Where was Toya?*

"Conrad Wagner, where are you?" Opa called. "Have you seen my grandson?" The old man kept moving, not stopping to get an answer. Hands pointed him toward the last place Rad had been seen working.

Finally, the silhouetted rider took on shape and form. Rad held up the lantern, waving him in the right direction. "Grandfather! Over here! I'm over here!"

Donner skidded to a halt in a billow of dried leaves and shriveled peaches. Rad ran to his grandfather and grabbed the horse's reins. "Are you all right, Opa?"

"*Ja*"—his gray head nodded—"but the wagon overturned. We broke a wheel and lost most of the remedy."

Disbelief echoed over the orchard among the pickers.

"Toya . . . is she—?"

"With Peter and unharmed. A little bruised but nothing broken." Quickly, Opa explained what had happened to the ill-fated cargo. "And do not be angry with her for allowing me to return for another wagon. I gave her no choice."

"How did you find your way?" Rad thanked God for seeing Opa safely home. Not for the first time, he wished he had listened to his instincts and sent Peter, or another escort, along with Toya when she first set out. Hesitation had nearly cost them their lives.

"Toya drew a map if I became lost, but"—Opa patted the horse beneath him—"Donner here is part pigeon. He headed straight for home."

Murmurs rippled through the crowd. Rad heard a mutter that they should have sent someone more experienced, someone better skilled at handling a team.

"Even the most skilled of us cannot command a team when it stampedes with fear," Rad said angrily. "I doubt any of us would have thought to pad the crocks. Her wisdom saved the remedy. Our concern here is not to cast blame but to hurry and replace the next shipment."

A collective groan tore the night air. They were all tired and too out of sorts to think clearly. There were not enough lanterns in all of Texas to allow them to continue picking this night, and he did not want anyone to be injured on their way home in the dark. "Go home, friends. Rest yourselves. We will renew our efforts tomorrow as we planned. Opa and I will go home and discuss how to proceed."

No one argued.

Rad grabbed Donner's mane and swung up on the animal's back behind his grandfather. "If someone will see my horse home, I would greatly appreciate the kindness."

"I will." Betina didn't wait for anyone else to offer. She moved into the darkness, then returned within seconds, mounted upon the huge Percheron.

"Danke, Fraulein." Opa leaned back into Rad. "I have come a long way and am too weary to sit the saddle much longer. It is good my oak of a grandson makes such a strong backrest."

"One last request," Rad added, reining Donner half quarter, "say a prayer for Toya and Councilman Stoltz . . . that they will finish what they set out to do."

"You have not spoken for the last mile." Betina rode alongside Rad, matching her mount's gait to Donner's.

"Opa is sleeping. I thought it best."

"But I can hear your thoughts from here."

"Oh? And what are they saying, big ears?" Though his tone teased, curiosity tinged his question.

"That you fear the wagoneer from Little Munich will believe they are not coming and will turn around and go back. That no one will be there to meet them. That Toya will not succeed in reaching Three Oaks Crossing."

"You have been practicing some of Opa's mysticism, I see."

"*Nein.*" Betina stared into the shadowed night, lit only by the lantern resting between her and the saddle horn. "I know you, Conrad Wagner. You ponder all twists of any troubled roadway. And I know your concern for Toya. She will not disappoint you. She *will* reach Three Oaks."

Rad's heavy sigh halted the katydids' buzz in the trees, yet Opa did not stir, leaning back into his grandson's chest.

"I know she will try everything in her power to see it through. But it is not what you think, Tina. My worry for Toya is not that she will disappoint me, but herself."

Betina faced him, though his eyes were in shadow. "Toya needed more than proving herself worthy of completing a task. She needed to be your most important consideration."

"You sound angry."

"I have a right to be. You played me for a fool, and I allowed it."

Rad reached out to grab her reins and stop their progress. "What do you mean?"

"You used me to get to know Toya. All those months you asked me questions about her. Made me believe that you would fight for the right to marry her. Yet when Peter returned, you allowed honor to keep you from claiming her heart. You used me to make Toya jealous. You used me to make Peter jealous. You used us all because you are too afraid to look Peter in the eye and make him face the truth."

Rad could not deny anything she said and felt ashamed for it.

"If y-you are truly my friend, if you honestly love Toya, you would demand Peter forsake his pledge and bow to the greater love you and Toya share. That is what I would want the man I loved to do!"

"Do you ever plan to tell Peter how you feel?"

She stared into the dark horizon, wondering how long Rad had known. "If they can return home without consequences of being out alone together, *ja,* I plan to tell him. I just hope I have not waited too long."

"How long have we ridden?" Toya complained, her back sore from having to sit the saddle in such a strange position. The only way they had been able to transport the crocks was to tie ropes around each one, string them over her saddle, and balance them on either side of her. If she moved, the crocks slid in the direction she shifted. "Is Three Oaks Crossing much farther?"

"There's a light ahead and a bank of trees. Perhaps that's the meeting place and the man we are to meet has supper ready and waiting."

Supper. The word sounded delicious. She hadn't stopped to eat that afternoon. Later she'd been so intent upon making the delivery and worrying about disappointing everyone, Toya realized only then that the hunger pangs rumbling in her stomach were real. "I hope you're right."

They forced themselves to resist the urge to spur their horses into faster gaits. To do so would upset the precious cargo they had safeguarded so carefully.

"It's a good thing Indians haven't threatened us. All we could do is slop honey on them."

Toya laughed. The image eased some of the tension bunching her shoulders. "Have I thanked you for caring enough to ride out and help?"

"It was mine and Conrad's idea that you needed an escort. We both were wrong. You managed to do quite well on your own."

Could Rad's resistance have merely been a need to protect and not an act of distrust? Toya reconsidered and wondered if she had overreacted. "Well, thank you for worrying about us, Peter. No matter what else we truly are to each other, I sincerely value your concern and our friendship.''

Peter urged his mount into a trot.

"Why do you speed up? You'll spill the cure."

"I hear one of your 'talks' coming on; and, frankly, speeding up is worth the risk."

"You are going to have to answer me, Peter. Better now than when we are among strangers you would prefer not hear. *Ja?*"

"You are a hard-headed, stubborn—"

"Mind your manners, Councilman. I happen to have a formidable adversary on my side now."

"Conrad stands his own . . . I will not deny that."

"I was thinking more of Opa." Toya hoped teasing him would put him in a mood to share.

Peter chuckled. "You are good for me, Toya. You make me smile when I am too busy to play."

"There is someone else who would love to make you smile in many ways." Toya silently thanked heaven for the opportunity to discuss Betina.

"Subtle, *Fraulein*. Did she ask you to speak to me?"

"Hear yourself, Councilman. Would Betina ever speak up for herself as long as she felt I would gain or lose in some way or that it might affect you adversely?" She halted and waited for him to catch up. "*Nein*. She will stand silent and bear the burden of her heart for the sake of being a true friend to us both. We owe her more than that. You owe her the truth."

"What truth? Betina and I have talked since I returned from Nassau. We both are clear on what must be done."

Toya looked at him in exasperation, glad she couldn't see the nuances of his face. She might have slapped him for Betina's sake. "Peter, do not play the village idiot. Betina knows, I know . . . *you* know . . . that you have failed at something important. This failure—"

"You're wrong," Peter interrupted.

"I am right," she countered, "or you would not protest so quickly. Whatever this failure you've committed, face it. Believe me ... I have failed in so many ways, I could not begin to tell you what I've left undone. But I offer you a sense of peace, Peter. Take one day and succeed at something. Tomorrow, try again and again. Until you stack up a pile of achievements. That is the only way to overcome what you cannot turn back the clock and repair. All this rescuing. Who is it you disappointed? Who has not forgiven you the mistake? Go to that person if you can. Ask them to—"

"I can't. She's dead. God knows I have tried to forget, but three years has not let me. No amount of time, no number of rescues, will save the one person I could not." The finality of his tone echoed into the twilight.

"Tilly? It is Tilly who causes you this pain?" Toya thought back to the last days of Tilly's life. "She *chose* to die, Peter. She *chose* to ignore our warnings and took off on her own. Nothing you could have done would have saved her."

"*Ja,* I could have. I was the reason she fled into the hills."

Toya reached out to touch him, but the balanced crocks prevented the horses from drawing together. "She was out of her head. The snakebite drove her insane."

Peter shook his head. "*Nein.* She was recovering. She told me so herself, plain and clearly. Tilly wanted to die because ... because she saw me kiss Betina. I did not mean for it to happen. I truly believed I was in love with Tilly, but suddenly I couldn't help myself. Betina and I ... we shared a picnic ... enjoyed each other's company, then it happened. How was I to know Tilly had asked your father to drive her along the river? How was I to know she would run away so she could escape the sadness. I failed her, Toya. I could not bear to do the same to Betina."

"So you fail Betina by demanding that I marry you? That makes sense?"

"We're friends. We can't hurt each other. A marriage between us would be good."

She sat straighter in the saddle. "Well, pardon me, Councilman, but I want more from marriage. I want sun upon my face, bluebonnets waving against my hair. I want the taste of honey on my lips." Toya smiled, the memory of Rad's love taking away the night's chill.

"And if I insist you honor the pledge?"

No threat filled his tone, assuring Toya that his words were halfhearted. "You will not ask that of me, Peter, and you know why. If you will put the past behind you, your own future is waiting back in New Genesis.

"Betina will never marry anyone else. She's too stubborn and much too in love with you to ever do that. But she will wilt and die a slow death because of you. Betina is a woman who loves to create beautiful things. How can she create beauty for others when the one beauty of her life is denied her? Betina needs your love, Peter, not protection from your inadequacy. Together, you can defeat anything."

Toya saw the flicker of campfire light and nudged her mount into motion again. "You cannot alter Tilly's fate, but you hold the key to Betina's. Lock away your past, Peter, and open your arms to her."

"Frau Hinger, what are you doing out here?" The tall man straightened from his bent-knee position, where he had been warming his hands near the campfire.

"Herr Wilhelm?" Peter and Toya proclaimed in unison. The same man who had brought the ill to New Genesis had been chosen to meet them for the cure.

"I am Toya Reinhart, Herr Wilhelm." Toya reined to a halt and dismounted. She stepped into the circle of light. "You called me that name before, but I am not this Frau Hinger you speak of. We must look very much alike, or, perhaps, it is the dark that hampers your vision."

Peter hobbled the horses at the edge of camp, where there were stands of buffalo grass from which to graze.

The man shook his head and insisted. "You must have taken the sickness too, Sonya. Is Dante back at home with Kirk?"

Toya looked at Peter for help. "Tell him, Peter, that I am not Frau Hinger."

"She is Toya Reinhart from New Genesis."

"You should be ashamed of yourself, Sonya. Leaving Dante alone with his father. All the other mothers await the cure. You should not have ridden out here to claim your share. We all agreed the families would draw straws and whoever drew the longest would receive the medicine first."

The man moved his head one way, then the other, trying to look past them. "Did you bring it?"

Peter quickly explained. Since Toya had been with the cureall through the entire process, she informed Wilhelm how it was to be administered.

Wilhelm peered at her harder. "You must be who you say you are, but I could have sworn..."

"Sonya Hinger," Toya repeated, wondering why the night seemed a bit chillier than it had been moments before. "Exactly like me you say?"

"She could be your twin."

Suspicion gnawed at Toya. "Then I suggest you take me to this woman's house so that I can see her for myself."

26

It took most of the next day to reach Little Munich. Mothers and fathers alike raced out to meet them, hope dashing instantly as they noted the few crocks that remained. Riding past the main streets of town, they took a path on the southernmost edge. A half hour out, they turned into a small lane that led up to a log cabin.

Wilhelm reined his wagon up short in front of the house. "Ho, the house!" Wilhelm called out. "Kirk . . . Frau Hinger, are you home?"

Toya slowed behind the wagon, noticing that the door of the cabin opened slight.

"Who's there?"

"Johann Wilhelm. May I pay you a call?"

"Herr Wilhelm." Relief echoed in the woman's tone. "God bless you. I knew you would come here first. Knew you would not let my Dante suffer anymore."

Recognizing the voice, older, more world-wizened, yet still the same she had heard every day of her life since birth, Toya dismounted and tied the reins to a post. Peter did the same. He finished before her and moved around to one side of the cabin, as if he meant to ambush the woman inside.

"Drawing those straws was absurd." The door swung open farther and the woman raced out into the light. "The medicine should go to the most needy. Where is—"

Toya moved closer to make sure her eyes did not deceive her. The aroma of baking yeast and herbs emanated from beyond the opened door.

"Hello, Tilly." Toya nodded at her sister, pulled off her riding gloves, and stuffed them into the pocket of her skirt. Words tangled on her tongue as emotions raged within her—joy that her sister had survived, anger that Tilly had deceived them all. She found solace with sarcasm. "You look particularly ... alive ... today."

"Johann, how could you?" Tilly accused the man as she rushed to the wagon and untied one of the crocks. "Is this it? Is this the cure?"

"*Ja,* but—"

Tilly untied one crock and rushed toward the cabin to return inside, but Peter now stood in the doorway, blocking her way.

Tilly tried to shoulder past him. "Let me inside," she demanded, ignoring Peter's steely gaze. "My child needs this medicine. Johann"—she shot the man a look of fury—"this is all your fault. Make this man move."

Johann climbed down from the wagon. "The Hingers are fine people, and you shouldn't be treating her like—"

"Sonya is my sister, Herr Wilhelm. I have not seen her for several years," Toya whispered, the pain of Tilly's betrayal more acute. "Step aside, Peter. We will all go in and she can explain while we heat the medicine."

Tilly glared at Toya, then moved past Peter.

Small wonder Johann thought Toya had lied about her identity. Other than her sister's figure being fuller due to motherhood, they looked the same. Following Tilly inside, she glanced around for sight of her nephew. "How old is he, Tilly?"

"Tilly?" Johann glanced from sister to sister. "Your name is Tilly, not Sonya?"

"Sonya is my nickname." She inhaled deeply as she poured the contents of the crock into a pot and set it on the already-heated stove. She let out a long breath as if she could blow away the resentment layering the distance between the twins. "Almost three," she finally answered.

Suddenly Toya realized that Tilly must have been carrying the child when she left the note saying she intended to go up into the hills to die. "Let that boil for about ten minutes."

Who was the child's father? Had she feared she would be cast out? Their strict German edicts left little room for motherhood without the sacrament of marriage.

Try as she might, Toya could not believe Peter would have left Tilly alone with a child. He was the sort who would have demanded the right to raise his own son. *Kirk.* That was the name Johann had called out when they first approached the house. Kirk was Tilly's husband. Toya would make a point to meet him before they left. But for now, there was someone far more important to see. *Dante.* "Where is he?" Toya asked softly.

Johann looked ill at ease. "It is clear the three of you have much to discuss. I will leave this crock with you and distribute the others—"

Tilly rushed toward the door. "What if it isn't enough? What if I need—"

"We'll bring more." Toya grabbed her arm. "We've already sent for another wagon."

"When you're ready to leave, Herr Stoltz, you can find me at the general store." Johann's gaze focused on Peter. "It is the building next to the Hingers' tailoring establish—er—next to Kirk's."

"Danke schön." Toya bid him farewell. "But we will be fine. We can return faster riding the horses. You will not need to see us home to New Genesis."

The two men exchanged a handshake.

"I shall see the boy now." Toya moved toward the paisley sheet that curtained off the kitchen from the rest of the living area.

Tilly moved like a streak of lightning to reach her son before anyone else did. She swept back the curtain and rushed to the small bed occupying one corner of the large, comfortable-looking room.

Amid the covers lay a dark-headed angel complete with a dimple on each cheek. Toya stared at the cherubic face, noting the pallor around his Cupid's bow of a mouth. "He's beautiful . . ." Toya whispered, the image now shimmering before her tear-filled eyes.

"My *nephew*." Sadness filled her tone where elation should reign. All she could think of was how Tilly had cheated her of knowing and loving Dante. "A beautiful, beautiful baby boy."

A glance at her sister reminded Toya she should also feel cheated by Tilly's lie. She should resent the grief Tilly caused everyone who loved her. Most of all, she should despise her sister for the precious time lost trying to keep that foolhardy and unnecessary pledge made to Peter. Toya decided she had every right to bring Tilly to task, but could not bring herself to seek vengeance.

Her sister was alive! For her own peace of mind, Toya vowed to know—to understand why Tilly felt the need to fabricate her death. "May I hold him?"

Tilly shook her head and pressed her hand against his brow. "Not until he is better." Worry etched her face. "Has it been ten minutes?"

Uncertain, Toya flared her nostrils to see if she could smell the peaches and honey yet. That was always a sign that the remedy was ready. *"Nein."*

A glance at Peter warned Toya that he was stewing and about to boil over. He spent years trying to overcome the guilt of her death.

All those days and nights long ago, searching the hills for Tilly's bones. Walking away empty-handed, glad to know there still might be hope. Horrified that none could be found and wondering if a scavenger had scattered them from here to the Llano Estacado. All those Sundays, keeping her grave site cleared of debris. Knowing no true bones lay there, but needing some place where she could talk to Tilly and seek solace from the loneliness that had become her life. *Ja*, Toya had a right to be angry. A right to demand an explanation.

"Tilly"—it took every ounce of Toya's will to keep her tone hushed so she wouldn't wake the boy—"I have to know the truth, and I can't promise it won't go beyond this room. Four lives depend on what you tell me, one of them being mine."

Peter reached out a hand to stop Toya's question. "No, please . . . let me ask. It is my right to hear this first."

Toya nodded, not entirely agreeing, but realizing that Betina's future happiness hinged on this answer.

"Did you ever love me, Tilly?"

At first Tilly didn't answer, and Toya thought he would have to repeat his question. But when her twin glanced up, Tilly looked as if she might cry. Toya knew the truth before she said a word.

Tilly straightened slightly and mumbled, "I never loved you. I was in love with Kirk and found out I was with child. But we both knew he would never be accepted into the community, and especially not our child. You see, Kirk is half Kiowa, half German. We knew Father would never have allowed us to marry."

"You never gave us a chance to know," Toya bit back. "So you plotted your scheme and left Peter and me behind to play out your lie to Father."

"I paid a heavy price. . . ." Tilly's chin lifted as her gaze boldy met Toya's. "I told Kirk to never, ever let me contact you."

Despite her anger, compassion urged Toya to place her hand on Tilly's tightly balled fingers. Her sister could have chosen to continue lying, yet she didn't. "It must have been hard for you."

Tilly's hands trembled beneath Toya's touch. "The hardest thing I've ever done."

"Peter loved you, but you never returned that love, did you, Tilly?" She needed to know if Betina's words were true. Had Tilly believe she was treated secondhandedly? "You agreed to marry him only because you knew it would find approval in Father's eyes. It is as Betina warned me— you wanted to be first in Father's eyes." Toya faced the hard truth of her sister's deception.

Tears bubbled over Tilly's cheeks. "I saw no harm. Father was so ill. You needed someone young and vibrant to take care of you. Peter was willing. It was Father's wish. What easier way for me to leave you if I knew that you would be taken care of in my absence?"

Toya was shocked. She sat back in her chair and closed her eyes, remembering all the nights that Peter went for a ride and did not return until long after midnight. She'd thought he'd gone into the night merely to think, but he'd been searching, searching for some hint of where she'd been laid to rest. If he could not rescue Tilly alive, then he would find her remains and return them to Toya.

"What about me?" Toya could hold back her anger no more. "Did you think so little of me that you couldn't tell me?"

Tears streamed down Tilly's cheeks. "What I did, I did because of the way I felt for Kirk and the child that grew within me. It had nothing to do with you. It was that damnable Betina Bram. Always Betina. Not only did she seek out your company, but the brazen—"

"Do not speak ill of my friend," Toya warned, "when she was the one who stayed by my side. Who would not even consider betraying my trust . . . even if it meant giving up the man she loved."

"If you had cared for me half as much as you did Betina," Tilly accused, "maybe I would not have felt so lonely. Maybe I would have not gone looking so hard for someone to love me.

"I know you don't believe me, Toya, but I missed you every day. I missed sharing birthdays and secrets. I even miss disliking the ways we are so much alike and being awed by the many ways we are different." Tilly brushed back her son's hair. "I can imagine what you must be feeling for me. I did not know how much losing someone could hurt until Dante became sick. A lesson hard learned, Toya. One I must pay for all my life, as I cannot even tell Dante about his wonderful aunt for fear he might accidentally mention your name and bring about unwanted questions."

"Does your husband know?" Peter walked to the door, looking out. "When will he return home?"

"A few hours at most. And *ja*, he knows all. I have told him. He has seen me struggle to live with my decision." Tilly reached out to press her hand over Toya's, and Toya allowed the touch. "Many times I have wanted to come to you, Sister. Many times I ached to tell you the truth. But I feared you would never forgive me. That you would never understand that I had to choose between love of Kirk and my child and love of my family."

How could Tilly know the way their father would react? Most of the tribes had treated the German settlers with cautious courtesy. In any new wave of immigrants, someone always chose to love outside their nationality. This time it just happened to be Tilly.

The smell of peaches and honey scented the air. "It is time," Toya announced, then met Tilly's gaze. "It is long past time."

• • •

No sign of either Toya or Peter. Rad wondered if he should have ignored Betina's reasoning and taken the next batch himself. They should have already been back.

Had Toya found the excitement she always yearned for in the arms of Peter Stoltz? If not, Lineva Pyrtle was raising enough controversy about the pair being out alone that if anyone found them, there might be a forced wedding before they returned. Rad could only pray that the townsfolk continued to believe his rationality that Peter merely offered escort . . . and at Rad's request. No one ever thought twice about Peter spending the night on the trail with women immigrants. Why consider he would be anything less than on his best behavior with Toya?

"Conrad, you look like you need some welcome news!" Albertine called from the seat of her buggy. A pale but much stronger Liesl sat between Toya's aunt and Betina. "Do you not think it a good idea to show everyone the merit of their efforts. If they see the child, you will lift lagging hopes."

"That is a fine idea, ladies. I'm glad to see you feeling better, little one. Perhaps they'll still be enough peaches left after the crisis to prepare you a strudel."

Liesl's eyes lit with anticipation, but her smile waned. "In a few days perhaps . . . when Peter returns. Why has he not returned, Herr Conrad? I am afraid he has taken ill too."

"We cannot have you thinking that, can we?" Rad latched on to the first legitimate reason for his leaving and not appear selfish or jealous. "I plan to deliver this morning's batch and find out what *has* happened to both Toya and the councilman. That is"—Rad glanced at Opa, who had wandered over to talk to Fredericka. Toya's younger aunt sat in the back of the wagon, propped on pillows and heavily blanketed—"if my grandfather will see that everything is handled here. We have picked all the peaches ripe enough to be of any use. Now all that is left is combining ingredients and seeing that they are stored properly in the wagons."

Opa leaned to one side to get a better view of his grandson. "Are you sure you want me to handle this for you. What if I forget? What if I cannot fulfill the task?"

"You must, Opa," Rad insisted. "Lives depend on you."

Like a master chef given full access to the world's biggest kitchen, Opa began shouting orders to anyone within range.

Betina climbed down from the wagon. "I shall be his memory until Toya returns."

"Good, then. It is settled." Rad checked the wagon to be driven to meet the messenger. "But if I should somehow miss them and they arrive back in town, tell Toya not to volunteer for the next wagon until we talk."

"Tell her yourself." Betina motioned to two horses topping the rise to the south. "No one sits a horse exactly like Peter does. I can only assume Toya rides beside him."

27

The duo reined to a halt alongside the driver's box. Rad fought down images of the time and possibilities shared between Peter and Toya.

"Good to see you back." He forced himself to include Peter in the greeting. After all, the man was guilty only of bringing Toya back unharmed.

"Were you able to make the delivery?"

"*Ja!* But there was too little left after the spill."

Rad couldn't be prouder of her and said so. "You did a fine job, *Liebling*. No one could have done better."

Toya beamed, reveling in the warmth of his praise. He raised his hands to help her from the saddle, and she slid into his arms with pleasure.

When Peter dismounted, Betina rushed up, fearing the worst. She grabbed his hand. "Please do not call Conrad to task. I know you feel you must marry Toya. Do not fight Conrad."

"I have no complaint with him." Peter turned to the crowd that had begun to gather and waved them to silence.

"But I do have something important everyone should know."

All hushed, awaiting his words.

"I shall not honor my pledge to Toya, for it has proven a false vow."

Lineva Pyrtle gasped. Speculation rippled through the crowd.

Assuming someone discovered that his and Toya's love could no longer be denied, Rad stepped forward ready to defend her. He was the one who had been unable to withstand the power of their love and had urged her into breaking her vow. He could not stand by and let her name be tarnished.

Expressions turned to surprise as Peter lifted Betina's hand and pressed a kiss upon it. "I want all of New Genesis, all of the world to know that I am sorry for the way I treated you for the past three years. I wanted to tell you, Betina Bram, that you were right. After Tilly disappeared, I blamed myself for her death. I chose to rescue others because I had failed miserably at protecting someone I thought I had loved. But I discovered something important on this delivery to Three Oaks Crossing."

Toya waited to see if he would keep her sister's secret. Tilly's duplicity would explain so much now. Would he use her to right the wrongs between him and Betina?

"I am tired of lying to myself. I did try to convince her not to run away. I did try my best, and that's all a man can expect of himself. I did not fail at trying to help her . . . I failed at loving her. For how could I"—his gaze swept over Betina—"when I have loved you from the moment my eyes met yours?"

"I should be really angry with you." Betina laughed. "But all I care is that you are here. I have been waiting so long to let everyone know how very much I love you too, Peter Stoltz!"

Quiet intakes of breath, gasps, and silent smiles coursed through the community. Betina flashed Toya a request for help, wordlessly asking that all was in order and nothing stood in the way of her proclaiming her love for Peter.

A wave of impishness engulfed Toya. She walked up to Peter. "You came back to marry Betina, not me. Is that correct?"

"Correct." Peter exchanged glances with Betina, but she merely shrugged.

"And you have now gained enough sense to know how much you love her? Is that also true?"

"And I have made it perfectly clear that the only man I will ever love, pledge or no pledge, is Conrad Wagner." Toya faced Rad and lost herself in the smoky blue of his eyes—eyes filled with love and longing, eyes that stared at her as if he were the bee and she his long-sought nectar.

Peter nodded. "You have."

With tears of happiness, Toya held out her hand, thrilled when Rad reached out to join hers with his. "Will you say it or shall I?" She shared a glance with him and a knowing smile.

"Let him, babblemouth," Opa suggested. "He needs to do some of the confessing, I am certain."

Everyone laughed at the old man's impatience.

"Then tell it I will. Toya and I give our blessings to Peter and Betina, especially since we have taken steps to ensure our own marriage."

"Taken steps? Taken steps?" Lineva looked like a pecking chicken, her head moving too swiftly to gauge everyone's reaction to the news. "Just what does that mean."

"It means, rattlehead, that I need to get these old knees working better so I can rock me a handful of great-grandbabies." Opa elbowed Aunt Fredericka, who grinned wickedly at her niece. "Told you, did I not?"

"Well, I told you about Peter and Betina, eh?" she countered.

"Why am I always the last to learn about these things?" Albertine complained.

"Because you are not curious enough." Frustration thinned Lineva's lips into a single line.

Toya hugged Betina. "I wish you all the happiness in the world, Betina. I hope you and Peter will become more than husband and wife. I pray you can offer him what I have treasured all these years—your friendship as well."

Betina returned her hug. "*Danke schön,* Toya. *Danke schön.* Whatever you said to him, however you convinced him to know his own heart, I can never repay your kindness."

"Just remain my friend, Betina. No matter where life with Peter may lead you."

"No matter where," Betina promised, squeezing her gently.

Rad offered his hand to Peter. The councilman shook it, forming a tentative friendship between them. "It looks like we'd better learn to get along if we intend to marry those two."

Peter nodded. "Or we will never hear the end of it, I fear."

"Is it true, then?" Liesl raced up to tug on Betina's skirt. "Are you and Peter going to be my mother and father?"

"If you like, sweeting." Betina nestled into the crook of Peter's arm, thrilling in the congratulations echoing through the crowd.

The Wagners and Reinharts stepped away from the best wishes being offered the town councilman and his soon-to-be family.

"Well done, Toya," Rad complimented. "Well done for everything—helping Opa, convincing Peter, delivering the cure."

"So I have finished several projects, have I?" Her tone matched the challenge in her eyes.

"*Ja?*"

"Then it is your turn, bee man. You left one thing unfinished."

"The cure will take several days, but we have enough now to—"

"I do not speak of the cure." She wrapped her arms around his neck and pulled him close. Toya brushed a featherlike kiss against his lips.

He chuckled, afire with the spark she had ignited within him. "I never left anything undone in my entire life."

Toya stood on tiptoe to whisper in his ear. "You promised we would make a baby who would have your eyes and my hair."

Rad dug into his pocket and pulled out the ribbon she had lost . . . had it only been weeks ago?

"And she will wear calico ribbons." His eyes darkened with passion.

"And will learn a healthy respect for a field of bluebonnets," Toya vowed, staring into eyes that promised a thousand seasons of love.

Rad laughed and swept her into his arms. "Will you marry me, Toya Reinhart? Right here, right now?"

"I thought you would never ask again."

"It's about time!" Fredericka and Opa shouted in unison.

"Finally, I can get some sleep," Opa said. "All that moonlight is hard on an old kettle like me. Might make me forgetful on occasion." He wrapped an arm around each aunt. "Would you like to wager that a little Rad is running around here next summer?"

Lineva Pyrtle gasped.

"Or a tiny Toya," Fred added.

"You know, Lineva, if you gasped one octave higher, you just might discover an actual note you can carry." Opa flashed Albert and Fred a grin. "If my grandson is anything like his great-grandfather, there just might be a Rad *and* a Toya.''

Both ladies blushed. Lineva actually found the note Opa predicted.

"Grandfather!" Rad laughed at the old man's feistiness.

Opa winked. "Well, that's one thing I *don't* plan on forgetting."

Epilogue

"Our lives have certainly changed since last spring." Toya glanced at Betina sitting next to her on the blanket spread over the field of bluebonnets.

"But one thing remains the same," Betina reminded her friend. "Opa refuses to decide which of your aunts he will marry."

Toya's foot gently rocked the cradle Rad had carved for their newborn twins. She leaned over to check her darling son and daughter, gently caressing each angel-soft cheek with her forefinger. She exhaled a deep sigh of satisfaction, then sat back to watch their father and godfather attempt to catch butterflies for Liesl.

The nine-year-old and other children of New Genesis and the surrounding settlements had not only recovered from Texas scurvy, but their numbers had increased by two Wagners and would soon rise by another Stoltz. It seemed *some* of Opa's predictions could be counted on. "How do you feel, Betina?"

"Hungry . . . always hungry."

The two friends laughed.

Betina's hand dipped into her pocket and pulled out the embroidered handkerchief given to her so long ago. She unfolded the kerchief and held it out to Toya. "Care for some pfeffernuss?"

The sight of the spiced cookies wrapped in her mother's kerchief made Toya's eyes burn with the sting of blinding emotion. "So you found it."

"It's a long story . . . about two young girls from Germany."

Actually, it is about three, Toya thought, carefully accepting the bundle. "I would like to hear it."

She took a bite of one cookie. The taste of true friendship was a wondrous gift. "These last forever, they say," she whispered. "No matter how hard they become or wherever life takes them."

The two friends clasped hands and smiled.

DeWanna Pace enjoys hearing from her readers.

DeWanna Pace
c/o The Berkley Publishing Group
375 Hudson Street
New York, New York 10014

E-mail: DeWannaP@juno.com.

FRIENDS ROMANCE

Can a man come between friends?

__A TASTE OF HONEY
by DeWanna Pace   0-515-12387-0

__WHERE THE HEART IS
by Sheridon Smythe   0-515-12412-5

__LONG WAY HOME
by Wendy Corsi Staub   0-515-12440-0

All books $5.99

Prices slightly higher in Canada

Payable in U.S. funds only. No cash/COD accepted. Postage & handling: U.S./CAN. $2.75 for one book, $1.00 for each additional, not to exceed $6.75; Int'l $5.00 for one book, $1.00 each additional. We accept Visa, Amex, MC ($10.00 min.), checks ($15.00 fee for returned checks) and money orders. Call 800-788-6262 or 201-933-9292, fax 201-896-8569; refer to ad # 815 (1/99)

Penguin Putnam Inc.   **Bill my:** ☐ Visa ☐ MasterCard ☐ Amex _____ (expires)
P.O. Box 12289, Dept. B Card#_____
Newark, NJ 07101-5289
Please allow 4-6 weeks for delivery.   Signature_____
Foreign and Canadian delivery 6-8 weeks.

Bill to:
Name_____
Address_____City_____
State/ZIP_____
Daytime Phone #_____

Ship to:
Name_____ Book Total $_____
Address_____ Applicable Sales Tax $_____
City_____ Postage & Handling $_____
State/ZIP_____ Total Amount Due $_____

This offer subject to change without notice.